IMPRESSIONS IN HALF-LIGHT

For my dear friend Betty,
the world's greatest human geographer.

Preston

9/2009

Fourteen Tales
from the
Underside of Reason

PRESTON FORD

Outskirts Press, Inc.
Denver, Colorado

Impressions in Half-light
Fourteen Tales from the Underside of Reason
All Rights Reserved.
Copyright © 2009 A Thousand Candles Press
V3.0

Outskirts Press, Inc.
http://www.outskirtspress.com

ISBN: 978-1-4327-3507-4

Outskirts Press and the "OP" logo are trademarks belonging to Outskirts Press, Inc.

PRINTED IN THE UNITED STATES OF AMERICA

Dedication

For Nick, Nancy, and Kevin at Auburn University Montgomery and thereabouts. Your early encouragement has proved indispensible.

Contents

Foreword   i

1. Thieves in the Temple   1
2. Back Country   20
3. The Big Finish   35
4. A Child is Given   59
5. Not Counting Hope   73
6. For Adele   89
7. One Too Many   100
8. H.E.R. and the Great American Famine   117
9. Being a Hero   128
10. Neptune Rising: The Return of Marty Larkmon   138
11. When I See Home   168
12. The End   172
13. Veteran's Day   183
14. The Thing   211

Foreword

Flying into space and walking upon other worlds is likely to remain a dream for most who long to do such things. For others, the mundane reality of flying in an airplane, or walking the streets of a foreign land is similarly a dream out of reach. This was true for me in my childhood, and I spent many summer vacations tethered to the distances I could explore on a bicycle before the street lights came on. Even so, I was more fortunate than many children because the public library lay in walking distance, and I had learned early on the joy that comes from reading. Because of the library's proximity, I spent many of those long-ago days unraveling murder mysteries, exploring the natural world, traveling to far off planets, or wandering the ruins of history.

The joy of writing seems inextricably linked to the joy of reading. Millions of people commit words to paper for millions of different reasons, but not all of them do so because they are experiencing the euphoria of the *idea*—the sudden, eye-opening insight or mind-expanding notion that makes one grab any pencil stub and scrap of paper at hand before one's clarity begins to fade. How similar that feeling is to the one that holds a reader transfixed, to the deep urge that makes one scramble after characters and events by flipping through page after page in something akin to frenzy. I, again, am among the fortunate who know both these feelings, and the pages that follow share my humble efforts to create a work that engenders this elusive and powerful sensation.

I have held off sharing these stories for quite some time. Most were set down on paper for the sheer pleasure that the setting down brings; few were begun with the idea that they would be offered for widespread viewing. Many have their origin in dreams, some obviously so and others less so. Here (perhaps understandably) is the real reason I have been reluctant to show them outside my own door. For better or worse, however, the time has come for them to see the light of day. Keep reading. Enjoy the journey.

Preston Ford
Hyattsville, Md. 2008

Impressions in Half-light

... There are regions of the mind that come unfettered when we sleep. Our first instinct on awakening is to order the landscape where our imagination has just run free. Despite our efforts, whether to make sense of what we have seen or to purge it from our memory, a moment of stark lucidity lingers like a bright spot on the retina...

...Such insights are not dreams in the strictest sense, but are more akin to ethereal notions caught in a supple medium, as fingerprints in warm wax ...

1.

Thieves in the Temple

The tent was huge, but the air inside was stifling. The folding chair wobbled and creaked each time I adjusted my weight. Dry grass that had been mowed before the tent went up speckled my shoes like flakes of dandruff along with a layer of dust. There had to be a thousand people packed in here. So many that chairs spilled out under the raised flaps. I guess the fire code didn't apply when there was just as much exit as enclosure. Mom and Dad had dragged my brother and me to outdoor revivals like this one when we were kids. It had been fun back then because we would slip out and play cops and robbers or spy versus spy among the rows of parked cars and busses. Being here tonight was a little like going back in time. An old woman sitting next to me used a cardboard fan to stir the humid air and hummed along with the organ music. The chiffon collar of her powder blue dress rose and fell with each puff of wind despite a double strand of fake pearls circling her neck. Like the others, she suffered the warm night with patience.

Your average tent revival ran for three to five nights, never more,

and ended on either a Friday or a Sunday. The average revival also
had at least one night or one speaker who brought down the house
and made the whole series of meetings worthwhile. Tent revivals
were seldom like the spit-shined crusades seen on television. They
were peopled with hard-core churchgoers and their reluctant friends,
relatives, and neighbors whom they would drag along at the behest of
the almighty. I had a feeling tonight would be the night that brought
down this house. A very strong feeling

Fire and brimstone rained onto the heads of spellbound listeners,
and dire warnings flowed like lava from the pulpit. The minister had
a riveting voice that smoldered and echoed in the canvas cathedral,
painting red and black pictures of doom and damnation.

"Modern thinkers," she said, "tell us that if the history of human
civilization was compressed into one twenty-four hour period, we
who are alive today would be living three minutes before midnight.
Midnight being the end of all things." She was referring to The
Doomsday Clock, the iconographic logo of the Bulletin of the
Atomic Scientists that was supposed to represent how close humans
were to doing themselves in once and for all. "It's good to know that
science and philosophy are finally catching up with the Good Book.
But I don't need today's so-called wise men to clue me in to the fact
that people are messed up; that the world is messed up; that the end
is near, and humanity's bill is about to come due.

"The scientists say man is about to destroy himself....
Humankind is about to be destroyed all right, but it won't be the
humans who do it. The hand of the Lord is poised like the blade of an
axe, and soon—very, very soon—that blade is going to drop.

"*Revelations*, the Sixth chapter and eighth verse, "*And I looked,
and behold a pale horse: and his name that sat on him was
Death...*""

There she stood, conjuring up hell-fire and Armageddon. But
here I sat, thinking only that she was the sexiest woman I had ever
laid eyes on.

She was the Reverend Mary Ruth Peoples, Evangelical Minister
and Spiritual Counselor. She was also a tall, buxom, small-waisted,
round-hipped brunette with the face of a cover girl. People, men
especially, did double takes when she walked past. 'What's Wrong
with This Picture?' should have been printed on a banner and strung

across the stage whenever she spoke. Men and women alike looked at that face and found it impossible to imagine her preaching of all things. Most people assumed a head that gorgeous couldn't have much inside of it. But when they *heard* her, when they focused on her words instead of her chest and her calves, the peculiarity of a gorgeous woman talking about the end of the world took a back seat to the dread and foreboding she was able to arouse.

I had seen unbelievers converted, had watched intelligent, confident people fall into worried introspection after being in her presence. She simply had a knack for scaring the bejesus out of people with her talk about the final judgment. It had even been suggested that she might be an angel, a lieutenant of the archangel Gabriel, sent with a vanguard of others whose job it was to prepare God's people for the Second Coming. The information flyer said she had received her calling at the age of fifteen and had started preaching at twenty. She was now approaching thirty and happily married.

"But, 'God is love,' you say. 'He's a just God, a forgiving God. We are his children and he loves us above the whole of creation.' Well people," she shook her head and chuckled. "I've got some *news* for you." She expelled the word with a sardonic hiss, almost spitting it at them. "God is *mad!* Mad, because you refuse to heed him. Mad, because you and your filth, your sin, and your iniquities stink like a mass grave at the height of summer! Mad, because you think you can sin now and confess later!"

Hands rose into the air. "Yes!" someone called.

"You think you can put in for a last minute reprieve. You're like a death row inmate who believes in miracles. You think a priest is going to come and kneel down beside your sickbed, call God's emergency number and get you off the hook at the last minute. 'I'm going to repent when I turn fifty,' you say, or…'if this test comes back negative'…. Any day now, Lord, just give me a minute. I've almost got lying and cheating and fornicating out of my system. First thing tomorrow I'm going to turn over a new leaf, turn my life over to you Lord, and start living according to the teachings of Jesus." Her voice rose with a song-like quality, with passion. "Just a few more days, just a little while longer. Ohhhhhh you fools. You insufferable, unholy fools who defile my Father's house!" she thundered.

3

Heads leaned together and necks craned to get a better look when she walked to the microphone. The place had quieted in anticipation. Her voice was strong and smooth, sexy like the rest of her. Even the other ministers on the stage followed her with their eyes and stole looks at her hemline. And I blamed none of them. I myself had not seen a better pair of legs in my entire life.

She had, of course, begun her sermon with a prayer.

"Dear Lord," her melodious voice intoned, "humbly we come unto Thee, asking that we might drink from the fountain of Thy wisdom." I looked around the tent. All heads were tilted toward the ground except hers. Eyes closed, her flawless face looked out over the congregation. "Speak, dear Jesus, to the hearts of these Thy people, that they might know the truth and serve Thee better. In the name of the Father, the Son, and the Holy Spirit, Amen."

"Amen," the crowd had rumbled, then settled back in the folding chairs to listen.

Her sermon had the quality of a summer storm. It started high up and far away with prophetic passages from the Old Testament stirring the air like a foreboding wind. She spoke easily at first, but something in the words aroused uneasiness, like distant flashes in a darkening sky, or a change in the quality of the air. In ten minutes, they were all hanging onto the edges of their seats.

They sat in rapt attention while she admonished them for their sins and laid their souls bare before heaven. Her words dug into the nooks and crannies of their consciences and drew out all their shameful secrets and transgressions. More and more hands reached skyward as the speech progressed, waving amid a cloud of "amens" and "praise God's." Loud clapping and outbreaks of *speaking in tongues*—the unintelligible vocalizations that were supposed to indicate direct communication with God—happened all around me. Some worshippers got to their feet, hands held high and faces turned heavenward. Her essential message was being taken to heart: every person in the place would do a swan dive straight into hell unless he or she confessed and asked forgiveness right this instant. At the apex of her delivery she stalked back and forth across the stage, jabbing the air with a manicured fingernail and hurling her words like bolts of lightning, damning them in order to save them.

The noise level rose in slow steady increments. Tambourines

jingled in the choir stand. The air sizzled with unnamable excitement, and I half expected to see bolts of electricity popping and whizzing between the tent poles. In twenty minutes, they were all clutched in her fist. And then, when their agitation was at its peak, she went for home, wringing them with everything she had.

She stopped moving and sank to her knees.

Her head fell forward, and a dark curtain of hair closed around her face. The noise level dropped for an instant and then surged with confusion and chatter. She was mute. Then she threw back her head.

Her face was twisted into an ugly imitation of itself. Tears coursed along her cheeks. She clutched the microphone with both hands, holding it tight against her breasts. She tried several times to speak and finally choked out the words "Dear God." Weeping openly, she said, "Dear God have mercy...have mercy," and rocked back and forth. Tears fell onto her hands and onto the cream colored lapels of her jacket. "*Save us....*"

Some cried with her in fear and exaltation. Hands waved everywhere as if desperate to get God's attention.

"*Dear Jesus, I'm...I am a sinner!*" she wept. The agony in her voice washed through the speakers with heart-wrenching effect. "...So unworthy...so unworthy...." A child on the seat behind me started to wail. His mother, wiping at her own tears, stooped and picked him up. The service came to a halt.

The presiding minister, a barrel-chested black man named Dobbs, got up from his chair and went to her. He knelt next to her and put his face near hers, a hand on her shoulder. The excitement was everywhere, crawling over my own skin as well as theirs. She could have traveled around that tent three times and never touched the ground so many hands were lifted up. On a signal from someone behind the stage, the organist began playing *Near the Cross* in soaring, majestic chords. The choir joined in, humming the melody and swaying to the music. Slowly, the happy chaos reverted to sounds of worship.

Rev. Mary took the handkerchief offered to her by Dobbs and got to her feet with his help. She walked back to the podium and stood behind it. Applause and cries of "Praise Jesus! Praise Him!" soared to the sagging fabric roof above us and continued until she had composed herself and was ready to speak again. Her nose was bright red and her eyes were swollen as if she had not slept in days.

"There is a man out there," she said in a thick voice, "who feels he's lost everything. You've lost your wife, you're snowed under with debt, everything's gone wrong. You feel you've had all you can take and you're ready to end it. You feel you've got no reason to go on living." And here her voice softened. "But it's not all gone. You still have the most important thing in the whole wide world. You still have the Divine Love of the Heavenly Father wrapped around you. You're still protected by the greatest insurance policy known to man: the Word of God, and the promise that He will lift you up and carry your burdens when the road becomes too rough." Her voice warmed. "You are safe in the arms of the Lord God Almighty, the Son of God who became the son of man, the Rose of Sharon, the Lily of the Valley!" She opened her arms and turned her palms skyward. "Jesus can turn it around! *Seek ye first the kingdom of God...* for the Son of God can do all things. *You* can do all things through Christ who strengthens you. But first and foremost, you-have-got-to be-lieve! Accept the Lord God and make him your own. He can heal bodies; he can heal lives. He can forestall the torment of Satan and bless you with life everlasting in heaven. But you must surrender and accept Him first! *John* Fourteen and six: *I am the way, the truth, and the light. No one,* no one, *cometh unto the Father but by me!*"

They waved their hands higher, murmuring "Jesus, *Jesus...*"

"*For I will open the gates of heaven and pour out upon thee blessings which thou hast not room enough to receive.*"

" 'allelujah!" a man behind me called out. The word echoed to my left and to my right.

"And there are others," she said, "many of you with special problems and special needs. There is a woman fighting against addiction, another who faces losing a son to prison. There is an elderly couple out there waiting for a diagnosis. Come," she said, opening her arms again. "Come and talk with the Lord."

And they moved toward her like a flock that had been lost in the wilds. Ones and twos in a slow trickle at first, then more and more until a steady stream moved in answer to her call. The sick and afflicted, the troubled and the weary, the broken hearted and dispossessed, every manner of unhappy and unredeemed soul made its way to the front. Like a great beacon showing the way to safety through pitch dark, she drew them to her until more people had jammed the aisles and packed the area in front of the stage than remained in the seats. And she went down among them and touched them all, laying hands upon one after another, filling them with the spirit of goodness, and ushering peace into their hearts.

It took awhile for things to settle down and for the crowd to return to their seats. After the last ones left the stage a special offering was taken. Dobbs said a benediction and the people began clearing the space. There was a tired, happy feeling in the air. While some of the adults dallied and chatted, children ran and played just outside the tent flaps. I walked outside and made my way to the white Chrysler Fifth Avenue parked with a small group of cars that sat away from the main parking area. I got inside, rolled down my window, turned on the radio, and waited.

A half-hour later I was woken up by voices and the sound of the passenger door opening and closing. I sat up straight and shook my head to clear it. I had dozed off. She was already settling into the passenger seat when someone spoke outside my window.
"How's that tooth brother?"
I looked up into Dobbs' face. Seeing the concerned smile, I forced a thin grimace of my own and reached to shake his hand.
"Not as bad as it was Reverend," I said.
"You be sure to get to a dentist first thing tomorrow now."
"Oh, don't you worry," I said, stretching the smile a little more.
"Are you two sure you can't stay just one night? It's absolutely no trouble for us."
"She's told you a dozen times already that she's got another engagement tomorrow." A woman's voice emerged from the darkness beyond. The Reverend's wife. "Now quit being a nuisance." She stepped up and hooked her arm through his. The two of them and the others who had escorted her to the car said goodbye for another ten minutes. While I began backing out, she continued clutching hands through the open window, finally waving when I turned toward the street. It was just after ten o'clock when we pulled onto the highway.

When we reached an empty stretch of I-70, she let the seat back and began undressing. First the jacket, then the shoes, then the pantyhose. She took them off and dumped them unceremoniously into the back seat. She leaned and reached behind me, unzipped a travel bag on the seat, and took out a pair of shorts, a sports bra, a loose-fitting tank top, and a pair of sandals. Shimmying out of her skirt, she first folded it, and then threw it into the backseat. She pulled the lightweight sleeveless blouse over her head and took off her bra. I reached over and rubbed her thigh, then let my hand travel up her flat stomach. She laughed and stopped it short.

"Eyes on the road," she said.

With her workout clothes on, she let the seat up and reached to change the radio station. Driving east on 70 toward St. Louis, I saw a million stars and the reflected glow of the dashboard in my window as the night sped by outside. When ninety miles of darkness separated us from the town of Wilkesville, Missouri, I decided to find a place to rest. A glow on the horizon told me we would soon be back in civilization. Another mile or so, and a green and yellow sign--a BP truck stop--came into view. Next to it was the bright yellow of a Waffle House. I got off at the exit and drove to the gas station. After I had filled up the car, we walked across the lot to the restaurant.

We went inside and took a booth near the window. Bright lights, cold air from the vents, and the smell of frying bacon drove away the sleepiness that was settling behind my eyes. She sat down on the padded orange seat and drew her legs up Indian style. The waitress, a young black woman with deep brown eyes and dimples came to the table with water glasses and utensils. She asked if we wanted coffee or orange juice, and said she would be back to take our order.

Mary Ruth unzipped the leather pouch at her waist and extracted a double fist-sized roll of bills. When the waitress came back, she was counting them out onto the table and separating them by denomination. The girl tried not to stare as she poured steaming coffee into the small porcelain cups. When she left the table, Mary Ruth let out a whoop.

"Fifteen hundred! Fifteen hundred bucks!"

Two men at the end of the counter glanced our way.

"Shhhh!" I said, trying to hide my own enthusiasm.

"Shhhh hell," she said. "Fifteen hundred for two hours work. *Seven hundred and fifty dollars an hour!* Damn! I'm good!" Her eyes gleamed and she laughed out loud, kissing a handful of the bills. "I am so good!"

I raised my cup in a toast. "Cheers."

We clicked cups.

When the food came, she laid into it like she had not eaten in days.

"Hey—hey," I said, "go easy. Can't afford to have you choke."

She grinned and kept on eating, talking through her food.

"Just a couple more months, three months tops and we start looking for a permanent location."

She meant a permanent location from which to base a television ministry. I shook my head and sighed.

"It's been a good night baby. Can we not talk about that right now?"

She stopped chewing and gave me a long stare. A very long stare.

I wished whole-heartedly that I had kept my mouth shut, or that I could turn back time. Five seconds was all I needed. If I could reverse time five seconds, she'd go on eating like a homeless person; I'd eat and keep my thoughts to myself. Just five seconds. But that's not how it works.

Her silence sent the jovial mood over a cliff—from celebration to *Christ, here we go again*, and since I had already stepped in it, I decided to cut to the chase and get it over with.

"Not now, okay? Let's not go there right now. Okay? I've told you a thousand times we're not ready. We'll be getting ahead of ourselves if we try to get into television right now. We need more money. LOT's more. We need a congregation. We need backers. And you are good hon', but a little more practice won't hurt your delivery."

"What do you know about delivery?" she sneered. The cup in her left hand stopped halfway to her mouth.

I put my fork down.

"I know that I sit in the audience every night. I know when they're really into it, and when they go along because they're in

9

church and think that's what they're supposed to do. How about that?"

She put the cup down. Taking some bills from her pouch, she leaned across the table and held them under my nose.

"When *you* start making seven fifty an hour, seven *hundred* and fifty, *then* you talk to me about delivery."

"So you had a good night," I said for the second time. She glared at me and shook her head. We were *really* going there now, no getting around it.

"Can you do it?" she spat.

"Jesus Christ..."

"Can you?" She asked again, tilting her head to one side. "Can you do one fucking thing besides sit on your ass and look up my skirt? You think your goddamn flyers are something special? I could get those at Kinko's in five fucking minutes. Can you get those people off their butts and make them give you a fucking dime? Can you?"

"No I can't, Mrs. Graham, but this was your idea, and you've been working this shit for so long, it's about time you got it right." I didn't want to fight with her, but the evil vibe spread quickly and took over. "Did we forget about New Orleans?"

Her eyes narrowed. Her lower lip trembled and curled backward against her teeth.

"What *about* New Orleans?" she said with a disgusted hissed.

I thought she might strike the table, or hurl her plate at me.

"How quickly we forget," I muttered.

In New Orleans, we had gotten onto the program for a revival at one of those mega-churches—a cross between a place of worship and a shopping mall. It had been her first time in front of an audience that size. The program was being simulcast on a local radio station, piped throughout the huge complex on closed circuit TV, being videotaped for a Sunday morning broadcasts, and audio recorded for sale in the church's bookstore. The bright lights, the roar of voices like the tide coming in, an ocean of people on the floor below her and just as many in the tiers of balconies above, the thought of still more scattered throughout the various centers, offices, and satellite buildings. She had choked. She stammered through the first ten minutes of her sermon and became light headed. When she was ushered from the stage to concerned applause, I told the platoon of attendants that she was pregnant and to be careful as they fought over who would wheel her to the five-bed infirmary just off the main suite of offices.

And all of a sudden I felt like a backstabbing bastard.

Her reaction reminded me how badly she had been humiliated. Still, she was just too goddamned impulsive. She had no qualms whatsoever about lowering her head and sprinting at a brick wall. Often, she wouldn't stop and think about how to approach a problem until after she was knocked on her ass. The television ministry thing was a perfect example.

"I'm sorry hon," I said with a sigh.

Thumb and forefinger curled around her chin, she glared at me with eyes like a diamond drill. Not just angry but seething, reliving the humiliation in her mind.

"I'm…" I wanted to say something other than "sorry," but I had trouble finding words.

The breath hissed out of her, and she turned her face away from me.

"I di—"

"Fuck you."

"—didn't mean that the way it sounded."

We'd been arguing about this for months. She was itching to get to the big time. A television ministry of her very own, her name glittering in Old-English script every Sunday. Loyal contributors raking together those dimes and digging out those singles every week, buying tapes and desktop magazines as fast as we could put them out. I knew we'd never—say—have our own university, as in Oral Roberts U, but I wanted us to build a solid foundation, one that would sustain us and let us expand in the future. After her weekly program was up and running, who knew? Maybe we would have our own cathedral some day. But all of that was still way in the future. Right now we had to stick to what we did best. When we made the jump to television, everything had to be perfect. It was almost funny when I looked back and considered that this whole thing had started on a bet.

She and I were sacked out in a crappy motel-cum-apartment building in southern California, tired of making love and bored as hell. I was flipping through the extraordinarily small selection of available channels when we came across a fat, sweaty preacher on the local cable access station. We watched for three minutes, then she blurted out, "That's guy's full of shit. I could do that." I changed the channel, but she grabbed the remote and flipped it back. "I could do that easy! Listen to him." I spent the next half-hour watching the man while she critiqued him. She had been a Mass Communications major or something like that back when she believed a college education would be her springboard to a comfortable life. She had dropped out the year before we met. Mary Ruth Peoples wasn't her real name, of course. Neither was Desiree Lynn, the name she had used to enter a wet-tee-shirt contest at a strip club outside of Long Beach (a contest which she won, by the way). That club is where we met. After winning the contest, she had gone on to work as a dancer. I hung out there most nights, having just gotten out of the Army, and I spent my days looking for work.

One night, a short, greasy-haired olive-skinned turd with an eye-pencil mustache, looking like he had just escaped from a Mafia costume party, came into the club. He sprinkled money all around the place, buying drinks and schmoozing with the girls, chatting them up singly and in groups. When he made his way to Desi, he bought us both drinks and, after complimenting her on her beauty and me on my taste, asked her if she had ever posed for nude photos. Somewhat taken aback, I nevertheless listened while he made his pitch. The money he offered was okay, I guess. Desi was capable of making her own decisions, so I took a long, long pull on my beer and held my reaction to a shrug when she agreed. I went with her to the "shoot" the next day, unsure why I had remained silent the night before. I was determined to see that everything was done on the up and up and gotten over with as quickly as possible. At that point, we'd been together for six months and I had started to feel a bit possessive. Not psycho possessive as in I owned her and she must do nothing that displeased me, but more like protective, with a hint of territoriality. She was my girl. I respected her independence and what-not, but she was my girl.

The "studio" was an entirely second-rate operation, perhaps third- or fourth-rate even. Imitation velour drapes served as a backdrop and were thumb tacked to a plaster wall. The sixties-looking camera equipment was bulky and worn; black paint flaked off in places and there was a dent in one leg of the tripod. A frayed area rug covered part of the linoleum, which had started to peel up at the corners. Everything looked cheap, including the junk jewelry they adorned her with and the splintering wicker furniture they propped her up on. Despite the extreme low-budget look of the place, it lacked the sticky ambience of honest-to-goodness sleaze, so I sat down and waited. Two people were there when we arrived: the photographer, and another so-called model who did Desi's makeup. The guy played the part of professional photographer well enough, and the girl did race around the entire time assisting him. When they were done shooting, the girl handed Desiree a roll of bills, put on a wig while the photographer reposition the furniture, and then got out of her own clothes.

Two weeks later, I was at the club waiting for her to get off when the turd showed up again. He schmoozed and glad-handed just as he had the last time, buying drinks, squeezing the girls' legs under the table, and generally spreading pomade all over the place. When he talked to Desi, he asked her to come down and do another photo shoot. When she hesitated, he sweetened the money offer, and when she looked to me, I gave her a long, disapproving stare. She told him she'd think about it. A day later, she went down without me and did the second shoot.

When Mr. Grease made his next appearance, he wasted no time with subtlety but went straight for the end zone.

"My customers still are sweating in their palms for you foxy, gorgeous body. I want you to make a little movie for me."

"Excuse me just a goddamn minute," I said.

The photos had been bad enough. I'd kept my prudish objections to myself and let her make up her own mind, but this was over the limit.

"I was talking to the lady," he said, sounding like a caricature of the big-time king of sleaze he so clearly wanted to be.

I had his polyester necktie wrapped around his throat before he finished making the offer. The bouncer, who had obviously been hoping for something to do, came leaping across tables and had me in a double arm-lock before I could do any real damage. He and the owner threw me out, and I wound up sitting in the alley behind the building until she came out. When she did, she told me the guy had offered her two and a half grand to do a short, tasteful love scene in one of his artistic ventures. A second couple would be in the scene, she told me, as if that would make the idea less repulsive. If she showed up, she'd get a third of the money right away and the rest when the scene was finished. He had promised her one take, straight sex, ten minutes max joy or no joy, all paid in cash.

"Is this a fucking joke? Are you out of your fucking mind?" I asked her and then told her if she went anywhere near that guy, I'd beat the crap out of both of them.

She knew I'd never lay a hand on her, and so she kept trying for a week to convince me. When she saw that there would be no changing my mind, she gave up and put her own foot down. She was going to do it with or without my blessing, and if I was going to beat the crap out of her, she wished I'd do it now so her face could have time to heal.

I had every intention of leaving her. There was no way I would spend the rest of my life sleeping next to a professional whore. She had a brain, but she had chosen to work as a stripper. That was bad enough. This was way over the line. I intended to slam the door behind me and take off without a backward glance. That was two years ago. Today, after all these months, I still can't put my finger on how she broke me down. All the attention maybe, all her assurances that her heart wouldn't be in it and it need not change anything between us. She had given me a whole load of porn industry horse shit about work being work and nothing more, and about how people in other professions used their bodies to bring home a paycheck. I wasn't buying it, but she stuck to her guns, and kept chipping away at me.

I was on the couch all day long the day she went on that shoot. With the lights out and the shades pulled, I drank from a bottle of Jack Daniels. It was dark outside, the lights and the TV were on, and she was in the shower when I awoke that evening and realized I'd passed out. When she came into the living room, still wet and wrapped in a towel, she went first to her bag then came over to the bed. She let a double handful of twenty dollar bills—with a few fifties mixed in—flutter onto my head. It seemed like a lot more than twenty-five hundred dollars. A whole lot more.

"No, it's not counterfeit," she said, reading my next thought. "I already checked."

"How much is it?" I'd asked groggily.

Five thousand.

The other girl had not shown up, so they'd paid her double to do the two guys at once. I got up and teetered into the bathroom where I threw up all over the sink and floor.

I had found a day job, and she was in the money, relatively speaking, for the time being. We had the one Volkswagen between us, and we managed the rent on this apartment, which we'd found through one of the bartenders at the club. Neither of us, however, would be able to afford both a place to stay *and* food for very long if we went our separate ways, so neither of us packed our bags that night. She had gambled that I would think twice before leaving her, but she had greatly underestimated the effect her little show business romp would have on us.

We passed the rest of that night in utter silence, and it was weeks before I spoke to her again. I don't mean *spoke* as in meaningful conversation, I mean it literally, as in *nothing*, as in not even saying "go to hell" when she asked about the rent or tried to make small talk about the weather. I did not say, "Pass the salt" when we ate, or even "no" when she asked if I wanted to catch a movie. Not a "damn you," not a "slut," not a single word from me to her for two and a half weeks. She grew accustomed to my silence and gave up trying to make conversation after the first few days. She continued to work at the club; however that one time, as far as I know, was her only adventure in filmmaking.

The silence ended on a warm Thursday when I came in from work For no real reason I asked her if she thought it would ever rain again in that part of California. When I had gotten up that morning I realized I was tired of being mad at her. Plain and simple. My anger was gone, and I wanted to talk to her again.

"Who cares?" she said and kept on washing the dishes.

She could have ignored me as easily as I had ignored her, I suppose. But there was something in her voice when she answered, and I knew she was glad the period of silence had ended. We made love that night like two people with long-simmering crushes alone together for the very first time. It was the same every night that week, and that week, it turned out, was the week we found the TV minister.

"Oh give me a fucking break," she had sneered and slapped her forehead. "Look at this guy! I could do that in my sleep!"

"Twenty bucks says you can't," I challenged.

That was the end of it I thought. But a week later, she came and sat down on my lap showing me a Bible highlighted and bookmarked with notes she had made.

"You are not serious," I'd said to her.

"Find me a church," was her reply.

The Reverend Mary Ruth Peoples was born (at first Mary Magdalena Peoples, but we discarded that because it was too gimmicky), and in four short months she had sheared flocks from Los Angeles to Miami.

She wiped her mouth and took a sip of coffee. "I'm tired of waiting," she said. "Why do we have to keep waiting? Why can't we just find a place and start making some *real* money? Now!"

"We don't have the startup capital," I began for the thousandth time. "We couldn't rent a studio for two days. We couldn't buy enough air time to…"

"Get somebody to donate a goddamned studio! Quit being so fucking--" The men at the counter looked our way again. She lowered her voice. "Did Jerry Falwell and Jim Bakker pay to be on TV? Hell no! They got paid!"

"*Everyone* pays for air time, for equipment, for production facilities, and for a shitload of other things." I'd done my homework as thoroughly as she had.

She tried to interrupt but I kept going.

"Listen, sweetheart," I said in the most appeasing tone I could muster just then. "You're the talent; I'm the brains. So far things have worked out fine. Haven't they? You just keep writing those sermons; let me worry about the business end. I'll get you on TV soon enough." I winked.

She persisted with the evil stare but I was firm. If she insisted on breaking into television now, the best we'd be able to pull off would be one of those home-spun *Community Evangelical Gospel Hour* shows that aired at four in the morning (on Saturdays no less), and she would be just another rank amateur. Just like the chubby preacher she had taken such pleasure in deriding so long ago.

She shook her head finally and relented. I went back to my food, which had gotten cold.

When I looked up again she was gazing out the window, lost in thought. I turned my head and saw our reflections superimposed on the cars in the parking lot.

"You know…" she began, but lapsed into silence.

"What?"

"Wouldn't it be something?"

"What, TV?"

She shook her head. "Wouldn't it be something if you could just get down on one knee and say, 'Lord, I believe in you and I'm sorry,' and everything would be okay? All your problems would be solved, all your sins forgiven. Wouldn't that be something?"

I looked at her with a raised eyebrow and asked, half joking, "You're not getting soft are you?"

"Nah," she said. "But…sometimes, when they come up…for prayer...you know? Sometimes when they come up for prayer, I can see it in their eyes. I can *see* it. They really believe some kind of miracle's going to happen. They're gonna get a fat bank account and go to heaven if I wave my arm over them. Wouldn't it be something if it happened that way?"

Pause.

"Is it that easy?"

"Yeah! *Acts* Second chapter, thirty-eighth verse: *Repent and be baptized. Romans* 10 and thirteen: *If thou will confess with thy mouth the Lord God and believe in thine heart that He is real, then thou shalt be saved.* Speak and believe. Say the magic words and win the grand prize. Eternal life and a French chateau in Waikiki. Great huh?"

"I cant' figure people out," I said with a shake of my head.

"It's freeze-dried Heaven," she said. "Paradise in a microwavable cup. No work, no worries, just add water. Just speak and believe, and you live forever, playing your harp and swinging with the Apostles."

I drained orange juice from my glass.

"As long as we know the difference," I said. "Long as we don't start believing the sermons."

Her gaze drifted out the window again.

"Do you think there's a hell?" she asked.

"I hope the hell not."

"Don't be funny, asshole. Listen. What if all that stuff in *Revelations* is true? What's going to happen to us?"

I thought a moment, and then told her she must be tired. "Why don't we get a room, take a nice hot shower and crash?"

She smiled, and I got the feeling she was glad I wanted to change the subject.

"Will you rub my feet?" she asked.

"Sure."

"And I can go right to sleep afterward, without you pawing me?" She raised an arched eyebrow.

"Of course not," I said, letting my eyes roam over the half of her that was visible above the table. I felt her toes on the inside of my thigh.

"You only want me for my body," she said in a husky, lascivious stage voice.

"Untrue, untrue!" I said, and banged the table top for emphasis. "Your body is only one of your many, many captivating qualities."

"Name another."

"Your smile."

"Yeah, right."

"Your eyes. Your razor-sharp wit. Your ability to speak in public."

"Yeaaah, bullshit," she said with a small laugh. "Come on, let's get out of here."

She put her sandal back on, stood, and dropped some money on the table.

"How much booze is left? Any?"

There was an unopened fifth of E&J Brandy in the trunk. Feeling tired and stiff myself, I looked forward to its giving us both a good night's sleep. My grandfather had told me long ago that there was nothing could be wrong with a man that a stiff drink, a fine woman, and a good night's sleep wouldn't cure. We'd crawl out of bed in the morning and hit the highway again. Our next big stop was a tri-state revival east of the Washington DC area, with two smaller appearances on the way. A few more months and we'd have enough capital to start working out of one location. Not enough for television, mind you, but enough to lease a storefront and get started. Until then, we had to keep moving. It was good there were so many, many sheep out there. Good because the sound of shearing was music to our ears.

2.
Back Country

Going alone to where the lions lived was a very bad idea. The native guides had told him this, and told him this, and told him this, a thousand times it seemed. The tall one especially, the Hutu man with skin so dark it looked purple in the noon sun. The Hutu (whose name he would never be able to pronounce) had warned him that going into the lion's domain alone was as smart as tying your head to a baboon. The old saying made little sense, but neither did going into the bush alone, which was precisely the Hutu's point.

Something inside him woke him up in the wee hours of that morning, long before first light, and he lay there on his cot trying to remember exactly what his boss, the Interim Head of Revenues and Benefits had said to him to make him travel half-way around the world on a glorified camping expedition. An expedition that might…just might…result in his witnessing the meaningless murder of an innocent dumb animal. Kendrick had been passed over for the job of Benefits Manager for the Borough Council of Northampton in Northampton shire. Kendrick was fully certified by the Institute of

Revenues Rating and Valuation and had kept current on all the latest licensing issues. He had not doubted he could do the job, but in his heart of hearts he had not wanted it when he was honest with himself. He was not content to remain in the position he had held for the last fifteen years, no matter what anyone else thought, but neither did he wish to take on so much responsibility that he would suffer a heart attack at the end of his first year. It might have been this seeming lack of ambition that had caused his boss to become cross with him. But Kendrick knew how to handle superiors who wanted to castigate him and grind him underfoot. He had put in for three weeks worth of his thousand-plus hours of accrued leave and jumped on a plane to Nairobi. After eight days in the wild both his boss—the little pus-headed twerp—and the insulting remark were a world away and their importance reduced to nothing by the distance.

The driver from Wild Ambition Safaris Ltd. had waited outside the Nairobi airport in a Land Rover while Kendrick found his bags and cleared customs.

"Mr. Charles Kendrick?" the man had asked with a huge smile when Kendrick approached the vehicle. Kendrick nodded and held out his hand. "Welcome to Kenya!" the man then exclaimed in a booming voice that drew stares from the other travelers, He had hopped out of the jeep, thrown Kendrick's bags in, and driven him straight through the city and out into the countryside. They drove for two hours through sweltering heat, swirling dust, and one mud puddle so deep, the jeep became stuck. At first, it seemed they would have to swim across, but the driver managed to coax the vehicle out with Kendrick gripping the doorframe and silently urging it on.

When they pulled into the permanent headquarters of Wild Ambition—three small buildings and something with a thatched roof that looked like either a shed or an outhouse—Kendrick wished for a fleeting moment that he could call his wife. This was strange because, were he at home in England, he would not have called his wife, nor wanted to call her. Celeste Kendrick was a frumpy, grumpy, ceaselessly irritable woman with a wicked tongue and a more wicked throwing arm. In the years they'd been married, she had broken an uncounted number of vases, glasses, mirrors and picture frames with her shoe, or her hairbrush, or any other "environmental weapon" which she could heft and hurl with one hand. She was adept at putting English on a thrown object and had more than once sent something whizzing past Kendrick's ear and broken an object directly in front of him. There were even times when she did it just to remind him she could. Kendrick did not know why his wife hated him so, nor was he certain why he hated her. Not simply because she threw things at him or cursed like a sailor. There probably was some deeper and altogether different reason why he hated her, but he could not put his finger on it.

Still, climbing out of the muddy jeep, he wished for a fraction of a second that he could call her. The night he'd blurted out that he was going to Africa for three weeks and might never see her again, her voice had softened and she had lowered her throwing arm, stunned, even though she had not believed him at first. When he showed her the brochure and the airline ticket that he had secreted away in his closet, she looked at him in a way she had not for many years. It had been a strange moment, and not another angry word had passed between them the entire week.

The owners of Wild Ambition Safaris, Ltd. were an American husband and wife who had run away from Western comfort and competitiveness so that they could Lord over the natives who came to work for them as guides. The first thing they did was have him sign a stack of release forms which said in essence that he, a petty bureaucrat in the local government of Northampton, being dumb enough to come to Africa in hopes of killing wild animals, was on his own in the event of injury or illness including everything from diarrhea and Sleeping Sickness to drowning and decapitation by crocodiles or hyenas. He might have been afraid if he had stopped to think about those things before he left home, but it was too late now. And did these two escapist hippies really think they could scare him? He was a grown man after all.

They served him lunch—barbecued antelope, or wildebeest—he thought, with American-styled baked beans and a cold, syrupy drink which was quite good except that it made him even thirstier than he had been and caused him to long for a glass of plain water once the beverage was gone. They had him lay out the clothing he had brought and augmented his own gear with a large canteen, a khaki vest for carrying extra shotgun cartridges, a khaki-colored pith helmet in place of his Sherlock Holmes deerstalker, a roll of mosquito netting, a sleeping bag, an inflatable mattress pad, a cake of unscented soap made in a nearby village, an Ace bandage to always carry in his pocket, a whistle, and a few other survival odds and ends. When his gear was re-packed, the driver loaded it back into the jeep.

"Why are you putting it back?" Kendrick asked.

The driver and the two owners smiled at each other.

"Camp site's a few miles up the mount-in, mate" the husband said and pointed. "Ya didn't think you were staying 'ere, did ya?" Kendrick wondered why the man wanted to sound like an Australian, since he was an American living in the middle of Kenya.

"We'll be here when you get back," the wife said unnecessarily.

Kendrick climbed into the jeep. The driver gunned the motor and the vehicle lurched away.

"G'day!" he heard the husband call through the swirl of dust.

He had been in the countryside of Kenya for just over a week now, soaking up more natural beauty than he had ever dreamed existed. He had ceased to miss his wife, had forgotten her altogether for long stretches. Had forgotten about everything back home until the night something woke him and he found himself first, unable to go back to sleep, and second, unable to remember what it was that made him come out here in the first place.

Then he started to think about lions.

There is a place on the outer edge of sleep where creativity flowers exponentially, where the mind becomes supple and amazingly receptive. One of the guides had told him the name the local people used, but he could not remember what the man had called it. In that stage of sleep, or near-sleep, the most outlandish notions seem plausible and entirely within the realm of possibility. The dreamer who finds himself in that place is hard pressed to understand why anything is impossible or ill advised.

He was not awake, although he had not been truly asleep for quite some time, when he started pondering lions and the possibility of bagging one and turning its pelt into a winter jacket. Seemed it would be easy enough, his mind told him. What? Get a rifle, some cartridges. Fill his canteen and take a handful of jerky from the stores. Why could he not drive out a few kilometers and scout for lions? The Hutus made it look no more difficult or dangerous than catching a cab late at night in certain parts of New York, say. For, he had heard that catching a cab in certain parts of New York after nightfall was a true test of a man's wit and resourcefulness. He had never been to New York City, let alone tried to catch a cab there, but he had heard all sorts of horror stories about people getting splashed, or being ignored completely, or almost getting run down by contemptuous, homicidal drivers. Yet people caught cabs in New York every single day. Since he had been here, in Kenya, he had heard tales of boys—*boys*—answering tribal custom by bringing down lions with spears. Why could he not bring one down with a Winchester? His eyes still closed, he saw lions pacing the open areas of the jungle, walking back and forth without a care and offering him a broadside shot if he had the nerve to take it. He saw lions lounging in the high grass at midday when the temperature was one hundred and twenty degrees—too hot for any living thing, even a lion, to do much more than lie down and wish it would rain. He saw lions strolling through city streets, lions swimming in pools and fountains, and lions eating in fine restaurants. He even watched a cute little stuffed lion yip and meow as it wrestled with a ball of yarn. When he realized his eyes were open and staring at the black roof of the tent, he said to himself, 'Why not? How hard could it be?'

His back felt the metal frame of the cot through the thin sleeping bag. Except for the buzz of insects, his breathing was the only sound.

He sat up and shook his head to clear it, and then he felt around in the darkness for his pants and boots. When he was dressed, he left his tent and crept to the truck where the guns were kept. From the racks, he selected a bolt-action rifle with a powerful scope, and took two handfuls of shells from an opened box. The eastern sky had changed from black to indigo, telling him there would be enough light to see by before long.

He decided he would take the newest of the three jeeps, the one he had rode in his first day in Kenya. It was tough and reliable, and he was confident it wouldn't strand him out on the veldt. He was sure they might all come running once he started it up. They might want to stop him.

He wasted no time thinking about *why* they might want to stop him. He only knew that they would and he had already made up his mind to go. He knew he could not push the heavy vehicle out of the clearing by himself, so he resolved to start it and let the clutch off quickly so that he'd be on his way while they were all deciding who should get up and look to see what was happening.

He walked around to where the trucks were parked and climbed into the jeep's high seat. Wedging the gun in next to him, he ran his hand over the dashboard until he found the ignition switch with the key still in it. Kendrick took a deep breath and turned the key.

The noise of the engine starting was like an explosion against the quiet of the countryside.

'Oh dear,' he thought, as he struggled with the gearshift and fought the jeep into reverse. It lurched backward, the powerful engine digging the wheels into the soft earth. He stopped, found the correct gear, and gripped the wheel as the tires bit into the soil a second time and sent the jeep surging forward. In a matter of minutes, he was away from the campsite and bouncing along the open grasslands that lay at the foot of Mount Kenya.

It was a glorious morning. If his wife had been here, seated beside him, he might have been able to say something pleasant to her, he thought. The broad sky rippled like a pastel river, its blue luminescence feathered and streaked with pearl-colored clouds and a double rainbow. Dark green bushes with broad, floppy leaves stooped low and glistened with dew in the growing daylight. Patches of low-lying fog hid dips in the land and swirled away from the jeep like frightened animals when it bounded through one furrow after another. The very air dripped moisture and was laden with a fresh, organic smell that soaked into his blood and energized him. How beautiful this place was. He could see now why the couple who ran the business had opted to remain here permanently.

What would his wife say if he telephoned her from Nairobi to say he was never coming home? Would she be dismayed? Surprised? Would she beg him to reconsider? Would she get on a plane herself and come to him? Would he welcome her if she did? Who knew? Who knew?

Thoughts of his wife faded as he bounced along the landscape trying to guess where lions might hide. He drove toward the rising sun for nearly an hour and found himself on an open veldt, a nearly empty plain of tall, yellow grass unbroken but for an occasional tree.

It looked very much like the type of grass lions might like.

Kendrick did not know why he was so certain, but he stopped the jeep and let the thrill run through him. The wind brushed the tall stalks back and forth. Yes, his hitherto dormant hunter's instinct told him. This was lion country. He worked the gun out of its resting place and stood up on the seat. Yes. Yes! This was where he would find his lion. He looked all around the landscape and saw nothing move except the grass. He couldn't see them, but he knew they were there. Crouching, sniffing, licking the blood from their whiskers and plotting. "Laying for him," as his grandfather would have said. He dug into his pocket and pulled out a wad of jerky. The dried meat tasted like seasoned gladiator's shoe. He tore off a tiny chunk with his eyetooth and put the rest back in his pocket. Perhaps it would taste better when he was hungry.

Perched on the seat back, he dug into his other pocket and drew out seven bullets. Kendrick knew nothing about guns except what the guides had been able to teach him. The gun he'd taken was lightweight, a manly looking weapon that had cost the owner nearly a thousand dollars but could fire only four rounds before it needed re-loading. He opened the bolt and pushed the miniature torpedoes into its dark tunnel. He worked the bolt in the opposite direction and savored the click that sent a round into the chamber.

Now locked and loaded, he felt like a great hunter in an old black-and-white movie, come to Africa to assert his dominance over her wild and beautiful lands, creatures, and native folk. He wondered what it would be like to ride in a sedan chair, high above the grass with his trusty rifle laid across his lap. He watched himself with his mind's eye, taking aim, firing at a bull elephant or a rhino that had stopped to watch him go past—a strange beast with a square body and four dark legs, each with two legs of its own farther down. The prodigious game would never know what hit them, having barely enough time to catch his scent before he felled each one with a single shot. Kendrick shifted the rifle to an awkward port arms and stepped down into the grass.

This was why he had been put on earth. This was why he lived. How sad that so much of his life had passed before he discovered the reason for his being. He was not a whipping-boy actuary in the local government of Northampton. He was not a hen-pecked husband. He was Charles K. Kendrick, Hunter, and upon this ground, he would win the respect and admiration of all who knew him, and of a great many who did not.

He crouched and took a cautious step, then another, and another. Nothing.

Not a sound except the wind. He continued moving in a straight line, staying crouched until his legs began to ache. He paused and then stood up straight. It was probably okay to stand normally, as long as he kept the gun at the ready. He checked again to make sure a round was chambered. The yellow brass of the shell casing winked in the morning sun. He scanned the horizon and sighted a far-off clump of trees.

That way, he told himself.

Kendrick fixed the location of the jeep in his mind and took off at a deliberate pace. The stand of flat-topped foliage had seemed a good deal closer than it actually was, however, he soon found himself able to pick out details of individual trees. He did not know the name of this type tree, and beyond the peculiar tops that looked as if they had been leveled by a gardener the size of Goliath, they were little different from other leafy, sturdy trees he had seen.

He felt his heart race and noticed he had begun to sweat, even though the air was still cool. Was it the short march from the jeep? Hardly, he thought. He looked down at his boots and saw they were stained a shade darker by the dew. Moisture trickled from his armpit and rolled down his temple. He took off the Pith helmet and wiped his brow. Did all serious hunters experience this? Was there some sixth sense—an early-warning system of sorts—that triggered these bodily changes to alert the hunter when his prey came into proximity? His hands shook as he drew back the bolt and checked again to make sure the bullet was in the chamber and ready. The shell casing glinted.

"On!" he said with a loud exhale. "Onward!'

After a hundred more paces toward the trees, Kendrick could make out a large, wooly ball of something nestled in the fork of a low limb.

He first thought it might be a bird's nest. And a very large bird by the look of it. Ostriches made their nests on the ground...an eagle, perhaps? Then he remembered eagles made their nests high in the rocks and used sticks instead of grass. So it wasn't an eagle's nest either.

What was it then?

He squinted severely, like a man who had forgotten his glasses, and tried to bring the thing in the tree into better focus. Something moved high in the treetop and he lifted his gaze to the upper branches. When he looked down again at the clump in the tree fork, he felt the air catch in his throat.

A long, golden brown torso stretched along the length of one of the lower branches. A stumpy finger of wood that poked out beneath the branch was not wood at all but a leg. He saw, all of a sudden, a long tail with a dark tuft at its end. His eyes moved along the animal's back, traveling all the way to the large tuft of wooly material he had first spotted. It was a mane. A fully-grown male lion had climbed the tree and stretched out on a low branch.

Kendrick's face morphed into a horrified grimace. His heart hiccupped and then pounded with such force, he was sure that he would die but that the animal would hear it first. An unbearable urge to wet himself squeezed out all thoughts but one: the horrifying realization that the lion had climbed up a tree. The massive, four-hundred pound body had been camouflaged by the leaves and the light. Now he could see it clearly, and, taking in its size, he was absolutely astounded to see it so high off the ground. Higher up than it could possibly have jumped. He could come to only one conclusion: a lion could climb a tree.

A *lion* could *climb a tree.*

It hit him like a biblical revelation. His eyes still glued to the lion's back, a startling sense of inconsequentiality, of insignificance, rolled over him like a wave. Really, what the *hell* was he doing in Africa? He was no hunter. He had not even realized a lion could climb a tree until just this moment. If that lion woke up, or smelled him....

Kendrick turned and tiptoed back the way he had come, holding the rifle in one hand like a leaky garbage bag. He had gone ten steps when he noticed a crease in the grass ahead of him. The stalks leaned out in a v-shape and twitched in a way that had nothing to do with the wind.

He pitched the rifle over his shoulder and ran in the opposite direction. He heard the grass rustle but he did not look back, not even when a throaty snarl cut the air behind him. His arms turning like a windmill, Kendrick raced into the tall grass, screaming as he went. The race continued for twenty yards, and then the earth opened up and swallowed Kendrick, to the cat's anger and utter bewilderment. One moment breakfast was only a leap away, the next instant it had vanished. She had seen gazelles do that, but this odd, tree-looking thing had been no gazelle. She stopped short when the meat disappeared, and by only the narrowest of chances did she avoid tumbling down the same hole that had snatched away her prey.

Kendrick curled into a fetal knot at the bottom of the hole and checked for broken bones, praying at the same time that the lion would not try to climb down after him. The ground was cool and damp. Roots stuck out of the walls here and there, but none seemed promising as a handhold should he try to climb out, even though climbing out was the last thing on his mind at that moment. He saw the lion walk around the hole, trying—he was sure—to figure out how to get at him. The drop was unnerving even to her, for she leaned her head down several times and dug her claws into the soft soil but pulled back when the dirt fell away. Kendrick felt the clumps of sod and tiny pebbles rain on him and shuddered each time they did.

How in God's name had he wound up here? Why wasn't he back at work, back in his cubicle where the world went on normally? How in God's name had he wound up at the bottom of a hole in Africa, with a hungry lion circling above him like a cat outside a mouse hole, wondering how to make a meal of him?

The lion disappeared and he got unsteadily to his feet. He could hear the swish of the grass above, even though the distance to the top of the hole was more than double his height. Should he try to climb out? Jesus no! He scolded himself. What sort of question was that? Of course he could not climb out. Climb out and be eaten?

He couldn't very well stay down here until he died, however. What would he eventually die of, thirst, exposure…starvation? Good God, it could take weeks for him to die of starvation.

What about the others? Surely they knew already that he was gone. Wouldn't they come out to search for him? Of course they would. Wouldn't they? Perhaps they would start searching when he did not come back this evening. That meant he would have to spend all day and all of tonight in the hole unless the lion went away and he could manage to climb out. If the others were true hunters and trackers and guides, they would be out at first light tomorrow combing the countryside. First, they would find the jeep, then eventually the hole with him in it. Maybe. What if someone was ten feet to the left or right of the hole but did not see it because of the grass? What if they only performed a half-hearted search? Or no search at all because he was just another silly, egotistical Englishman who had watched The Lion King and a hundred Tarzan movies and so thought all the wildlife in Africa would bow down to him just because he had a shiny gun and a pith helmet. Dear God.

The lion reappeared and growled into the hole. Kendrick shuddered. He could see that some of its teeth were as long as his index fingers and as sharp as the serrated edge of a steak knife. He sank to a squatting position, putting an additional three and a half feet between himself and the beast. She growled again, much louder this time and took a swipe at something Kendrick could not see. Her growl was answered by a louder, deeper, fiercer retort. The lioness took another swipe at whatever it was then leaped straight across the hole. Kendrick's stomach knotted and he felt his bowels try to surge into his shorts. The cat cleared the hole, and for a moment he saw nothing but blue sky. Then a new female leaned over the opening. Directly across from her, the maned head of a third lion—a very large, male lion—appeared and looked down at him.

* * *

"The news is bahd boss," said the Hutu man with a smirk. " 'e tuk *your* jeep, *ahnd* your *hrr*rifle."

The Excursion Coordinator, called the "Head Hunter" behind his back by his men, muttered a curse in Swahili. He had worked twenty-one years as a park ranger and game warden in the Nairobi Wildlife Preservation & Game Reserve system before going into partnership with the two Americans. Having seen far more than his share of misguided adventurers over the last eight seasons, he looked at the sky and thought again about quitting.

"My owhn, *personal hrr*ifle?"

"Yes boss. Sorry."

The man cursed once more and kicked a clump of sod with his boot.

"Shall we go to fhand 'im then?"

The boss frowned.

"Let me think about it."

* * *

'Our father who art in heaven....' Kendrick whispered to himself at the bottom of the hole.

There were now *seven* lions in all. Five females, the alpha male (which he could still hear barking despite the quarrelsome noises of the others), and a second, subordinate male clustered near the hole. Each had tried to get at him—some by lying down and extending paws in his direction, two by easing themselves an inch at a time over the lip of the precipice until they almost tumbled in. Kendrick's heart had paused and jump-started itself so many times he could no longer raise his head without feeling dizzy. When one of the cats leaped across the opening and landed only its front paws on the other side, he had cried out. It had clawed the earth and struggled until its hind legs were back on solid ground.

After an hour Kendrick was exhausted, never having been so thoroughly and unrelentingly afraid for so long in his entire life. Every fright he had ever suffered blended together would not have come close to the murderous terror of this one morning. He thought about God and his wife, about his mother. He felt pangs of longing for his desk and the oppressive coziness of his cubicle. If only he could get out of this hole in one piece. His mind looped memories of every Discovery Channel program he had ever been bored enough to sit through at home. Each time he thought there was no more fear to be squeezed out of him, one of the lions would snarl at him or send a clump of dirt tumbling onto his head. And each time he began to believe he no longer cared if they did get down there and eat him, one would peer over the edge and lick its whiskers. Depleted as he was, he sensed in his heart that he had scarcely begun to know what tired would feel like. By the time he was rescued, his body would be in a wholly different universe of exhaustion. *If* he were rescued.

31

As if he needed one more thing to think about, he began losing control of his bodily functions. He sat down gingerly, but stood up again, the effort of bending at the waist putting added pressure on the balloon inside his pelvis so that he felt it might pop any second. It was a miracle, he thought, that he had not wet himself—or worse—the instant the first lion came at him. He cursed himself again as he looked at the bottom of the hole. Whatever he put down there he would likely end up sitting in, so he had better dig a bit at the very least. Using the heel of his boot, he did precisely that, shaping a crater the size of a salad bowl in the soft earth. His insides rumbled and quaked, as if the sight of the hole had encouraged his intestines to loosen their floodgates. He looked up and then shut his eyes when he saw that four of the lions had stopped clawing at each other and were watching him. He gingerly undid his buckle and released the fastener on his pants. The large male licked its front paw and its whiskers. Kendrick eased the zipper down and, feeling oddly like a zoo animal, squatted over his hole.

At the first sound, the male stood up and rumbled, and then they were all clustered around the hole again. He had never felt so peculiar in all his life and he wondered if it would feel any different to lower his pants and climb into the fountain in the downtown square back home. The male barked at him, and a chorus of growls went around the pride. He wished he could stop, but his body was on autopilot now, and he was only along for the ride. Their noise grew, and it became obvious that by relieving himself he had given them new resolve. It seemed one of them would fall—or finally jump—in on top of him any second now. He hunched his shoulders and covered his head with his arms when an ear-splitting roar sounded and made his heart skip another beat. He had always assumed it was the smell of blood that sent wild animals into a killing frenzy. Who knew it was this smell? The growling intensified—grew into full-fledged, full-bodied, full-throated roars. They were fighting! *'Oh Jesus God...'* He heard savagery and murder in the chaos above his head. Rocks, dirt, and tufts of grass rained down on him. He was afraid to close his eyes, and doubly afraid to look up.

Then it happened.

He was already as low in the hole as he could get without lying down. A sudden rain of noise and dirt made his muscles tighten and forced his body into an even smaller knot just before the weight came crashing down on top of him. His scream was stifled by the avalanche of animal smell and hot fur, by the crushing bulk that landed square on his back and drove the air out of his lungs while it mashed him into the mud he'd created.

* * *

Three of the men had taken a second jeep and set out on the trail of the first after a breakfast that was longer and much more leisurely than what the Head Hunter normally allowed them. By the time they left camp, the sun had claimed the sky completely and was beating the savannah with all its strength. Once they set out, it took them less than an hour to find the abandoned jeep.

The missing man's trail pointed from it in a straight line to a stand of trees in the distance. All three shook their heads knowing that the fool must be off playing "Great-White-Hunter" or some derivation thereof, and wondering if the Head Hunter would send the idiot home and keep his money. When they came to the spot where lion spoor crossed the man's trail, they shook their heads again, knowingly and with more seriousness this time. They also took a moment to make their own rifles ready, just in case. The Hutu saw the lions first, saw and heard them tussling over something hidden by the grass, and assumed he would have to search through the mess of remains to find some identifiable trinket that could be sent back to the man's wife. He noticed, though, that there was no blood on the animals coats or faces and tried to calculate if they had already had time to eat the man and clean themselves.

The driver stopped the jeep while they were still thirty yards away. The Hutu nodded to the man in the back seat, who then stood with his rifle and drew a bead on a female standing in profile. The man squeezed the trigger, felt the kick of the rifle, and was startled to see the lion pitch over and disappear from sight.

They drove the pride off by firing into the air while the driver revved the engine and honked the horn. The big cats, annoyed by the racket, and temporarily cowed by the sudden loss of one of their number, began moving away. When the last one disappeared in a shimmer of heat and waving grass, the men climbed down from the vehicle and walked to the spot the animals had abandoned.

A hole.

The Hutu surveyed the crushed vegetation and clawed earth. Not a drop of blood anywhere. He stepped carefully to the edge of the hole and looked down into its depths. A pair of eyes blinked up at him.

"Mr. Kendrick!" he said loudly, "what have you done with the boss' *hrr*rifle?"

3.
The Big Finish

I t came to him in a dream. Just as Handel's *Messiah* revealed itself during a nap, just as Coleridge had dreamed *"Kublai Khan,"* and just as Bohr saw the structure of the atom in a dream, he first saw it all in the sable corridors of sleep. On the morning that his greatest work was conceived, on the day that would give birth to his magnum opus, Marty Larkmon, composer, conductor, and borderline genius, sat straight up in his bed and said: "Wow!"

"Wow!" he said again, remembering vivid colors and rhapsodic harmonies pouring from an orchestra under his baton and filling the world with music and light. He heard in his mind the thunderous roar of thousands, upon thousands, upon thousands of people clapping and shouting a standing ovation that went on and on for nearly an hour.

"Ho-lleeee Jesus!"

He threw back the sheet and scrambled out of bed, stepping into the cereal bowl he had left on the floor the night before. He dug up the telephone and punched in a number.

A sleepy, female voice answered.

"Honey, guess what!" he said excitedly.

"What is it Marty?" the woman mewed in mild irritation.

"I HAVE IT!" he shouted.

"Oh my God!" He heard her sit up. "Do I have it too? How do you know? I swear it wasn't me, Marty! I'd never—!"

"No, no! I've had an inspiration. It's huge! It's so big, even I don't believe it."

An exasperated sigh wafted through the receiver. "That's great Marty. Call me when the check comes."

The phone went dead in his ear, but he was too caught up in the fever of inspiration to care about her sarcasm and rudeness. She'd find out.

He dressed quickly and grabbed his composition notebooks, the ones that had all the little lines and spaces printed and ready for an inspired hand. He ran out of the door, realized he had neither his coat, nor his keys, and ran back in. He had to hurry to Orchestra Hall before the freshness of the vision wore off.

Late that evening he was a trembling wreck. He had sat in a tiny, soundproof room for almost sixteen hours and had not had food, drink, rest, or fresh air the entire time. The room's only furnishings were an upright piano, a stool, and a near empty wastebasket. He had pulled a ketchup-smeared McDonald's bag from the wastebasket, flattened it out, and written on it when every inch of every page of the composition notebooks—including the inside and outside of the front and back covers—had been decorated with musical notation and stage directions.

It was precisely eleven-thirty p.m. when he slid from the piano bench to the floor and burst into tears. The sore, cramped fingers of his right hand shook as he wiped at his face and hugged the notebooks and the white paper bag to his chest. He struggled to his feet and kissed the ink pen that had served him so well and then, stumbling out of the building, made his way to a nearby bus stop, having forgotten where his car was parked and feeling too weak to drive anyway.

Six days later, Marty walked into the Music Director's office carrying the finished score like a holy relic. He laid it gently on the velvet blotter, his eyes damp with emotion, and said, "When you have time" and then turned to leave. Outside the building, he broke into a bright, bubbly laugh, and then he broke into tears again, so full was he with the joy of being alive.

It was hard being a genius.

Marty was in his late thirties and had suffered the stigma of unusually high intelligence and astounding creativity his entire life. Like geniuses throughout history, he had been scorned, cut out, and marginalized by children and adults as far back as he could remember. He was only nine years old when a knuckle dragging, mouth-breather of a graduate intern at his elementary school had given him an IQ test and botched the math when she calculated the score. Adding insult to injury, she had marked the boy down on his written response because the handwriting was unnecessarily loopy and somewhat effeminate. As a result, Marty had placed a meager one half of a percentage point below the exalted *American Academy of Perspicacious Excellence*'s cutoff score for certifiable genius. As the boy grew, he obsessed over what turned out to be the defining event of his childhood. In time, he came to despise psychologists with a passion that could only be expressed in guttural Klingon slang.

Like the greatest of great thinkers and creators, Marty had an unshakable faith in the soundness of his ideas. He had always believed he was put on Earth to accomplish something groundbreaking, awe-inspiring—something that would shake the world to its very foundation. This new work of his–his first full symphony–had to be the thing. The Music Director would already have examined the score, and by the time Marty reached home, the man would have called and left a message on the answering machine.

"Marty, you're a genius!" the Director would exclaim. "I—I—I…" or some similar nonsense would follow, then he would say, "I am calling together the appropriations committee as I speak so that they can begin to arrange funding! Call back on my private line the moment you get this message!"

A broad smile blanketed his face. Life was grand beyond measure.

"Marty!" The Director's British accent leaped out of the answering machine. "You must have lost your bleeding mind! We've had some damn-fool ideas from you before, but this...this is...! You should immediately seek medical help my boy! I doubt rather seriously that we will be able to renew your contract at the end of the season."

There was a long "peeeeeep" and then a mechanical voice saying "No-more-messages."

Marty was puzzled. How could the man have said such a thing? How could he not have appreciated the vision that created this work? This could be the greatest performance ever conceived. Couldn't the man see that? He hefted his copy of the score, which lay on the coffee table. The typeface was plain, the page unadorned, but the words, the words embodied such strength, wielded such power, conveyed such learned authority:

Manfred Phillip Morganthol Larkmon
Symphony No.1 in A-Sharp minor, Opus 16:
"A Bloody Mess"

He flipped it open to the introduction.
It would cost a lot of money.
An awful lot.
And it would be big.
Very, very, big.
This was bigger than anything ever dreamed of, let alone attempted. Mahler, Wagner, Tchaikovsky, Strauss, none of the great composers, even those who had loved lavish productions and great, big, stupefying sets could come close to this. For starters, Marty would need a one thousand-piece orchestra and a choir of no less than four thousand singers. The piece would unfold in two astounding parts, two strikingly original dramatic performances that would give physical form to the music and add the critical sensory dimensions of movement, ambient sound, and smell to it. The first phase involved a one-hour motion picture, the second a live action set-piece battle that would be talked about for decades to come. He would need an entire regiment of Abram's M-1A1 main battle tanks and a squadron of armed AH-64 Apache helicopter gunships. He

would need seating for two hundred and fifty thousand people, and at least one and a half square miles of open ground. Last but not least, he would need one low-yield thermonuclear weapon with a hand-held, remote detonator.

Perhaps he should go to the funding committee himself.

It was no matter that one man didn't believe. Life was still good.

* * *

The following Monday, he sat outside a conference room and whistled while the orchestra's appropriations committee reviewed his proposal. Inside the room, the eight men and women read it, promptly tore it up, and slipped quietly out a side door. An hour passed before Marty realized they had ditched him.

He was seized for an instant by an emotion that was alien to him—despair. That people whom he knew and had worked alongside for season after season should abandon him. That they should mock him and vandalize his score.... That they should turn on him so abruptly and unjustly.

Then he became furious. Furious and more determined than ever. He had not expected his groundbreaking work to run up against such closed-mindedness. Each time Marty looked into a mirror (or any really shiny surface) he saw the flame of genius blazing behind his eyes, blazing and yearning for outward expression. He pounded his fist into his palm. With God as his witness, he would not cease. He would not give in to naysayers and Philistines, to people so shortsighted they might as well be blind. He would find a way, and his music would be heard in the end.

It so happened that that very night he saw a taped interview with the billionaire tycoon and philanthropist Mo Earl. Sullen and disgusted, Marty watched while his girlfriend did her nails. When the oil magnate (who was just under five and a half feet tall and who actually wore a white hat) agreed that arts and humanities were important for school children, the genius in Marty stood up.

"I've got it," he said.

"Again?" said his girlfriend.

"I'm going to call Mo Earl."

"Sure you are."

"Watch me," he said.

"For God's sake." She got her purse. "Let me know when the check comes."

The check came three weeks later. A big check. With a long letter signed by Mo Earl himself. He would back Marty with every resource at his disposal. He would stand beside him and march in lockstep for as long as Marty needed him. He would make public service announcements. He would urge his friends to invest. He would have to claim at least seventy percent of the gross receipts to offset his risk, but the lawyers could work all that out.

Marty read on.

Earl's company, Continental Oil, was sending a team to help with the legwork. The enclosed check was made out to Marty for three hundred thousand dollars and was meant to get him started. Marty just missed bashing his head against the coffee table when he fell to the floor. When he came to, he called a printing company and made arrangements to have the score mass-produced. Rehearsing, feeding, transporting all those musicians would be a logistical nightmare. Turning it over in his mind, he could not contain his joy.

One week later he met Mo Earl in person, and the two of them stood on a gently sloping hillside overlooking the lower sixty thousand acres of Earl's Montana ranch. Through high-powered binoculars, Marty spotted a butte several miles away. The ground between this slope and that pillar of rock was perfectly flat, and the rolling hillside on which he stood stretched away from him in both directions and curved until it enclosed the ground on three sides. It was a box canyon, Earl told him, and it would make a natural arena.

Perfect.

He would put the orchestra and choir here on the northern slope. The audience would occupy the eastern and western slopes. A shuttle bus system, lots and lots and lots of port-o-johns and waste receptacles, souvenir booths and concession stands, first-aid stations—it would work. It would all work like a charm. The minor details had fallen smoothly into place.

The major details were another matter.

Marty's procurement committee ran into trouble on the tenth day. Forming the thousand-piece orchestra had been a breeze. Finding four thousand singers had been a walk in the park. The tanks were not so easy.

The United States Army wasn't Midtown Motors and did not sell its tanks to just anyone who walked in off the street. It never had, and it never would, and forget what you heard in the liberal, fag media. It most assuredly would not sell to persons in the private sector. Not even the oldest, most dilapidated tanks in its inventory. Not even for a landmark theatrical production. Not if Shakespeare, Mozart, and Pavarotti came in together and signed for them. Not "no," but "hell no." And get the hell off this base unless you want to talk to the MPs.

Buying a low-yield nuclear weapon had been even harder. Agents from the FBI, the Nuclear Regulatory Commission, and half a dozen other government agencies questioned the Continental Oil people for a week and a half non-stop. After their tax returns, their credit records, their college transcripts, their driving records, their medical records, their high school exit exam records, and several other aspects of their personal histories had been checked and re-checked, they were forced to say the Pledge of Allegiance over and over again and sign loyalty oaths before being released on their own recognizance.

It was Mo Earl who suggested they try one of the wealthy but politically unstable nations of the third world. It turned out that a number of these nations had hopes and dreams for low and medium yield nuclear devices, but none had ever been able to get its hands on fissile material or a good set of plans.

It seemed they had run into an impassable roadblock.

Marty was highly bothered and ready to switch to dynamite and converted earth-moving equipment when, out of nowhere, the tank buyers made a breakthrough.

A disgruntled General in the Ukrainian army made an entire regiment of cold-war era Soviet T-62 tanks and other vehicles available along with a detachment of helicopter gunships at what he thought was a very fair price. For a few dollars more, he would throw in the crews to operate them. For a mere fifteen million additional U.S. dollars, he tapped his contacts in Moscow and came up with a bonafied, honest-to-goodness, 1-kiloton battlefield nuclear weapon and an out-of-work defense ministry engineer who wired the device so that it could be armed and detonated with a simple, universal television remote control. At first, no one believed this could be done. The engineer explained four simple modifications to the electronic detonator within the bomb and explained that they would, of course, need an intermediary receiving station to boost the signal and then transmit it to the warhead. But if control and precise timing were what they wanted, this would give it to them, and if they still doubted it would work, just give him a thirty-minute head start and then push the button. Someone asked him why not a simple black box with one red button or something like that instead of a television remote control. He told them they could do it themselves if they didn't like his idea, and that settled the matter.

Marty was drunk with joy.

In the months that followed, he flew to every major U.S. city and rehearsed with individual groups. On the night of the performance, he would conduct and direct both choir and orchestra from a podium raised high into the air. The motion picture would reveal the origins of the great conflict explored in the music. Gigantic, football-field sized rectangular screens spaced around the floor of the canyon would show the movie drive-in style, and when it was done, a squad of tanks (with the help of explosive charges placed in the support posts of each screen) would tear the screens down and leave an unobstructed view of the open ground that would serve as the battlefield in part two. The opposing armored forces, along with their supporting helicopter gunships, would then mix it up in real time using genuine, high-impact training ammunition. There would be real fires, real smoke, real damage, and real injuries if someone got careless. The audience would be up on the canyon's sloping sides, so maybe none of them would get hurt. The nuclear device (which Marty nicknamed "The Big Finish") would be placed on the very top of the far-off rock formation he had spotted, and Marty himself would detonate it at the climax of the battle. Knowing he was dealing with a modern audience, he had carefully structured the piece so that it ran exactly ninety minutes. Even greatness had to bow to the short attention span.

Continental Oil hired several independent consultants to study the potential effects of a hypothetical, above ground nuclear explosion on the unspoiled plains of northern Montana. They wanted a guarantee that the crowds of spectators would be safe, and that there would be no long-term damage to the environment. Each consultant they contacted was happy to provide whatever assurance the company wanted so long as it was done on condition of anonymity.

In all, nearly two thousand VIPs from government, industry, academia, the arts, the sports world, and the world of entertainment were invited as distinguished guests. The remaining two hundred forty-eight thousand tickets would go to paying customers. Mo Earl and Continental Oil could not contain their joy when they added up the potential profits from ads and merchandising. There would be so much bonus money floating around, even the window washers would have to hire accountants.

* * *

Because of Continental Oil's media blitz, the nearly quarter-million tickets sold to the general public were snapped up in just under sixteen hours. By chance, sixteen hours was about how long it had taken Marty to pen the first draft of the symphony. Knowing it meant nothing, but seeing a chance to draw in even more paying customers, Continental Oil played up the coincidence and offered another sixteen thousand tickets at auction. These too sold out in record time.

* * *

Nine months after the dream, and six weeks to the day after the first ticket went on sale; Marty dragged himself to the mirror and checked to make sure the flame of genius was still burning in his eyes. Immortality was still several hours away and already he had gone a day without food and three days without sleep, subsisting entirely on coffee and Rolaids. The alternating bouts of crushing fatigue and caffeine-induced euphoria left him in a perpetual daze. But all was in place; every detail had been checked, rechecked, and checked again until there was nothing left to do except wait for that day's sun to go down.

The fact that nothing could possibly go wrong meant without a doubt that something would. Marty, who should have been sound asleep in his suite of rooms in the Earl Mansion, decided shortly after one p.m. that he would fly over the area and inspect the preparations. His advisors assured him there were already enough people doing exactly that, but Marty was adamant. A helicopter was made available, and Marty found himself darting over swelling crowds of spectators, hovering above swarms of men climbing over helicopters and armored vehicles like ants over chunks of bread. Things were fine until he ordered his pilot to land. He wanted, he said, to talk to the soldiers up close and give them some last-minute pointers on creating dramatic effect from inside the tanks. Every soldier he talked to listened and grunted until Marty moved on to the next man. They had no idea who he was because he had no entourage with him, only the helicopter pilot. He had reached the fifteenth vehicle in a long line of gigantic, ferocious-looking machines when the man in charge of it told him in Russian to shut the fuck up and get away from his crew so they could get some work done.

Marty—who understood Russian—was shocked and infuriated into complete silence. When they got back to the helicopter, he found his voice, got someone on the radio, and shouted into the microphone until whoever he was talking to agreed to come out and fire the offending tank commander. When the soldier reported that he had been fired, all the men in his crew rebelled, and their rebellion spread until someone called back to production headquarters and told them that if one man was tossed off the set, they would all walk. Marty, who was again airborne by that time, screamed and beat his head against the helicopter door. All right goddammit. They had him, but he wanted that man's name. He would deal with him *mano a mano* once the show was over.

He had the pilot set down twice more, each time among the civilian spectators. He felt like a god, despite the rudeness of the soldier whom he was sure as hell going to set straight just as soon as he left the podium tonight. And like a god, he felt duty bound to descend and walk among his followers, allowing those who were most awed to bask in his actual presence. There must be thousands who ached to ask him questions about his vision, and he imagined it the height of arrogance to keep himself aloof from them. On the chopper's second landing, he saw every size, shape, color, ethnicity and walk of life among the unbelievable numbers who gazed skyward with mild wonder as the vehicle slowed and hovered, and who then scattered when it lowered itself onto a patch of green that, moments before, had been the sight of a touch football game. Through the windshield, Marty saw people pointing at the helicopter. Someone even jumped up and down and waved both arms. They knew who he was. They knew him and they were excited because he had chosen to land among them. He was awed, because he did not think his face so easily recognizable. His name, of course, but not his face. Yet they knew him, and they loved him, and as the blades stopped spinning, they came across the grass toward him. He got out of the helicopter and walked toward them with his arms outstretched, ready to embrace them all and be smothered in their embraces. A beautiful black woman in denim short shorts with a tie-dyed tee shirt knotted above her belly button led the approaching group. Marty wondered if she, under the influence of his god-like visage, would sprawl on the grass and offer herself to him. He was not sure he should take her right out here in public, but if she really wanted to be taken, they could be back at the Earl Mansion in a matter of minutes.

"Hey you moron!" the woman shouted from several yards away. Marty froze. "You could've killed somebody!"

"Whaaa--??"

"Idiot!"

"Asshole!" someone else shouted.

A football flew past his head.

The crowd broke into a run and came at him. Something inside his head shook him awake and he darted back to the helicopter.

"What the hell'd you say to 'em?" the pilot asked as people banged on the windshield.

Marty made him take off and put down again, in a safe area this time, and then he walked to one of the many areas where rows of concession stands sold souvenirs and food.

A much more conservative Marty approached a large group of people who had watched him walk from the helicopter. Smiling his best, he held out his hand and introduced himself to the first couple he came too, a pair of seniors standing in line for ice cream.

"Hi. I'm Marty Larkmon."

The man and woman glanced at each other.

"Marty Larkmon," Marty said again, still smiling his best. A few people nodded; others began turning away.

"Well, good to meet you," the elder man said. "I'm Sam Greenberg, and this is my wife Sally." Marty shook hands with the woman.

Marty and the Greenbergs stood there awhile and waited for the line to move. Finally Sam said, "Well, we've got to go," and took his wife's hand and pulled her away. "You enjoy the show now." They left, and the other people continued ignoring him. Flicking an embarrassed wave to no one in particular, he turned and went dejectedly back to the helicopter. Once he was aboard and the craft took off, his heart sank into his shoes. This was nothing more than a day at a theme park to these people.

The helicopter flew low over the crowds, and he could see where a college fraternity had scraped out a shallow pit for a female mud wrestling tournament. A throng of peace activists had chained themselves together in front of the VIP grandstand and thrown red paint all over its walls and all over the ground in front of it. These were just two of the things he saw as he flew from one end of the arena to the other.

He watched these and other goings on, and prickly heat began to bite beneath his collar.

It was more than the fact they were indifferent, even hostile, to him. It was more than the legions of opportunists about, using his performance to further their own agendas. It was more than the reality of temperamental soldiers and their pretend dedication to his endeavor. It was the fact that they—every accursed soul out here–had put his music second to picnicking and tee-shirts and things of that nature. Here they were, mere hours from witnessing an unprecedented performance, about to listen to the first ever, and quite possibly the *only* ever, live performance of the most important piece of music he, Marty Larkmon, had ever created. And all they could think about were hot dogs.

Profound anger swept over him.

"Goddamn it…" he muttered, "I'm the reason they're here." His lips quivered; his hands clinched and unclenched. His skin reddened.

He grabbed the pilots arm, sending the helicopter into a steep bank. "I'm the goddamned reason they're here!" The pilot fought the craft back under control and regarded Marty's red face with terror. Marty turned away, lifted the handle on his door and—to the pilot's utter horror—leaned halfway out.

"I'm the freakin' reason …!" he screamed at the top of his lungs.

He told the pilot to circle the area so that he could let those sonsofbitches on the ground really know what was what. Leaning out the door again, he shouted, cursed, and poured abuse onto the oblivious heads of the people below. The pilot was all too happy to land and put Marty out at his limousine. When the composer was gone, the pilot radioed his boss and said he would quit before he would ever fly another celebrity around.

From his limo, Marty phoned around until he found the show's head of acquisitions. He was a young man fresh out of graduate school and had obviously gotten the job through nepotism. Instead of using his own name, Marty invoked the name of Mo Earl and told the man he wanted The Big Finish moved from its position on the mesa miles away and brought into the arena itself. He wanted it placed in the very center in fact, and he wanted it done right now.

"Ahb—ahb—ahhhhhb…but sir? Isn't it a…a *bomb*?"

"Of course not you idiot! Don't you read your freakin' memos?"

"But sir…"

"Are you questioning Mo Earl's judgment?"

"No sir. No sir!"

"Well then you get that goddamned package moved! On the double! Mr. Earl and I are going to do a fly-over in one hour. If we don't see that you've relocated that device, I swear to God you'll never work on this continent again!" He was screaming into the phone. "Do you read me!"

"Yes sir! Yes sir! Moving it right now sir!"

Marty slammed the phone down and went back to his rooms to wait.

* * *

Continental Oil had spared no expense in producing the show.

Continental Pictures, a wholly owned subsidiary, had snapped up last year's Best Director and all the people who had worked with her on a film that had won six Oscars. They had put together the one-hour movie segment of the performance in record time, and then screened it to hearing impaired audiences in seven states. Since the movie would have no sound of its own, it made sense to test it with people who could not hear anyway. If the story went over with the test groups, it would likely go over at the performance. And go over it did. One critic told a deaf reporter in sign language that there was so much tension in the film, if it had gone on longer than one hour he would have wet himself. That was good enough.

On the night of the show, the choreographed arrivals of various VIPs would take close to an hour. They would make a big deal of the arrival of the musicians with a long train of custom busses convoying to the arena and disembarking at the amphitheater seats built especially for them. Mo Earl and his family would arrive by helicopter along with the CEO of Continental Oil. Last of all, after the hundreds of VIPs and the thousands of musicians were in place, when the spectators had once again settled in their places on the hillsides, Marty himself would be flown in.

Among the many thousands who had had to pay for their tickets were the Music Director who had called him a nut and threatened to fire him, and the finance committee who had thrown away his proposal and not given him the courtesy of a face-to-face turn down. Earl's ad agency had done a phenomenal job of promoting the performance if not Marty himself. Across the U.S. and around the world, hundreds of thousands more people tuned in on PBS or cable and satellite pay-per-view. CNN, the BBC, and other news organizations from all over were covering the event.

With so many people involved in the unfolding production, it was exceedingly strange that no one seemed concerned about the warhead. Only two people besides Marty, it seemed, even remembered there was a warhead as time ticked away. One was the young executive, whose familial connections had gotten him his job, and the other was Bob—a pudgy regional manager from Continental Oil who had been temporarily assigned to Marty as an executive assistant. And it was Bob who took the call when the other man phoned to report the device's successful relocation.

"You moved it where?" Bob said aghast.

There was a pause.

"Uhhh, dee huh ahmmm…"

Bob felt all the blood drain from his upper body and settle around his knees.

"What is your name?" he asked slowly and quietly, so as not to further excite the stuttering man on the other end of the phone. The stuttering man hung up, raced out of his trailer, and threw himself into the first vehicle he found with keys in it. He tore away from the cluster of pre-fab buildings that served as production headquarters and headed for the interstate highway as fast as the truck would go.

Bob clutched the dead phone with a perspiring hand. He didn't know the exact time, but he could see two helicopters warming up on the manicured expanse of lawn below the balcony outside the opened window. A small group, including Mo Earl, made its way toward the nearest one. Marty stood on the other side of this bedroom suite in front of a mirror while the butler adjusted his cummerbund.

"Ahm, Marty?"

"Yeah Bob?"

"You got the remote?"

Marty patted his pants pocket.

"Got it right here."

Pause.

"Ahh…shouldn't you keep it someplace…safer?"

"Like where, Bob?"

"I could hold it for you."

Marty laughed and turned from the mirror. He gave Bob a toothy smile and said, "Now why in the world would I want to do that?" He turned back to the mirror and played with his hair, looking at Bob over his shoulder. "Shall we go?" he asked, and laughed in his throat.

Bob bolted from the room and ran out onto the balcony. He leaped over the railing, found that there was a concrete patio directly below it and not grass, then he got up and limped to the nearest helicopter, whose door was just closing. Bent at the waist, Bob waved his arms wildly and circled toward the front of the machine. A door opened, and Mo Earl leaned out gesturing furiously at the blades.

"Mr. Earl!" Bob cried, "Mr. Earl we've got to call it off! He's nuts!"

"Speak up boy, I can't hardly hear ya!" Earl shouted.

"It's the *bomb*! He's had the bomb moved into the arena!"

Earl climbed down from the helicopter.

"What in the hell are you babblin' about!"

"It's the bomb! Larkmon had the bomb moved right into the arena! He's nuts Mr. Earl. We have to stop the show!"

Mouth agape and eyes slowly widening, Earl listened as Bob told him about the phone call and what was sure to happen if Marty made it to the podium. In his mind's eye, Earl saw first the explosion, and then the entire valley disappearing into a wallowing wall of fire. He climbed back into the chopper.

"Can't ever trust city folk," he shouted to his wife, and then told the pilot, "Point this thing to'ard Canada and get me the hell outta here!"

The pilot jabbed at his ear indicating he had not heard.

"I said get this bird the hell off the ground sonny! Head north or east or some damn where but don't go near that arena!"

Bob grabbed Earl's coattail.

"Wait! You're responsible for this! You have to help me get that remote!"

"The hell I will!" Earl shouted and slammed the door on Bob's arm.

Bob howled and collapsed to the grass, cradling the injured limb between his thighs. The helicopter lifted off, and Bob struggled to his feet. He glanced backward over his shoulder and his jaw dropped when he saw Marty trotting towards him with a hammer in one hand. Bob hobbled to the second copter, opened the door, and climbed into the seat.

"Take off! Take off!"

"What the...I can't take off. I'm supposed to deliver the conductor."

Bob reached for his gun, realized he did not have one, and so grabbed the pilot with his good hand.

"The hell you will. Get this thing the hell off the ground, and head for that arena! Now!"

The pilot took Bob's arm and twisted it until he screamed and stumbled backward out of the cockpit. His foot caught on the doorframe and he tumbled to the grass. Marty stepped nimbly over him and climbed into the seat.

Bob got to his knees and grabbed the tail of Marty's tuxedo with his good hand.

"Come back here you crazy sonofabitch!"

Marty raised the hammer, considered, then tossed it out the open door and slammed the door on Bob's arm. Bob collapsed with the other wrist between his legs. The strobes beneath the helicopter blinked as it rose into the twilight. He struggled to his feet and hobbled stiff-armed back toward the mansion. He would have to find a corner that would be safe from the blast.

* * *

South of the tycoon's estate, the encroaching night was driven back by the miles of halogen lights that stretched around the arena's perimeter. Thousands more floodlights illuminated the orchestra and choir, the VIP grandstands, and the dense crowds of spectators blanketing the inner slopes of the hills. Every bug in the northwest had zeroed in on Earl's land.

They flew for fifteen minutes and circled the performance area twice. Twenty-one minutes after he sprained Bob's other wrist, Marty climbed down from the helicopter and set foot on the hallowed soil of immortal fame. He walked to the base of the three-story tall, pyramidal platform from which he would conduct and received his ivory baton from a white-gloved attendant in a full tuxedo with tails. He then disappeared through a door in the pyramid's base. Atop the structure was a broad stage with a podium at its center. As an elevator lifted Marty up the inside of the structure, a panel at its very top slid aside, allowing him to reappear moments later, poised and with great dignity, his arms hanging confidently at his sides. He paused to look all around him, and then he stepped off the lift and strode to his podium at the top of the world.

The general noise of the crowd turned into applause like the roar of a tsunami and grew louder and louder as he stood there. Marty felt the thunder in his chest and could not hear himself think after the first few seconds. It filled all his senses and flooded the deep caverns of his soul. This was it. This was it! Below him, arranged in a great semicircle like a mammoth folding fan were his orchestra and his choir. Cameras flashed across the landscape as far as the eye could see, glittering like a ripple of shooting stars. His heart overflowed. Tears pooled in his lower eyelids and spilled down his cheeks.

'You bastards,' he thought.

'You ignorant, despicable bastards.'

Not a single one of them was clapping because she appreciated Marty's genius, or because he grasped the full implications of what was about to happen. Even their applause was a programmed response. The glitterati—the celebrities, the wealthy, the famous— had come because the public's attention would be focused here tonight. The learned and the powerful had come to rub elbows with the famous. The stupid, pretentious working classes had come hoping to glimpse the wealthy and the powerful from afar. Lowest of all were the mindless cretins who had come out simply to see machines get blown up. It was Bull Run all over again. Idiots with picnic baskets sauntering out to watch the cannons fire, ignoring the fact that they would be sitting in the middle of a war.

He lifted the microphone headset from the music stand and fixed it over his ears. Then he took the remote out of his pocket and laid it next to his score.

The ocean of lights dimmed.

According to the Guinness Book of World Records, no one had ever attempted to show a movie—drive-in style or otherwise—to a quarter of a million people in one location at one time. When the words *"Years ago..."* appeared on the screens, Continental Oil and Continental Pictures were jointly credited with assembling the largest movie audience in history.

The piece began with a haunting fanfare—a cacophony of horns slammed against the night sky in rich, intricately syncopated flourishes. The notes interlaced themselves, weaving one about the other until goose bumps blossomed on the listeners' flesh. The fanfare went on for a full minute, ranging across the chromatic scale and running up and down the rows of brass instruments like a gleeful spirit released from captivity. When it came to its end, there was an instant of awed silence, then all two-hundred thousand plus spectators were cheering insanely. Five minutes elapsed, and Marty had to step away from the podium before they quieted enough for him to continue.

When he took the podium again, a smattering of applause in the distance threatened to start a new ovation, but before it could take hold, an avalanche of eight hundred male voices began a grave, rumbling, prayer-like refrain that drowned it out, sounding for the entire world like the beginnings of an earthquake.

On the screen, the worry-lined face of a gray-haired man in a dark uniform appeared. He gazed intently at a large map spread out on a table, and then he looked into the faces of a group of men standing nearby. They all looked as if they saw the end of the world coming.

The low tones dug deep into the soil and vibrated through the landscape. Marty raised his left hand, and a whirlwind of female voices enfolded the bass and baritone surges, melding with them and lifting them until the hills rang with a thirty-two part cantilevered harmony.

The image of the elderly General in gray was supplanted by that of a group of younger men in khaki, their chests and shoulders festooned with ribbons, medals, and ceremonial braid. They looked at the same map the old General had seen and grinned like wolves at a lamb's carcass.

For fifty-five minutes the audience watched both sets of men—those in gray and those in khaki—draw lines on maps, point fingers, hustle along corridors, shake their fists at televised images of one another, and stand before large windows with thoughtful expressions etched onto their faces. The silent shouting and the unheard threats and counter-threats reached the boiling point finally, and one leader spoke something into a red telephone while the other scribbled his signature on a long piece of paper and thrust it at his jack-booted aide. The audience was tense and disconcerted, as evidenced by the never-ending background chatter that Marty had not anticipated even from contemporary movie goers. A sudden, jarring bang that shut them up for half a second was followed by laughter and even more excited chatter. A second explosion, followed by a third and a fourth and then a whole series of them made the giant projection screens rock on their supports. To the audiences' utter delight, tanks began rolling out from camouflaged positions and driving straight through the screens' metal supports and steel anchor cables. All six screens went tottering to the earth like prefab buildings in a major earthquake.

Downrange on the canyon floor, sand-colored tanks began rumbling into position.

A new version of the opening hymn began. Sonorous bass and baritone voices stronger than pillars of concrete and iron rooted themselves in the very earth while cloud-like wisps of soprano splendor polished and honed them to sharp, aching beauty.

Though he tried with all his might to focus on the performers in front of him, Marty could see people waving and milling about, and he could hear quite clearly a backwash of clapping, *while* the goddamn choir was singing. He ground his teeth but kept on going.

The mesmerizing song continued until all four thousand voices in the choir were involved. He waved his arms in a wild, wind-milling gesture, and a sea of violins and oboes took up the melody, exalting it and lifting it until its glory rained on the landscape like the heavy dew of autumn. Wave after wave after wave after wave of unbelievable music pulsed out from the orchestra and rippled over the throngs. It was beautiful…even if Marty said so himself…so beautiful, and….and why the *hell* wouldn't they be quiet! Dabs of spittle collected in the corners of his mouth where bursts of air escaped his pursed lips and grinding teeth. He played on.

After several minutes, the music changed, lost its glow and effusive sparkle. An ominous chord spread through the stringed basses then found its way into the percussion and lower brass. Out of nowhere came the disembodied chop of helicopter blades, rising in volume though no helicopters could be seen. The crowds craned their necks and looked all around, then roared with approval when a phalanx of heavily armed gunships appeared above the grandstand on the northern slope and zoomed toward the canyon floor. A mighty "ooooooooooh" rose to the sky when the first red lines of tracer bullets zipped through the air. The tracers were answered by thunderclaps and powerful, reverberating bangs as tanks let loose rounds from their main guns. Dust clouds and smoke hovered above the field like a legion of phantoms. The forty-odd helicopters paired off and climbed in a long line toward the darkness above the arena lights.

Piped through hundreds of sound amplifiers, the evil music—meanwhile—grew louder, while the tanks fanned out in staggered formations. Tension seized the audience. For a moment, there was only the disturbing thrum from deep in the orchestra and the far-off growl of diesel engines. Then six helicopters swooped out of the darkness and lit up the battlefield with more tracers and with rockets this time. An entire row of tanks vanished in a cloud of smoke and dust, but even as the gunships dove, several more tanks opened up with turret-mounted machine guns.

"Aaaaaaahhhhhhhhhh…!"

"Ooooo hooo hoooooooooo…!"

Marty bit his lip. The singer who was to solo at this point stood at a microphone, but she was trying to see what was happening out on the field and missed her cue. Marty shouted a curse at the woman, who could not have heard him even if she had been paying attention. She glanced up at him finally and started her solo eight measures late.

It went on like that, the crowd "Oooooo-ing" and "Ahhhhh-ing," until Marty was ready to stab himself in the leg with the baton. The tanks and the choppers had really begun to mix it up. The reek of burning fuel and scorched metal lay over the landscape in a smoky, acrid haze that made people cough and rub their eyes. Piercing shrieks raced through the choir and the sound system when a helicopter strayed in close to the grandstand. The downdraft from the rotors was strong enough to make Marty stumble against the platform railing; it also whipped the score from the lectern and blew the lectern over.

The audience cheered.

Far downrange, a second formation of tanks appeared and took up positions behind and alongside the first. Finally, a third group emerged and opened fire on the first two. Now, the remaining helicopters that had been held in reserve were loosed, and the night exploded in an all out air-land battle. The crowd went crazy.

Marty grabbed the remote and shoved it into his pocket, then he set the lectern upright and picked the score up off the platform floor. He found his place and tried to regain control of the mammoth group. His heart sank, however, when he saw that many of them had stopped playing altogether and were craning their necks to look down the field. The dust, smoke, and flames, the thunder and the brilliant explosions that boomed from the warring machines and echoed along the canyon walls had transfixed the entire woodwind section, along with great swaths of the choir. He looked around at the spectators and, of the many thousands that he could see plainly, not a single one was paying attention to the music. He saw towels spinning like propeller blades, places where something that looked like "the wave" was happening. Even in the VIP grandstands, hundreds of people were on their feet pointing and gesturing, shouting, cheering—doing everything but listening.

That was it.

That was the last goddamned straw.

The anger coursed through him and set his skin ablaze. His blood boiled like the inside of a pressure cooker. He tore off his jacket and flung it over the side of the platform. He broke the baton in two and flung the pieces at the choir. Grabbing his score from the lectern, he ripped out pages by the handful. When he could not tear the binding in half, he hurled it to the floor and then kicked it over the side. He hefted the lectern and pitched it over the side.

Having seen the jacket go fluttering to the ground, many of the musicians who had zoned out came back to their senses and re-focused on the conductor. They quickly melded back into a performing entity and continued Marty's masterpiece of despair, which was absolutely heartrending to anyone who could hear it over the noise of the crowd and the battle.

Marty's hair was wild and drenched with sweat; sweat was in his eyes and on his tongue. Shouting curses at the orchestra, the choir, and the audience, he raised his fists to the sky and let out what (in a quieter place) would have been an earsplitting howl. That sound was carried away in the torrent of music that swelled up the canyon walls, cascaded over the grassy hilltops, and flooded the darkened countryside beyond. His jaw set, he took out the remote, pointed it, and hit the power button. He punched in the first set of numbers to awaken the transmitter and send the power-on signal to the device.

He punched in the second set of numbers that told the device to arm itself.

The orchestra plowed headlong into the finale without Marty's guidance. The music writhed and contorted like a chemical fire; it surged through him and fried his nerves, boiled away his insides. Broken by rage, unable to contain his fury, he threw back his head, pointed the remote at the transmitter, and pressed the last three buttons: one…zero…ONE!

Nothing happened.

He looked at the remote, shook it, slapped it against his palm.

He tried again.

One…zero…one—holding the last button down with both thumbs. The orchestra and choir gave up trying to follow him because interpretive dance had never come up in the rehearsals and his jerking about was murdering their timing.

Marty had forgotten the orchestra. He shook the remote and pounded it furiously, squeezed it in a death grip. Why didn't it work! Why was the red light not coming on! Why—! He flipped it over and found the little latch on the bottom. He pushed down on the arrow and watched the little door pop out.

No batteries!

No freaking batteries!!!

He hurled the plastic device to the podium and jumped up and down on it with both feet. His music rose higher and higher in the night, swelling in an ever more heartbreaking crescendo until a single, dramatic chord hung in the smoky air. The sound broke off, repeated itself once, and then faded away into the night. Marty sank to his knees and wept. Something had told him to buy batteries.

It was the greatest standing ovation ever given. The Canadian Prime Minister wiped tears from his eyes and told his staff to have someone approach Marty about becoming a Canadian citizen. A noted scholar and music critic proclaimed in a post-performance interview that Marty Larkmon must be the world's greatest living composer. Three members of the Nobel Committee, each of whom had watched the performance via satellite, wrote independent proposals suggesting that a new category, Arts and Entertainment, be added to the achievements for which the Prize is given, and suggested that Marty Larkmon should be its first recipient. A Playboy Playmate (who had posed for the upcoming centerfold atop a tank turret) and a Penthouse Pet (who had posed beside a helicopter) got into a cat fight when each heard the other say that she wanted to be artificially inseminated and bear Marty's child. The stage technician who retrieved Marty's jacket after he hurled it from the podium smuggled it out of the arena and sold it to a fence, who eventually ransomed it back to the Metropolitan Symphony Orchestra (of which Marty was made Music Director and Composer-in-Residence) for an undisclosed sum. It was later enshrined in the lobby of Orchestra Hall. Continental Pictures fell to work the very next day producing "A Bloody Mess: The Life of Marty Larkmon," with Tom Cruise as Marty and Paul Newman as Mo Earl.

"The Big Finish" was airlifted to a spot several hundred miles north of the Hawaiian Islands and detonated on the sea floor. Scientists said an underwater volcano caused the sudden seismic disturbance. Everyone who knew better was smart enough to keep quiet.

The awards, the gifts, and the fan mail that poured into his office helped Marty get over his disappointment at how the evening had turned out. After gauging the reactions of groups around the world, the National Endowment for the Humanities published a paper that concluded Marty had indeed created a new art form, one that combined elements of grand opera, the traditional symphony, performance art, and motion pictures. Sadly, it was too big and dangerous for anyone to ever do it again. They agreed that in a single evening he had become one of the most important musical figures of the twenty-first century, adding that he probably had no idea how close he had come to making his name a permanent part of world history.

And when he read that last part, Marty could not deny himself a full-bodied roar of hysterical laughter.

4.
A Child is Given

Still wearing her bedroom slippers, Carrie Neal closed the door to her apartment and waited to hear it lock. This was a secure building but a person could never be too careful. The tall, carbon fiber-based composite panel was actually stronger than steel, and its polyurethane outer surface projected the 3-D appearance of an oak door, right down to the varnished grain and three-dimensional brass numbers that floated above its surface. Only by touching the door could one tell it was actually a flat surface. From the inside, she could make the door project a full-length image of the person standing in the hallway, a feature that made it much easier to decide not to answer certain knocks. As she listened, a mechanism whirred inside the panel, sliding the lock into place and causing the green LED above the knob to flash. Satisfied, Carrie walked to the end of the corridor and clip-clopped down the echoing stairwell. She figured she could be halfway to the first floor by the time the elevator arrived, even at this time of day. Besides, walking helped her prepare herself.

She was chanting under her breath when she reached the rows of mailboxes in the building's lobby. In the first week of waiting for a final yea or nay, she discovered that saying the words "it-is-not-there...it-is-not-there..." got her ready; it turned down the gain on her expectations and blunted the hurt she felt each time she opened the box. The whole chanting thing was contrived and went against her true wish—to see a gold-colored envelope with her and her husband's names on it—but it seemed to work, so she kept it up. There was no doubt they would be approved. They met every single criterion and passed every test with flying colors. Still, dread hung over their lives like a jungle canopy, and disappointment crouched inside the mailbox every day, waiting to grab her when she reached in.

Why the hell was it taking so long for their confirmation to arrive? She would open the box and find crap from every corner of the earth, everything but the coveted golden envelope, and it made her want to scream and tear her hair out. It was all she could do some days to keep from ramming the box back into the wall and ripping up whatever mail she did find. Why did they do this to people? Why not send an ordinary electronic notification? Why not a telephone call? Even a call with a pre-recorded message would be better than waiting weeks and weeks and weeks for a paper envelope that could be lost, stolen, misdirected, or God knew what else. If a person tried to submit an income tax return or a passport application on paper, not only would she have been laughed at, she almost certainly would have been fined. So why did the most important notice the government sent out get mailed in a stupid paper envelope? It was a mystery right up there with the meaning of life. Carrie did not like bad-mouthing the government, but the whole thing was ass-backward. Why didn't they just send the things out on horseback?

"It-is-not-there...it-is-not-there...it-is-not-there..."

She stopped at her box and took a deep breath. Placing the pads of her fingers in the recessed slot that also served as a handle, she waited until she felt the lock release then pulled the aluminum door toward her. The mail slot tilted forward, and she stuck her hand inside.

"It-is-not-..."

Her fingers touched a single envelope, which she lifted out.

"…there."

The holographic postmark of the United States Government glinted in the light flooding the lobby. A jolt raced up her arm and coursed through her body, slamming her heart into high gear and sending waves of weakness through her legs and feet. Tears pooled in her eyes and blurred her vision before she could blink them away. She eased herself to the floor and pressed the envelope to her breasts, holding in the wild thrills that caromed through her.

"Mrs. Neal?"

A gruff voice spoke from her left. He was a middle-aged Caucasian man in dark blue coveralls pushing a utility cart full of potted plants and gardening tools. One of the maintenance workers, he had stepped off the freight elevator in time to see her slide to the floor.

Carrie recognized him. She held up the envelope, unable to speak.

The man blinked twice, and his blue eyes widened when he realized what she was holding.

"Oh my goodness," he said, letting go of the cart's handle. He knelt, stripping off a soiled glove, and placed his hand on her shoulder. "M-y-y goodness! Well you let me be the first…"

He gave her an awkward hug and then helped her to her feet. "Now you calm yourself, young lady. You got plenty of time to celebrate. Don't go making yourself sick." His face was ruddy and wrinkled, as if he had spent years frowning at broken winches on a sailing ship. His kindness struck a note inside her, and she tried to breathe deeply as she raised herself from the floor.

"I'm all right," she said once she was standing. "Really, I am."

"Can I get you anything?"

She shook her head "no" and wiped her nose.

"I'm okay."

Inside the apartment, she sat down at the dining room table and played with the idea of not opening the envelope until her husband got home. He would be in the city until well after six. But this was the biggest, the most momentous day of their lives; this was something they should share.

Even as she considered it, she knew there was no way she could hold out. He'd understand. He'd do the same thing if they were in each other's places, she figured. With trembling hands and infinite care, she worked the flap up, careful not to tear the envelope or damage the precious document it contained—a single sheet of heavy bond paper marbled with latte' colored wisps and bearing a government watermark. She drew a tissue from the box on the table and wiped her nose again. The letter read:

United States Department of Population and Demographics
Bureau of Reproductive Licensing
Washington, D.C. 20010-8692-77-1

Mr. and Mrs. Christopher and Carrie Neal, Case No. 6040119-5995
1500 5th Avenue #16
New York, NY 11213-1601-34

February 22, 2094

Dear Mr. and Mrs. Neal:

After careful review and evaluation, your application for authorization to conceive and parent an offspring is approved, and you are hereby authorized to obtain immediately all reasonable medical assistance necessary for successful conception.

You must report to the B.R.L. Regional Office located at 1 Empire State Building within forty- eight hours of receipt of this letter to be photographed and to have your permit and license issued. Please call the telephone number below for a list of documents and other items to bring with you. Congratulations on your approval and best wishes.

L.G. Harrow
Director of Reproductive Licensing

H. Monroe Silverdine
Secretary of Population and Demographics

The raised seal glittered under the track lighting. She hugged the letter with both hands, rejoicing in the soulless, utilitarian odor of government stationary. Whom should she call first? Her husband or her mother?

She was blinking, nearly batting her eyelashes, when his face appeared on the screen, and he thought for a moment that she had called to flirt with him. When she held the letter up for him to see, making sure the raised seal was visible, he reacted with stunned silence, then a yell tore out of the small screen. Faces crowded in behind his, then she saw him spin around in his chair. People whom Carrie had never met sent her glowing smiles and warm congratulations. A young woman waved her congratulations from across the room and turned her face away after doing so.

These announcements always spread a bittersweet cloud. Invariably, people with children and those who had won approval celebrated with the new licensees, while those who had been denied coped visibly with the pain of having that wound re-opened.

She watched her husband gather his things even as his coworkers patted him on the back. He blew her a kiss and told her he'd get a cab rather than wait for the train. If there were one to be had in the middle of the day, he'd be home in a couple of hours. After they hung up, she called her mother.

Carrie was in a golden glow by afternoon. She sailed through the apartment dusting and polishing everything her dust cloth could reach, humming as she went. She even pulled out the stepladder and dusted the cameras.

The bathroom camera was mounted in a corner above the tub, so she had trouble reaching it. After a moment's consideration, she climbed onto the side of the tub and grasped the mount with her free hand. Leaning against the wall for balance, she wiped the dust off the top and polished the lens, moving the camera slightly as she did so. A sharp, steady beep sounded up the hall in the living room. She climbed down with a sigh and walked out to the wall-mounted screen above the old-fashioned telephone table in the front hallway. The word "RECEIVE" blinked at her from a pale blue background. She touched the screen and the beeping stopped. The letters ghosted into the background and were replaced by a message:

"[cdx773-1] ZONE: BthR2—CAMERA HAS BEEN REORIENTED. DO YOU NEED ASSISTANCE?"

The screen waited.

She touched "NO" and waited while it flickered.

"THANK YOU" appeared after a pause.

The screen went dark.

Jesus Christ.

She hated that damn thing. Let a fly land on any camera in the house and it would start honking like a goose in a bear trap. If you took a hot shower and steamed up the bathroom the first thing you'd likely hear coming out was this thing cheeping and chirping. It was nerve wracking. And if you didn't respond to it, uniforms would be at your door in five minutes. The federal home monitoring law was up for renewal next year and would not only pass, but would likely be expanded. Carrie sighed and shook her head. The price one paid to live in a child-safe country.

Standing in the spotless kitchen a half hour later, she recalled for some reason that as a teenager, she had always felt a vague uneasiness when she undressed to take a bath. Oddly enough, the bedroom camera had never bothered her. No normal person paid any attention to a bedroom camera, she guessed. But the bathroom camera was different. Maybe it was because the bathroom was smaller, because it had no windows and felt like a cave. She'd had no idea really. But every night from the time her breasts had started to develop, Carrie had felt things crawling over her skin when she disrobed under its eye. She had been sixteen and a half when she finally told her parents about the feelings. The therapy had been brief and highly effective. Her quiet dread of being alone in the bathroom with the camera watching had faded into memory, until recently.

Despite her own past difficulty, she had supported any and every measure the government took to protect children, including home monitoring. Yet, it had bothered her to hear last week that lawmakers were closer to outlawing privacy walls around toilets. The lowly toilet cubicle was—under current law—the only indoor place that was exempt from monitoring. The back of Carrie's mind had already begun turning over the idea that she might someday have to go back into therapy.

She took a bottle of wine from a low cabinet and placed it in the fridge. After tomorrow, it would be a long, long time before she was allowed to drink again. Taking a head of lettuce from the crisper, she plunked it into the sink. If the Government *really* wanted to watch her pee... She supposed she would learn to live with it. The child-safety benefit was worth the additional sacrifice.

In some countries, even some English-speaking countries for God's sake, they allowed bathrooms, bedrooms, whole buildings to go unmonitored! Jesus Christ, a person could do anything to a child in those heathen places. She knew one thing for certain, even though she did not want the toilet cubicle outlawed, did not want to do her business in the open with the camera watching, she sure as hell would never set foot in some backward, uncivilized country that did not have reliable government monitoring. Let those fruitcakes in the so-called Progressive Party go there. In fact, put them all in a boat.

Carrie had never had much use for the Progressive Party, the legions of whining, tree-hugging, dope-heads who still, even in the home stretch to the Twenty-Second century, wanted to hand the country over to foreigners and losers. She still longed to meet a Progressive who could talk three minutes without bitching about the educational system (which now worked, because the government had stopped throwing good money after bad trying to provide schooling for every damned crack baby, Hop baby, and unwanted "Ethner" that turned up in a dumpster or a public restroom). Every school system in the country required upfront tuition for every child that passed its doors. Carrie was not an insensitive woman, and she understood how a job loss or a major illness could render genuinely good families incapable of paying for school, even for high school, which was the cheapest by far. But life was tough. If a family couldn't pay...

Decades after the slide had started, economists and others still marveled at how the cost of college had plummeted once people had to pay to send their kids to grade school. Changes in educational laws had prompted changes in educational attitudes, and vice-versa. Congress now poured so much money into colleges and universities that, if a family could keep their kids in school through twelfth grade, chances were they would get a world-class college education for little or nothing. The trick was paying for the first twelve years. If she and Christopher lost their income and were unable to afford public school, Carrie would simply sit down and teach her child herself. Of course, parents who weren't responsible enough to have jobs that paid enough to cover the cost of school probably would not care if their children learned anything anyway. That was the real reason some people stayed stuck in low socio-economic pits. They didn't work hard enough. They didn't work hard, and they spent too much time and energy complaining.

Carrie hated to go shopping. It was not the shopping that bugged her but the impossibility of stepping outside without being avalanched by complaints about this law or that law. People complained about having to pay for schooling, about having their homes monitored, about forced drug rehab, about mandatory contraception, about reproductive licensing, land set-asides for business and industry, limits on travel, bans on immigration, the government's refusal to support the endless parade of Fill-in-the-Blank-Minority Heritage Months. There were complaints about every frigging law passed in the last forty years, the very laws that had made this country a safer place. Good God. Every inter-vision bandwidth beyond spectrum thirty was a wasteland of talking heads and tiresome, black-and-white films about the Holocaust, or slavery, or God-knew-what else. *Slavery* for Christ's sake!

She always had to shake her head on that one.

They were still whining about slavery in 2094! Nearly five hundred years after the fact, people wanted Carrie and her husband and good people like them to feel guilty about ancient history. Why? What could Carrie possibly have done about slavery? She had no more control over slavery than the slaves had had. And she was sick unto *death* of hearing about it. They never talked about the inconvenient little fact that from the time they were set free, the lot of them had done nothing but bring the country down intellectually, economically, morally…and genetically. They had jobs, but they complained about the jobs they had, and they accused other groups of "perpetuating a class structure that kept them on the lowest rung of the social ladder."

She snorted.

Even after there had been a Black President, they kept dragging that line out.

If there was so much inequality, how had Wilson W. Enright become President? The Progressive Party had—of course—put together a textbook-friendly answer to that one: a grateful nation elected him because then *General* Enright succeeded in subduing the

Middle East and central Africa—something four Presidents and a truckload of generals before him had failed to do. But Enright had not won the election because he won a war. There had been Black generals before him, and there had been plenty of White generals who had won wars and not had a chance in hell of becoming President. Enright had won because America truly was a color-blind meritocracy. Racism, prejudice, all those things that some people swore kept them out of good jobs and good schools were all things of the distant past. But good people like Carrie and her neighbors could not escape name-calling because they had made something of their lives. Wilson Enright had, of course, been the most inept President in history. But if even one of them could become leader of the Free Americas, why couldn't they all—at the very least—work hard enough to send their kids to public school? That was the touchy part. It took hard work. Her husband had worked hard all his life, and now they enjoyed a comfortable existence because of it. But those people...all *they* wanted to do was chew Hop and lay around at what they called protest rallies. Instead of wasting their time protesting, they should use those hours to find a second job. *Then*, they'd be able to send their kids to school. And if their kids were educated, maybe they would contribute to society rather than weigh it down.

She shook her head.

Why was she thinking about such things on the happiest day of her life? Good God. It was as though she and Christopher had won the lottery. That's how big a deal this was. Getting a parenting license was as involved as getting a government security clearance. It would be easier for a seventy-five year old smoker to get life insurance (if tobacco were legal) than it was for a single person (or even a couple married less than three years) to get a parenting license.

The front door chimed, and Carrie floated into the hallway, grateful that something had broken her train of thought. She stopped in horror, however, when the door illuminated and showed the person on the other side.

"*Ahh* shit," she muttered.

An Arab—or Spanish or Indian, Gypsy, wop, dago, wetback, redskin—woman (Carrie forgot which) with huge, dark eyes and wavy, black hair stood on the other side of the door. It was their neighbor from across the hall. The woman was considered a great beauty in her own country, Carrie guessed, and she and her husband probably had sex like two ferrets at the height of mating season. She was glad the woman couldn't see her expression—annoyance mixed with mild disgust—because she really did not feel like pretending something else had made her frown. Even neighborly people like she and her husband didn't feel like accommodating every half-breed who rang the bell. They always smelled like garlic, this woman and her husband, and Carrie could not imagine why the woman was at her door. She touched the eight-by-ten rectangle set into the door at eye level, and the woman on the other side was able to see her face.

"Yes?" she said.

The woman beamed a flawless smile at her. "I am sorry to disturb you Mrs. Neal, but I was just downstairs and I heard the wonderful news. I wanted to offer you my congratulations!" The excitement in her voice was barely contained.

Carrie was thrown off her guard for a moment. Good news certainly did travel fast.

"Thank you. May I ask how you heard?"

"Oooh Mr. Jessup. Mr. Jessup is so excited he is telling everyone who will listen. He says he himself has not seen a newborn in three years! He cannot wait to see the little bundle when you bring it home!"

Good God, Carrie thought. Could she get pregnant first?

"I want to tell you how happy I am for you," the woman continued, clear eyes sparkling under long black lashes. She was clearly on the verge of tears. "My husband and I…" She wrung her hands; the words poured out in a warm gush, "my husband and I were also approved!"

Carrie considered opening the door. For an instant she wanted to hug the woman, who did not look dangerous, even though she wasn't American, and you never could tell…

The woman clasped her hands in front of her, bright-eyed and beaming, bemused at Carrie's insistence on talking through the door. Her smile drooped minutely as Carrie watched, and she began rubbing her palms together self-consciously.

"Perhaps you will join me for a cup of tea?" the woman asked.

Carrie considered. She knew in her heart that she could stand to be even more neighborly than she already was. And this *was* a secure building. The hallway, the stairwells, every part of it was monitored for motion, audio, and video. It was not as if the woman could hit her over the head and drag her down to the basement and kill her. More importantly, this was the happiest day of Carrie's life. This was like Christmas, only the feeling lasted forever. She was so happy she actually would have hugged the woman, despite the strange dress (a cross between a bed sheet and a curtain) she had wrapped herself in. Perhaps...

"Mrs. Neal...?"

Carrie blinked.

The light in the woman's eyes had dimmed noticeably. Her smile, shrunken to an embarrassed smirk, returned when she had Carrie's attention again. She sheepishly re-extended the invitation to tea.

Carrie hesitated.

"Uuuuuh...it sounds nice, but my husband is on his way home and uuh... I think I should wait until he gets here."

The woman's face softened with disappointment.

"I am sorry..." she began. "You want to first share your happiness with your husband. How silly of me..."

"Well, yeah, you understand," Carrie said. "Can I ask you a question?"

"Of course."

"How long did it take you and your husband to get approved?"

"Almost eleven months," the woman said.

"*What!*" Carrie exclaimed despite herself. Less than a year? Two lopes from the dark side of the world had gotten approved in less than a year? When it had taken nearly two and a half frigging years for her and Chris to get approved. "*Eleven months?*" she finally asked aloud.

The woman shrugged. "Yes," she said softly. There was awkward silence. "Perhaps another time...." Her voice trailed away.

"Sure. I'll call you," Carrie said and switched off the panel before the woman had a chance to respond. Standing in front of a switched-off door felt vaguely like cleaning ones nose in front of a two-way mirror. Head lowered, the woman shrank away from the other side and disappeared.

It occurred to Carrie that the woman might not be foreign at all. Perhaps she was Native North American. Now those were beautiful people. Every painting, every movie Carrie had seen growing up showed the long wavy tresses tied with leather cords, the perfect noses and prominent cheekbones, the flawless skin. Fat chance that she was though. The 2090 Census had officially put the United States Native North American population at fourteen thousand, with most of them living on Reservations. In a country of three hundred twenty million, a person almost had a better chance of meeting an extraterrestrial than an Indian. Still, there were plenty to take their places. The AAD's for example, Americans of African Descent, as Enright had re-christened them during his first campaign for the presidency. There were so many of them that they were never going anywhere.

The clouds under her feet continued to float her about for days. Her mother and father wept when they got the news, as did her in-laws. The happy couple had spent that first night out on the town, celebrating, as they had not done since the first night of their honeymoon. To think that they *would* be allowed to have a child. It was too much to believe. The two hours they had spent at the BRL office actually getting the coveted documents passed in a blur. From the office, they had gone directly to a local hospital to register as parents-to-be. Then began the long series of tests and examinations, and the treatments that would remove the universal male-female contraceptive from their systems and make them temporarily immune to it. Now, they could drink all the water they wanted and it would no longer suppress her ovulation or his sperm production. She even felt excitement at the prospect of taking classes again. There was a full slate of parenting courses that they would now have to take as a couple. A home inspector, an AAD woman, had come to their apartment and approved the mandatory renovations to what would be the child's room. The air filtration system, the padding around the lower third of the walls, the separate climate controls, the sound management, and low-UV lighting system had all passed. Barely a month after the letter arrived, everything was in order. All they needed now was the baby.

The front door chimed a week later as Carrier went about her daily cleaning. Dust rag in hand, she walked into the front hallway. The door illuminated as she approached, showing a mail carrier on the other side.

That was odd.

Why would he bring the mail to her door rather than place it in the mailbox? Unless it was Special Delivery?

She smiled.

It was her cousin in London. She and her husband had received the news, and this was their congratulatory surprise. They had been promising Carrie and Christopher a trip to the British Isles since they themselves had moved there. Travel tickets!

She went to the door and touched the talk panel.

"Yes?" she said, excitement taking over her voice.

"Mrs. Carrie Neal?" the mailman asked.

"Ye-e-sss," she said again, singing the word this time.

"Special Delivery."

Carrie opened the door. She jabbed her thumb squarely on the ID pad and took the envelope the man held out to her. She closed the door, watched it go dark, then hurried to the dining room where she plopped down at the table and tore open the envelope.

United States Department of Population and Demographics
Bureau of Reproductive Licensing
Washington, D.C. 20010-8692-77-1

Mr. and Mrs. Christopher and Carrie Neal, Case No. 6040119-5995
1500 5th Avenue #16
New York, NY 11213-1601-34

March 18, 2094

Dear Mr. and Mrs. Neal:

Your previous authorization to conceive and parent is herewith and immediately withdrawn pending further notice. This action is being taken in light of additional information uncovered during a follow-up investigation and which you failed to disclose during the interview phase of the certification process. Information currently on file with the United States Department of Defense indicates that a period of 15 days restriction was imposed upon Neal, Christopher 772-08-9897, beginning 03 Jan 2080 and ending 18 Jan 2080 in accordance with

United States Navy Regulation R-14645 Sub-paragraph 188 governing moral standards and conduct among persons in service to the United States. It was further found that Neal, Christopher, the above named, did bring a female companion not his lawful spouse into a dwelling proscribed under due authorization of the local command authority for use by Naval personnel only. Moreover, that he then engaged in activity of a sexual nature with the same, such activity being prohibited by the above cited Naval Regulation.

You may appeal this decision. Your request must be received in writing at the issuing office of both your permit and this withdrawal within five working days.

The Bureau of Reproductive Licensing regrets the necessity of this action.

L.G. Harrow
Director of Reproductive Licensing

H. Monroe Silverdine
Secretary of Population and Demographics

Her mouth fell open.

She was still sitting there, staring into space, when her husband came home.

5.
Not Counting Hope

The old Chevy pickup trundled toward the hilltop with twelve of us chained together in the rear. We pitched forward and back as it bumped along, and I allowed my body to move with the rolling bed of the vehicle while those packed in next to me held me upright. It was a clear California day, dry from the Santa Ana winds. Sparse clouds dotted the horizon. The promise of rain in the dry season brought nearly the same joy as the rain itself did. But that rain was still a long, long way off if, indeed, it ever reached us. In contrast, a fine layer of red dust coated the truck and everything in it, people and pioneer tools—the pickaxes, sledgehammers, and shovels—that lay in the bed. We looked impassively at each other as we bounced along, no one wanted to speak.

The three women with us were all dark-skinned and had their hair tied away under blue bandanas. The bandanas did not provide as much protection from the sun as the baseball caps the men wore, but they were handy for wiping sweat out of the eyes, and for soaking with water and applying to a burning face or neck. The women wore the same tough boots that we wore and the same simple outfit—navy blue work shirt and pants without a belt. If they had had lighter complexions, they would have been allowed to work indoors stocking shelves or cleaning, minding children, serving food, perhaps answering telephones—even if being lighter made them no prettier. As they were, they had to labor outdoors or in factories alongside men.

I fed my mind idle thoughts so that it would stop torturing me with the knowledge my wife had disappeared. She had been gone for two days now, and I had no idea where she was. There was an empty ache in the hollow of my chest, a slow panic that I had at first kept control of but that was now becoming unbearable. She had not run off, because she would not have gone without me, of that I was certain. I had waited all weekend for her to show up, listened for the click of her heels on the porch. When the first bell sounded this morning, she still had not come home.

She is very fair. Perhaps not fair enough to pass for white but very close, and she has thick brown hair that hangs past her shoulders. She is also educated. Not merely literate, as we all are more or less, but educated. I first saw her two years ago inside the main house. She was sitting barefoot in a bay window that was awash in sunlight. The book that she held on her lap was as thick as a sofa cushion, and she later told me it was the dictionary and she had been reading it. Her handwriting is a beautiful intermingling of calligraphic alphabets and Arabesque curls and loops. She can calculate interest, percentages, and even do long division in her head. She would bring a handsome profit to a kidnapper, but God forbid she should fall into the hands of some ignoramus who would put her to work on an assembly line or behind a cash register. God forbid it, for doing such work would kill her just as surely as falling off a cliff would. She cannot tolerate tedium and repetition.

Even worse would be to place her in a private residence, for there is no doubt she would face the greatest danger of all, the one far worse than boredom.

Darling (that was her real name, Darling Teresa Lavascoli, given to her at birth and changed to Grimes when she came here three years ago) was paradoxically vain and yet fearful of the regard of others. She preferred to wear loose-fitting pants or long dresses and skirts to work because they hid her legs. She has beautiful legs, and they have always brought her attention she would rather have avoided. She never wore shorts beyond our front door, and she seldom wore blue jeans or garments of any sort that stopped above her knees. She told me more than once she would kill herself rather than submit to rape. And if she could not kill herself beforehand, she would kill him (whoever he might be) afterward. She had warned me that I must always be prepared to go on without her, that that's how life is for us and those like us.

The ache inside my chest was acute and dug its way inward like a knife in a wound. A feeling of anguish, a powerful need to cry out in fury, circled inside me like a trapped animal awaiting the time when it would no longer be denied, the moment it could no longer be caged.

Not my Darling. Please dear God, not her.

I thought of all the other wives I knew or had heard of who had suffered that awful fate.

Was my own mother one? I never knew anything about her, and it had bothered me more and more as I grew older. Every year on my birthday, I would stare into the mirror and wonder how much of what I saw was her.

I know my father well. Not my real father, I guess I should say, but the man to whom I was given to raise. He was handyman, mechanic, gardener, and chauffeur on the place where I grew up, and he told me that he had been given a second wife shortly after I came along and my mother was sold. Was he my mother's husband then, I had wondered? He had never answered when I asked him that, telling me only to mind the present and not go worrying about the past.

When my wife did not come home for dinner two nights ago, I imagined she had been kept at the office. She worked in the accounting division of Grime's corporation at an office park less than a mile from the estate. Chiefly because of her complexion, the police would have been lenient with her if she had been out after curfew. She would have told them she had worked late, and they would have allowed her to go on her way with a minimum of questioning. Not so for the rest of us, but then, Darling wasn't like the rest of us.

Besides her complexion, she had other tricks that helped her get her way. She had considerable poise and could affect an air of regality that made nearly anyone she encountered, white or black, pause before addressing her. Three months ago, we had spent a Sunday afternoon at the markets. When we were ready to head home, Darling, instead of getting into the long line that waited for the bus, walked to a taxi stand and put her hand out.

I tried to stop her.

Generally, blacks could hire taxis if they were in uniform or could otherwise prove they were on their way to work, and if no whites were waiting. There was no law to this effect, only the imposing weight of tradition. The official policy, in fact, said the opposite: that a worker who has committed no breach of the peace must not be unreasonably delayed in reaching an assigned destination. The bus, nevertheless, remained the customary mode of transportation for us.

She refused to leave the taxi stand, so I stood next to her, trying not to let my nervousness show. It had been a good day and all I wanted now was to get home without incident. She told me not to worry and waved at an approaching taxi. A policeman came along just as the cab slowed to a stop in front of us. He asked us for our ID cards and gave Darling a venomous stare when she held hers up between thumb and forefinger but refused to relinquish it to him. When he was sure that she too was black, he asked us if we thought ourselves too good to ride the bus and reached for Darling's elbow, ready to turn us away from the curb.

She drew her arm away and, peering at him above her glasses, told him not to touch her.

I watched the ire flood into his face and knew right away that we would both be arrested. We hadn't broken any law, but the policemen wouldn't let something like that pass. If he had to, he would fabricate a reason to arrest us.

She pushed the glasses up on her nose and gave the man another scathing look. First telling him the name of her "employer" (she would not use the word "holder"), she then quoted the city ordinance that allowed her to hail a taxi whenever—as she interpreted it—she pleased. If such a simple thing as this were blown out of proportion and even remotely affected her prompt arrival at work tomorrow, her "employer" would make certain that he, the patrolman, and everyone in his chain of command appeared before the Mayor's council to explain the police practice of harassing innocent workers who only wanted to get home before dark. The policeman had stared hate at her and then walked off muttering under his breath.

If a bondsperson who worked the day shift were out after nine o'clock without an authorized pass to a specific destination, he or she went straight to the tombs—the catacombs of holding cells below the city—until the holder or a representative came to post bail. Most "employers," or holders ("owners" actually, but that term had fallen into disfavor during the Human Rights Movement of the late 60's) passed the monetary burden on to the worker through demotions, extra work, or any number of other ways including punitive rationing and sustenance withholding, which were illegal, and even beatings, which though not talked about in polite company and denied in the media, still occurred.

It would not have taken her more than an hour to walk from her office even had she decided to do so, but I—idiot that I am—did not go out to look for her until it was almost ten.

The truck hit a dip in the road and lurched to a stop. Red dust swirled around us.

The doors opened and two men climbed out of the cab. One was young and stocky and wore a black goatee to add years to his cherub face. The other, the older of the two, had a red mustache and wore a tropical camouflage Special Forces hat with a wide, floppy brim and a leather drawstring that dangled under his chin. He was our overseer.

It seemed to me that he did not like this job. I guessed he did it because he lacked either the skills or the connections to gain a position that would give him the same level of authority over free people. After walking out a few feet and surveying the landscape, he told the other one to lower the tailgate. He then spoke to us saying, "Okay folks, on your feet."

We climbed down from the truck one-by-one, moving awkwardly around the digging tools. When we were all on the ground, the younger man freed us from the stainless steel wrist manacles but left us chained together at the ankles.

"I'm sorry about the shackles, gang, but Mr. Grimes has been in a strange mood all week. And what the boss wants, he gets." He paused as if he expected us to show our appreciation for his plight and thank him for his words of comfort.

The younger man nodded his agreement.

"Anyway," the first went on, "what I need from y'all is a slit trench. About a foot-and-a-half wide and four foot deep…from that orange marker way up there," he pointed. "All the way down to that trunk pipe."

We followed his gaze down the side of the hill to a spot nearly two hundred meters away. He was going to use twelve people for two entire days to dig a trench that a backhoe could make in just a couple of hours. *How stupid is this?* I thought, but kept it to myself. The slope was a bit steep, maybe they thought it too steep for a backhoe, or maybe Grimes was just too cheap to hire one, which also made no sense because the contractor who supplied the pipe would undoubtedly be equipped to lay it.

The overseer looked at me, and I wondered if my face had given away my thoughts.

"It's gonna be rough going in spots because of the boulders. When we come across one, we're gonna have to team up and break it out. Until we find the first one, I want four of you to start with picks and the other eight with shovels. We'll trade off after a while."

Grimes was an idiot. We all knew it, and we knew that *they* knew how we felt and felt the same way. Why in God's name did the man want to irrigate a hillside filled with boulders? The overseer started toward the truck then stopped and said, "Probably would go quicker if we'd brought in a backhoe, but it's good we got plenty of work to keep everybody busy." He was saying the more work we did, the less chance someone would be sold at the end of the quarter.

Minutes later, we trudged up the hillside and set to work.

I took up a pickaxe and for the rest of the morning both the noises in my head and the pain in my chest subsided. Hard physical labor is a wonderful stress reliever…depending on how much stress there was to begin with and whether or not the tools of ones work readily change into weapons. My muscles worked like well-oiled machine parts though embers of distress still smoldered in my gut. I lost myself in the work at hand, but slowly, insidiously, the diminished ache inside me crept up again. Four hours and forty-one meters down the hillside the chattering in my mind resumed, despite my labor. At the same time, our rhythm was broken by a considerable chunk of rock buried in the dirt. The goateed cherub brought sledge hammers from the truck and we pounded it to pieces. When we had cleared its jagged remains from our path, I took up the pickaxe again. On my second swing, Bailey, the man chained to my left leg, threw himself to the ground and pulled away from me.

"Heeey man! Watch how you swing that damned thing!"

They all stopped and looked at me.

"Sorry," I said and offered my hand to help him up. We went back to work, and I tried to handle the tool more carefully. After a few strokes, however, I caught myself grunting like a madman with each swing, and I realized I was slinging the blade as though I intended to cleave the planet into two. The howling, the screaming in my mind that had spun up slowly like a hurricane, grew until it drowned out all other thoughts. The anxiety lodged in my chest began to spread like poison from a ruptured organ. Now, I was hurling the pick with such violence that it lodged in the ground on every other stroke. The others gave me as wide a berth as the chains allowed.

"William! *William!*"

It was hot now, incredibly hot.

I heard my name being shouted from far away and looked up, dazed.

"You trying to kill somebody?" the overseer asked. He and his assistant stood nearby, but out of range of the pick.

"I've got work to do," I said breathlessly. "Leave me alone."

"You're gonna give yourself a heart attack if you don't take it easy," the overseer replied. "Why don't you take a break? It's almost time for lunch anyway."

The others watched me.

"Leave me alone," I said again.

I swung the pick and buried it up to its handle again.

"Dadgummit! You're gonna break that thing if you don't quit swinging it that way!"

"Hell with it," I said. "He'll just buy another."

"Okay. Lunch!" the overseer called.

The others continued looking at me.

The temperature had been mild that morning. Now the sun blazed like a planet-smelting furnace. I had worked the entire time without noticing the heat, but now it hit me all at once and overwhelmed me. I leaned on the pick handle and tried to slow my thoughts, to grit my way through a bout of dizziness. My forehead and temples throbbed with pain. A high-pitched whine that grew sharper by the second pierced my eardrums; my lips tingled and my hands began to tremble. I shook my head but could not clear it. One moment I was angry but fine physically; the next, darkness pressed at the edges of my eyesight, seeping inward until all I saw was a blurred circle of light. I heard Darling's laugh, and for the first time since realizing she was gone, I surrendered to the urge to cry out.

The ground swayed and I fell to one knee clutching my head. I was sinking into a well of blackness, but my whole mind was fixed on my wife. Hands grabbed me, held me up even as I tried to lie down. Where was she? Where was she? Some sonofabitch on this place knew what had happened to her. Wasn't I worth a sideways whisper letting me in on the secret? If she was kidnapped, didn't that fucking bastard Grimes care enough to notify the authorities at least? Wasn't she worth that much?

"Help him. Take his arms."

"Move him out of this sun."

She could figure decimals to the fifth place *in her head*. Were they going to let some dirty fucking trafficker steal her and drag her off somewhere to count boxes, or sort eggs, or clean fish?

I found myself lying face-down in the dirt, water draining from my nose and eyes. Where was she?

" 's heat," someone said. "The heat got 'im."

They called my name, and pressed close around me.

"Get on the radio and call for doc. No, wait…unlock him first."

From far off, I felt the manacles let go of my leg. A cold, wet cloth touched my forehead. I grabbed the hand holding the bandanna and felt another stroke my hair. More hands touched my back, tried to comfort me.

"Let it out…" a woman said. " Let it out."

She knew something.

Was she the only one who missed seeing Darling the last two days? Many of the women hated her because she worked indoors and wore stockings every day. She got a new business suit once a month—not a cast off either—brand new from a department store.

She went to meetings with Grimes and sat in when his business partners came to the estate. She and I were the first to have a color television and a phone. Where other estates worked, we got Memorial Day and Armistice Day off because of her, yet the others hated her. They must have known something. They *had* to know she was gone. They had to. But they said nothing because they were glad.

Anger flared alongside my sorrow; still, I clung to the woman's hand as if it were Darling's own.

"Doc's on his way up," the younger man said.

The overseer knelt beside me. "It's gonna be all right," I heard him say. "Margaret, Tess, go on and get something to eat. He'll be all right."

They put me in the back of doc's station wagon, and he drove me down the hill and back to where the residences were, stopping at the large shed that served as a dispensary. "Doc" was actually a registered nurse, which was smarter than having no qualified medical personnel at all on an estate this size, but cheaper than having a real doctor. He checked my blood pressure and my pulse, listened to my heart, then drove an IV needle into my arm and connected it to a bottle of saline.

"So what happened up there?" he asked.

Doc's manner was just right for a medical person: he cared but he didn't care. He'd move heaven and hell to get you past an illness or injury. But if Doc saved you or if he lost you, he'd go home, eat his dinner, perhaps drink a beer, and fall asleep in front of the television.

"You wanna talk?" he asked when I said nothing. A picture of Grimes hung on the wall above his desk, the same picture that tainted every one of our living rooms. Starring at it in undisguised wrath, I cleared my throat and spoke.

"Someone took Darling."

He checked the IV.

"Who's Darling?"

He was still new here, had been on the place less than a month, but he should have known who she was. There was concern in his voice, but I reminded myself it was part of his job.

"My wife," I said. "Someone took my wife."

"How do you know?"

I moved my gaze to the ceiling tiles and shook my foot, struggled to keep my voice under control.

"Why else would she not come home for two nights?"

"Did you call her job?"

My foot moved faster. Perhaps he meant no harm. But how stupid was that question? If his wife had been missing for two days, would he not have called her job?

"I called," I said finally. "She's gone."

Doc said he would see what he could find out and sent me home on one day's bed rest later that afternoon. That night, the clock in the hall chimed twelve, and I lay wide awake on the bed, clutching Darling's bathrobe and gazing at a corner of the ceiling when a knock rattled the glass panes in the front door. I went to the door and saw the overseer standing like a jaundiced statue in the urine colored light from the yellow bulb that pledged not to attract insects.

"William? How you feeling?" he asked when I opened the door.

"All right I guess," I said flatly.

He cleared his throat.

"I came to give you some news. She ain't kidnapped. She ain't hurt or nothing either."

My heart jumped in my chest. His words were like cool water on a scalded patch of skin. She was okay. I nearly smiled with relief but caught myself. Where was she? What else did he know?

I waited for him to go on.

"Mr. Grimes took her with him when he went down to San Diego on Tuesday." He paused, probably thinking I knew what he'd say next.

I waited.

He exhaled and scratched his chin.

"Well…he left her down there William. Traded her…"

A great iron bell clanged inside my head.

Traded her? Grimes had traded her?

He *sold* her. The black-hearted sonofabitch *sold* my wife.

He sold her.

No matter how this man dressed it up…traded, transferred, optioned, re-assigned…it meant the same thing in the end. They bought and sold people the way they did pets and furniture. As if a person were nothing more than a stack of wood, or some trinket in a jeweler's case. As if Darling herself were nothing more than an adding machine. And the man standing before me could not even bring himself to say the word, could not keep himself from sugarcoating her fate.

"You can call her," he added and handed me a scrap of paper. "I'll have one of the others check in on you tomorrow. Be ready for work on Wednesday, zero-five-thirty." He turned and stepped off the porch without a backward glance.

I closed the door and hurried to the kitchen where I snatched the phone from its cradle and dialed the number. It rang and rang and rang until I wondered if he had written it down wrong. I was about to hang up and try again when a soft, tired voice answered.

"Women's dorm."

I spoke rapidly, not sure if the woman on the other end would understand me or even care about what I was saying.

"Hold on," she said when I paused. The phone clunked onto a hard surface and I waited, listening to a long silence that unnerved me. I was *this* close to hearing her. What was happening on the other end?

"William!"

Her voice jumped out at me; her breath whistled into the line. "Oh William, William...." She was crying. "William...you have to come...you have to get me out of here."

"Where are you? Did they hurt you?'

She hiccupped.

"Talk to me," I said. "What happened?"

"You have to get me away from here. You have to talk to Mr. Grimes."

"Darling, tell me what happened. Where are you?"

"S-San Diego," she said. "I'm at a plant in San Diego."

She quieted herself enough to talk and told me the whole story. Grimes had taken her with him to meet the president of a company that manufactured professional sports attire. She had come upon the idea of making high-quality look-alike garments for youths, and setting up Grimes' retail outlets as the sole distributor. The man had been so impressed with Darling that he offered Grimes a queen's ransom for her when their meeting was over. Although he valued Darling, Grimes was not given to sentimentality when it came to business. Moreover, he was a greedy piece of filth who would have sold his own children had they been black. Grimes had "traded" Darling to this man, who wanted her not only as an accountant but as his *personal assistant*—a common, paper-thin euphemism for a mistress who could actually do meaningful work during the day. She was to be both his bookkeeper and his plaything.

Darling was outraged and told the man she was a human being and a married woman, not a toy for his amusement. He might as well shoot her right then and there if he thought she would ever be his concubine.

She had then told Grimes, pointedly, that she was ready to come home.

No one with enough money to acquire her would be stupid enough to do her real harm no matter how she behaved, but the man Grimes left her with had little tolerance for insubordination and even less for talk of "rights." Minutes after Grimes was gone, he'd had her taken to the plant that made the synthetic cloth for his garments.

When she arrived, she had been forced into a storage room and stripped by a male guard while another watched from the door. Her outer clothes torn to shreds and snatched away from her, she clung to the remnants of her slip and used it to hide herself from their leering smiles. Without a word to her, the two men left her, locking the door from the outside. An hour later the door swung open and one of them threw a smelly, grease-covered set of coveralls into the room. He stood in the door and watched as she fought down her revulsion and pulled them on over what was left of her own garments. As she struggled with the zipper, the man stood aside and a gigantic blonde—a stocky, broad-shouldered, Nazi frauline of a woman in denim pants and a heavy work shirt—stormed in and grabbed her by the hair.

The woman dragged her barefoot out of the room, down a flight of metal stairs and across a concrete floor to a long, open area lined on both sides with stainless steel vats the size of above-ground swimming pools. The two-thousand-eight-hundred-gallon tanks were used to cook the resins that formed the base of the synthetic fabrics. After each use, the tanks had to be scraped out by hand with a large rubber tool that looked like a squeegee without a handle. There were twenty in all, and each vat was topped with a heavy lid that connected it through flexible hoses to a series of pipes in the ceiling.

The air reeked of chemicals. A sharp, stabbing odor filled her nostrils though exhaust fans whirred in the ceiling and pulled the noxious fumes up chimneys that dispersed them into the atmosphere.

The twenty or so people tending the vats wore respirators over their mouths and noses. None of them stopped working to watch as Darling was pulled to the far end of the room where three of the monstrous cooking pots sat with their lids raised. The woman caught the eye of a female worker and made a gesture that encompassed Darling's bare feet. The worker scurried off and returned a minute later carrying a pair of rubber boots, rubber gloves and a respirator similar to her own. Her eyes glistened as she bundled the objects into Darling's arms and turned back toward her own workstation. The blonde woman had grabbed the back of her collar, spun her around, and made her fit the respirator over Darling's face. Seeing the thick hair interfere with the straps on the breathing apparatus, the guard yanked the apparatus off, untied a bandana from her own sweaty neck and draped it over Darling's hair. She then shoved the respirator against her face and savagely hauled the straps over the bandana. She made the other woman wrestle the boots onto Darling's feet. When she was fully dressed in the alien outfit, the woman showed her the metal rungs that ran up the side of the vat and made it possible for a person to climb up and inside.

Darling fumbled her way up the rungs while the woman shouted at her from below. When she reached the top and leaned over the opening, she saw gluey residue caked to the inside walls. Here the smell was concentrated and powerful, so much so that it caused her head to ache. After only a few minutes inside the tank, she began to cough and rasp despite the respirator. Her stomach constricted and she vomited before she could get the mask off her face. Despite her distress, she was aware of her glasses tumbling into the muck at her feet. When she got her mouth and nose clear of the mask she gulped in a mouthful of the fume-laden air and retched again as it clawed its way along her windpipe and seared her lungs.

They made her work non-stop the entire first day, and she had fallen asleep on the break room floor at the end of the evening shift.

She had been allowed a cold sandwich from a vending machine for dinner and was told she could get water from any sink off the factory floor. The following morning, she had sheepishly asked about coffee and the woman had slapped her.

The people who raised Darling and those who worked her had always had one thing in common: they protected her. She had always been favored, had always been given first quality and first pick; she had never, ever been struck as far as I knew. Now she wept.

"She *hit* me! All I did was ask…"

They had not allowed her to call home, nor given her two minutes to scribble a note to me so that I would know she was alive. Friday evening and Friday night, all day Saturday, all day Sunday, all day Monday, they had worked her mercilessly. This was her first night in the workers' dormitory. It was just after midnight, and she would have to get back up at five a.m. for the morning shift. The abject misery in her voice made my face burn with rage.

"They treat us like dogs…they're going to kill us…"

She couldn't help being the person she was. She had always been willful, true, but she was also unaccustomed to ill treatment. If she were kept there, she might toughen up over time.

But she should not have had to. It was not right what Grimes had done to her. To us. There was no power in heaven, in hell, or on the face of the earth that could make me accept this and allow her to rot away in that place.

I would kill Grimes.

I would kill every cop, every guard, and every wealthy degenerate who dared to get in my way.

I would die if I had to.

"I'll come," I said, not knowing where we would go from there, but knowing I had no other choice. I had been given all of tomorrow for bed rest, so I'd have one day, or nearly a full day's head start. I knew I wouldn't be able to get on an airplane. And how many checkpoints could I get through if I stole a car and tried to drive? A bus was the only thing that would get me anywhere near her. After I found her, where could I take her so that we would be safe? Mexico? Obviously. But, how many people died in the southwestern deserts each year trying to slip across the border into Mexico? It would be much easier to cross the northern border into Canada. But Canada was so very far away. There were old tales about a network of sympathizers who had helped people escape to freedom in the 1800s when parts of the U.S. still outlawed slavery. Folklore said that Abraham Lincoln, the sixteenth President, had prepared an Executive Order freeing all slaves but had torn it up when every state in the south and five in the Midwest threatened to secede and declare themselves an independent nation. If those networks had ever been real, they had long ago disbanded or been shut down. There would be no one to help us. Once we cleared the fence, so to speak, we would be on our own and would either find freedom or die. Captured fugitives had the shortest life expectancy of any people on earth. Most died mysteriously while in police custody or "accidentally" at the hands of bounty hunters. Some "committed suicide" shortly after they were returned to their holders. It was widely held that runaways were too much trouble. Better to get rid of them once they started running.

"I'm coming," I said again. "You hold on. I'll come get you."

"Get off that phone!" A ferocious female voice cracked like a whip in the air behind her. "Hang it up. *Now!*"

"William help me! Hurry!"

I heard sounds of a struggle, someone trying to wrestle the phone away from her.

The line went dead, and I gripped the receiver like a thing I wanted to strangle. A blister of pain formed in my throat and stuck there like a dollop of molten metal. I slammed the receiver down on the countertop. Then I did it again, and then I pounded it and pounded it there until it cracked in my hand. I ripped the base off the wall and hurled it across the room. There were four chairs at the small kitchen table and I grabbed one, hefting it like a two-handled club. Walking to the living room, I laid into the portrait of Grimes, again and again and again until the floor was littered with broken glass, chunks of plaster, and bits of splintered wood. I kept on until gaping holes yawned in the walls and the chair itself splintered against a beam in the sheetrock. I threw it aside and went around the room destroying everything: shelves, lamps, the bookcase, the other pieces of furniture, the television, everything.

I slumped to the floor at last with my back against the overturned sofa. Dark spots vibrated in front of my eyes; my shaking hands clutched at my heart as it slammed against the wall of my chest. A minute passed, then two, and then I got up slowly and made my way to the bedroom where I found my pants and pulled them on. What hope did we have? I first had to get myself to San Diego; then I had to find her. I would find the place, but after I found it, how would I get her out? I didn't know how we would make it to Canada, or even to Mexico, without a miracle.

Hope was wasted, I knew. Wasted and useless. And, not counting hope, not counting on a distant and uncaring God to help us, what else did we have? Nothing.

I put on my shirt and boots, gathered all the money we had in the house and shoved it into my pockets. All I knew was that I had to find her. I had to get her away from that place, or I had to die trying.

6.
For Adele

In the real world, it is late December, long past midnight and freezing cold just beyond these walls. Dry air blows through the vents, and I toss about in bed unable to sleep for memories that will not release me. After an hour of tiresome turning, I get up and click on the radio. Soft music fills the room and I begin to relax. Before long, I feel my conscious mind slipping away, sliding down into the caverns beneath the blanket, out of my body, and into the world of dreams.

I am lost inside an ancient structure, hurrying, running as fast as I can through dank hallways and past doors that open into darkness. The walls bristle with hidden life; the wood itself seems to moan with consciousness. I round each corner with mounting dread, wary of what lies in front of me. I do not believe in ghosts, or haunted houses, but I do not know where I am, and I sense that something is terribly wrong. I go as quickly and as quietly as I can, my fear of what waits in the murk ahead at odds with my fear of what is coming behind me. I must get out of here. Quickly.

I go down a narrow staircase and find a heavy door. Once, twice, three times it swings open without my having touched it. Behind the door, a musty passage trails away into blackness.

Apprehension weaves itself around me like a shroud, exciting the hairs on my neck and all along the length of my arms. 'It is only fear,' I tell myself. Fear of the stale breeze, of the tomb-like odor that rushes through the opened door. It is only fear. Yet I hesitate, wondering if whatever is behind me will prove a harmless nuisance compared to what waits in the darkness ahead.

'Hurry,' a voice whispers to me, and I cross the broken threshold. I know in my guts that I must pass through this stretch of darkness if I am ever to find the thing for which I search, and above all else, I know that I must leave this place, soon.

I come out suddenly into bright sunlight. A brilliant cobalt sky soars above a stand of healthy pine trees. Through the trunks to my left, I see a long strip of sand and the ocean. Looking all around me, I see that I have somehow emerged from the trunk of a tree—a thick gray oak stippled with black and choked with webs of Spanish moss. It stands alone in a clearing, separated from the other trees by a barren circle. The pines are tall, green, vibrant things straining toward the endless blue. But this oak...this old oak tells of illness and death. Its branches are wrenched into bizarre angles, jutting this way and that like broken bones. Its yellow leaves, splotched with disease, flutter half-dead among the malformed boughs like a moribund flock of cadaverous birds. The stone-colored bark is riddled with hernias and forms a ring of tumors wherever branches meet trunk. Its roots clutch the earth in gnarled fury—an ancient, dried-out hand clinging angrily to life.

I do not understand what has happened. My mind fills with questions I cannot answer, so I turn from the oak and face the strip of land beyond the trees. But before I have turned completely, out the corner of my eye, on the periphery of my senses, I feel the old tree moving. A surreal sensation twists in the air around me, swirling like droplets of fog, stinging my eyes and coating my tongue with the taste of copper—the taste of fear, I realize. I turn back and watch in amazement as the injured branches wither and retract, crumbling as if squeezed between giant hands. When the skeletal boughs have crushed themselves into kindling, I turn away a second time, more eager than ever to leave these woods and touch the sand below them.

Yet something...something will not let me be and forces me to turn back once again. Now there is nothing save a jagged stump, its upper half blackened as if by fire.

I hasten down the hillside, stumbling and sliding through rocks and undergrowth, until I come at last to the empty beach. I am overcome with relief, but I see no one and sense that I am as alone as if I stood on the surface of the moon. I call out the first name that comes to my mind: Adele.

I am convinced it was the medicine that caused it. The doctors have told me otherwise in the time since it happened, but I believe it was the pills.

The phone rang just before six a.m. A male voice with an accent so thick I could barely understand it spoke into the receiver on the other end. The Spanish lilt, the static in the background told me the call came from very far away. The foggy discernment of early morning made me infinitely uncertain of what I had heard. My wife, I was told, was in a hospital in Buenos Ares, her condition critical. She had been severely beaten among other things. Could I come? There might be time if I hurried.

There are nightmares that come to you in sleep. They leave you sweaty and shaking, wondering how a thing so insubstantial as a picture in the mind could torture you and pitch you back into the waking world with a scream on your lips. And then, there are nightmares that spring at you in the light of day. These are of the ground-shaking, soul-wasting variety and are far more potent, for they ride on the chaos that breaks down lives and sometimes unmoors sanity. One minute you are sound asleep, the next minute you are being told your wife is hospitalized in critical condition; that she is seven thousand miles from home in a foreign country. Her companion—a man, the voice tells you—is already dead.

In the gloom of daybreak, I reached for the bedside table, stretched out my hand to touch something—anything—solid. Anything that would tell me I was awake, and that the world around me was real. Yet, there was no way it could be real, for I had spoken to my wife on Thursday. Today was Saturday; she was in Boston with her sister; she would be back in Seattle on Monday. Something unreal was happening. Searching for words in the half-light, I could only say over and over again, *"what?"* until I sounded, even to myself, like the scratched recording of a dunce's voice.

The woman told me she was a grief counselor.

She looked like a Revlon model behind the wire-rimmed glasses and the French roll that hid most of her black hair. She was easily five-foot nine or ten in her plain, low-heeled shoes. They and the rigor-mortis styled pantsuit she wore did much to conceal the fact she was a woman. She must have had difficulty getting people to take her seriously as a shrink.

I took her seriously. To me she was serious as the end of life itself. I told her this, and then I told her to get out because I had absolutely nothing to talk about with her.

It was a rainy afternoon when an attendant showed Adele to my hospital room. I say "hospital" because that is easier then explaining the true nature of the place where I was sent just weeks after my wife's death. It *was* a hospital of sorts; sick people went there to get better. But there was no emergency room, and when patients arrived by ambulance, it was never with lights and sirens going. There was very little noise there, very little confusion—just an endless procession of quiet days and long, long nights.

I still do not remember arriving here. My last memory of the world before the hospital is centered on my old office.

I know that I had lost track of the days. I know that I had begun rising each morning and making my way to work mechanically. On some days, I arrived and found the building locked. On other days I found myself wondering what I was doing there, and that there was something I desperately needed to talk to my doctor about although I could never quite put together what it was.

The day that stands out most clearly, the one I will never forget if I live until the pyramids crumble, is the day a beer-bellied man with a blond mustache and blond eyebrows, who smelled like corned beef and Old Spice, leaned over my desk and frowned down at me. Breathing like a bull who had the matador cornered, he had slammed a handful of papers down in front of me and asked—no, hurled—the same question at me again and again, "Do you realize what this is gonna cost us?" Did he mean the papers? He could not have meant the sheaf of papers he held out, could he? How much would the papers cost?

Someone tried to pull him away, whispering to him in an urgent tone; something that I thought included the words "*his wife.*" There was more whispering, louder the second time, and then I heard something that sounded like "*for Christ's sake!*"

A very strange thing happened then.

My arms softened and began to wriggle inside the sleeves of my jacket. My hands drew toward me, as if the limbs had shortened, and disappeared inside the cuffs. I watched, amazed, and tried to push them back out. My arms continued to move slowly from side to side in the sleeves, and I could see the fabric of the jacket rippling along with them. I tried to lift them from the desk, but this only made them wiggle more violently. The fat man with the blond moustache glared at me with undisguised wrath, his blue eyes glittering behind his glasses. The other man, the one who had whispered "*…his wife…*" and "*…for Christ's sake!*" looked sideways at me and kept trying to pull the first one away.

I looked back and forth from my sleeves to the angry man with the curled fists who looked like he wanted to hit me.

My heart was beating fast enough to hurt, and my mouth was suddenly so dry I could neither swallow nor speak. *What was this?* What in the name of God was happening to me? Was I dreaming again? The medicine they had given me after the phone call helped me sleep, but it gave me dreams I neither spoke of nor cared to remember. Was this real? Was this possible? A voice inside me tried to answer, but the man standing over my desk, hissing like a leaky steam valve, leaning closer, and closer, and closer, until I could see the veins in his eyes had me frozen and terrified. I watched as foam collected in the corners of his mouth, and then, Christ almighty, two pointed teeth descended from his upper jaw and cut the skin of his lips as they slid into place.

Far away at the end of the tentacle that had replaced my right arm, a hand—my hand—snatched a letter opener from the desk and rammed it into one of the ears. The huge man bellowed like a wounded animal and withdrew, but the arm—my arm—recoiled like a rattlesnake and rammed the opener against his temple before he could get away. The bloodied opener shook in my fingers. A hurricane of shouting and movement erupted, and suddenly people were holding me in my chair even though that thing had scared the piss out of me, literally. I flailed and fought against them at first, but then clung to the nearest person while the others scurried about and shouted orders at each other.

In my mind, there is a vague memory of standing outdoors in the pouring rain wearing only my underwear and pacing back and forth on the sidewalk in front of my neighbor's house. I can recall that the rain that day was warm (much like the rain on the day I met Adele), and that it came down in buckets amidst thunder and lightning, but I cannot recall when or if it really happened, and I have no idea why I was out there, or where I intended to go.

I had told her that I did not need a grief counselor. That I felt no grief, and even if I did, I could damn well grieve all by myself. I didn't need someone holding my hand and telling me it wasn't my fault. I knew damn well it wasn't my fault. Was my insurance supposed to pay some med-school dropout to tell me I wasn't responsible for my wife being raped and beaten into a coma two days after she chose to have a romantic getaway with another man? I didn't want to "work through" this woman's psychobabble, her daytime talk show bullshit about acceptance and healing. I didn't care.

What was I, I asked her during our first meeting, a drunk? Did I need this? Did I need to be in this place? How about all these people leaving me the hell alone and letting me rest? How about stop trying to comfort me. If I cry, I said to her, would you get out of here and go tell someone else it wasn't *his* fault.

She asked about the man I had wounded with the letter opener

"It was the medicine," I said. She knew damn well it was the medicine. What kind of a shrink was she if she couldn't figure that out? Adele had listened. From the very beginning, she had listened.

She sat in a chair near the window in my room one Thursday and wrote while I ranted and raved and threw questions at her. Wasn't she supposed to ask me questions about my childhood? Wasn't she supposed to find out if my father had walked out on the family, or if I'd gotten up one night and caught my mother servicing strange men in the living room? If I had been locked in a closet, or chained up in a basement, or left behind on a bus or a train, or some other such nonsense? Mondays and Thursdays she came and sat in my room, listening and writing in her genuine all-leather portfolio while I went on and on about that bitch who had slipped off and gotten herself killed, who had not had the decency to say so much as a "go to hell." Who probably had left home without even a backward glance?

She had picked one hell of a nice way to earn a living I told her another time, although, she was a bit overdressed to come sit in my room and watch me watch Seinfeld. And I knew she got tired of listening to me, I told her. No matter how well she hid it, I knew it was there. I knew it grated on her nerves, hearing about the stupid, heartless cunt whom I had wasted so many years of my life on, hearing me talk endlessly about how good I'd been to her. I must have wondered aloud a billion times how the woman could leave me the way she did—without a word, so that I'd wind up stumbling through life like a blind man, or like someone who had to keep learning the meaning of up and down, right and left. If I was not an irritation to this woman after the first few weeks, I said, I had no idea what would be. But, she kept coming, and she kept listening, writing endlessly in that portfolio of hers. Our visits followed that pattern for months it seemed. Indeed, for a long, long time.

On a Monday, six months after I was sent there, two o'clock came and Adele did not arrive. I sat in the chair next to the window and watched for her, but she never came. Three o'clock, four o'clock, five…six… I knew by then that I would not see her, but I stayed near the window and kept looking.

I still do not understand what went on, but I doubt I slept five straight minutes that entire night. My mouth was dry when I went to bed, and I felt not butterflies but crayfish and millipedes crawling in my guts. When I closed my eyes, I heard my heart thumping and felt my body move with each beat. I flipped from stomach to back and from back to stomach until the sheets were wrapped around me like newspaper around a flounder. I would force myself to lie still until some part of me began to forget I could not sleep, and then something inside my head would shake itself, realizing I had dozed off. Although I wanted to rest, my brain fought to stay awake, and at two o'clock in the morning, some idiotic part of me went on looking, waiting for her and hoping she would come. Far into the pre-dawn hours, images of Adele seated in the chair next to the window, legs crossed, glasses sliding forward when she looked down to write, floated across the darkness behind my eyelids.

I call out to Adele again and again.

The only answer is the "whoosh" of wind moving through the distant trees.

The beach, the ocean, and the sky are all sucked away suddenly, spiraling downward into nothing as if sucked into a drain. I find myself standing in my own kitchen, looking down, and watching while the tan and the blue mix into an evanescent purple before vanishing. Now, a new song comes to me, borne on the sound of waves and punctuated by the call of seagulls. A new picture swirls up from the drain before me, like a filmstrip running in reverse. I am seaside again, standing in the foam of the incoming tide. The wet sand shifts beneath my feet while mollusk shells and tiny pebbles gently grate against my skin. Over my shoulder, in the distance, I see the skyline of a great city. Now it is almost perfect. I am immersed in nature, which I love, and yet not far from the bustle of civilization, which I also love. I feel a sense of peace so profound I can find no words to describe it. Then I see Adele sitting on an elegant, straight-backed chair. She wears a strapless cocktail dress made of black velvet. The creamy almond glow of her skin contrast sharply with its midnight color: she looks amazing. Her long legs are crossed and she folds her hands in her lap. I wave, but it seems she cannot see me.

Fifteen months came and went.

The fall equinox approached and brought with it cool nights and stark blue skies in the daytime, a welcomed relief from the dry heat of a changeless, monotonous summer. Adele and I would walk beside the man-made lake in the late afternoons and early evenings talking about sports, the weather, our favorite wines. We had long ago ceased sitting and watching television when she came, but spent every minute we could outside the room, out on the grounds of what I now called "the resort." We spent more hours sitting, taking in the sight of Canada geese and other wild birds that had not migrated. The sound of leaves being raked into piles and the smell of wood smoke, the feel of frost on the air made the passing days seem like a retreat at a picturesque mountain hideaway. She had moved me to the bottom of her rounds a while back, and it seemed she stayed later and later when she visited, until eleven o'clock one night. In the long months since I had been committed, only two days mattered in the week for me, Mondays and Thursdays. All the others drifted past like ships on the edge of sight. Distant and vague, they had no real bearing on my life. I did not join the wider world until Adele made her visits.

She seemed not the slightest bit surprised when I told her one evening that I had uncovered a cache of feelings for her, that our relationship—in my mind—had transmuted into something I did not understand; that I thought I loved her, in other words.

Standing on the verandah, gazing into the crisp, indigo night, I told her that I would not have lived if she had not come into my life. In the long weeks after my wife's death, the devastating reality of her absence and the wrenching knowledge of her betrayal tore into me at precise intervals, twin machetes wielded with demonic strength. I awoke precisely at daybreak each morning and lay there until it ran over me like a train; I could never, ever say good-bye to her; I could never ask her why. The knowledge would envelop me and cling until I could not stand it, until I wanted to peel the flesh from my own body to save myself from suffocating. At the lowest point, I found myself believing that death could not be worse. I found myself wishing that a wall would collapse in the night, or that I could summon the courage to aim my car at a cliff. But I had not died—not on the outside, not physically. I had melted into catalepsy instead, faded to a state of incompetence and incoherence. When she came to me, all that was left was a walking, breathing shadow.

Unlike the trauma surgeon who rushes in and, in a flurry of blood and suturing, stops with his hands the ebbing of life from a mangled body, Adele, in the manner of the shaman almost, had healed me without lifting a finger, without seeming to, in fact. She had drawn out the mind-breaking confusion, shaping it and nullifying it as it emerged, diffusing and dispatching it like the rain of summer washing away a forest fire.

I took her hand in mine and felt the warmth of her fingers, the hardness of her tapered nails that glistened with clear polish. I brushed her hair aside with the tips of my fingers and touched my lips to hers. She gave me a light peck then swiveled her head so that my lips rested against her cheek while I breathed her perfume. She squeezed my hand, and I knew suddenly, with blinding insight, that I could go on without these visits, without her, even. I saw too in that moment that the woman who had died in Buenos Ares had been nothing more than a stranger to me, though for many years, I had been convinced otherwise.

The weather cooled more in the weeks that followed, and my discharge day came at last.

It was sunny and cold when she came by that morning cradling a brightly wrapped package in her arms. I was told not to open it until I arrived home, and the smile in her eyes said something more that I could not read. Perhaps she knew how much I looked forward to our follow-up meeting. Perhaps she did as well.

One of my former neighbors had come to drive me to my new place.

At the curb outside the main entrance, with staff and other patients watching surreptitiously, I said my good-byes to the resort and so long to her. I did not wish to embarrass her, so I did not try to kiss her there, under the bright sun, before so many eyes. Even now, in my heart, I question the worth of assembly-line therapy. I do not want to believe in the healing power of talk, or of the other touchy-feely nonsense that takes the place of getting up after you fall. But I hugged her as though my life depended on her, for it had. I sensed her heart beating in time with my own, and I said, "I love you," against her cheek. "I know," she whispered back, smudging my ear with lipstick.

* * *

Hours pass in the real world. The nighttime changes shape like the surface of the sea. It rolls lazily toward the dawn and the music from the radio changes. The pictures in my mind follow suit.

I am surrounded by trees again, in a park this time, and all the trees are touched with autumn red. A little boy who resembles me is here also, and I tell myself that this must be my son. I look at my hand and see no ring, yet I know that I belong with the woman who helps him climb to the top of the jungle gym. She has soft brown eyes, and her skin is the color of honey. Her hair is a glorious fusion of earth tones, flame, and burnished copper. Her smile radiates warmth and dazzles me like sunlight caught in the facets of a great diamond. She is not Adele, but she is every bit as beautiful as Adele was to me in those pained, empty days that I have left behind.

The two of them, my son and she, play together like old friends. He hangs on her leg and gazes at her with an intense affection that rivals my own. We take turns making faces at a disposable camera, and he wants every picture taken to be of her. As I watch them, I think briefly of my former wife and of the other women I have loved, of those who walked out of my life and of those whose lives I walked out of. I say I am sorry and good-bye to each of them. May they each find a peace and a happiness that approaches the peace and the happiness I have found, and may there always be angels like Adele in the world.

7.
One Too Many

It was Greg, one of the guys in the office down the hall, who first showed him the website: *SeeNoEvil.com*. He grinned and told them to get back to work, and then he went to his desk and continued to swim through city hall's spreadsheets.

At home it was different.

"Consenting Adults Do It Better," the banner proclaimed. He saw that he could browse until he found a picture he liked, plug in a credit card number if he so desired, and send a confidential message to the siren of his choice. If you got a response, the disclaimer told him, go get 'em cowboy. If you didn't, tough shit. Try again tomorrow.

It wasn't his Catholic upbringing that made his forehead wrinkle as he scanned the column of photos; it was plain old disbelief.

This was a scam. It had to be. Many of the photos had the head cropped off or the face blacked out, but from what he could see; there wasn't a crack head or a truck-stop hooker in the entire bunch. This was obviously a very upscale club. He saw bodies that looked like they belonged to tennis pros, all with the aura of well-to-do lifestyles.

It was hard to believe any woman who looked this good would resort to a website for swingers, even if she wasn't getting it at home and needed some extracurricular pampering. Among those who had the audacity to show their faces, he saw dazzling smiles and expressions that were oh so easy on the eyes. What tickled him were the profoundly uncreative headlines that he saw with some of the ads: "Hi Daddy," "DV8," "Are U Up, Big Boy?" They sounded way too dumb for the products they were meant to sell. This had to be a scam.

Greg, or one of his frat-boy colleagues, was probably sitting on the other end of that web page at that very moment waiting to see if his name would pop up.

But at least the photos were nice.

In five minutes he found among the co-eds, housewives, and professional women at least a dozen whom he would have taken home to meet his parents just because they were so good looking.

Those assholes must think I'm an idiot.

He browsed until he came across a busty, drop-dead gorgeous figure draped in soft, see-through material the color of emeralds. Her body was bare beneath the short, green garment that was loosely cinched with a satin belt. Her face was turned so that the yellow hair which hung past her shoulders obscured her profile.

He read over the pitch points again.

Pay a flat fee to send messages for one month. No moral judgments, no drawn out mating rituals. If you scored, if you hooked up… *if…* then you were no-doubt in for a memorable ride. Of course nothing was guaranteed, and he, the subscriber, assumed any and all risks associated with meeting other guests face-to-face.

No kidding?

He thought a moment.

It was too good to be true, he told himself. Then he typed in his card number. They could only steal his identity once.

Six days later when he logged onto the site, he saw a small number "1" next to the mailbox icon. The message purported to be from the emerald-clad beauty who had mesmerized him and said this was the only message he would receive until after she saw a photo of him. Sitting in his apartment the next night, he thought it over, and then he emailed one. In turn, he received a bathing suit photo of sorts—four women sipping daiquiris at poolside. Three of them had blond hair.

*Oooooooookay...*he thought as he studied the faces. Actually, if she truly was any of the four this was still a no-lose proposition.

Let us proceed, he thought.

Her headline had read, "Blah Blah Blah. Come Lick Me." Her ad went on to say: "Skip the small talk. Clean, D/D free hetero female ISO similar male non-smoker thirty or under. Leave your resume, relationship stories, vacation photos, etc. at home. Looking for fun and excitement. Nothing more or less."

In her follow-up email to him, she'd asked: "What exactly are you looking for? Want to screw the office temp in the copy room (so to speak)?"

He'd written back: "Actually, I'd like to screw the boss' wife in the copy room (so to speak). Looking for the same things you are: no games, no drama, no strings. If she happens to have hair down her back, a small waist, and pretty legs, well, you get the picture."

For two weeks they negotiated a face-to-face meeting, then it was 12:30 in the afternoon on a Thursday, and he was buying a hotdog from a sidewalk vendor at the edge of Griffith Park downtown.

He felt like he had walked into a cheap spy novel. She told him to buy a hotdog at the cart on the northwest corner of the park, walk to the fountain at the park's center, and sit on the bench closest to the statue of Tennessee Williams. Obviously, she would be watching, deciding at the last minute to reveal herself, or not.

"Shall I tie a yellow ribbon in my hair?" he'd asked.

"Do it and I'll meet you. Don't do it, and I won't," she'd said.

So he sat down under the gaze of Tennessee Williams and bit into the hotdog.

While he still chewed the first bite, a woman in a business suit got out of a taxicab on the far side of the park and started toward him. She had a classy, corporate look, and as she drew closer, he could see that she certainly had a face to match the body he had begun to fantasize about. She flashed a smile at him and walked past without stopping.

Figures.

He checked his watch and settled back against the bench's wooden slats. He bit the hotdog again then turned and tossed it into the nearby trash bin and straightened his tie. When he turned back, he saw a pair of well-shaped legs sit down on the other end of bench. She wore a green skirt with a matching jacket and carried a calfskin briefcase in her left hand. In her right she held a bottle of Evian with her fingertips.

"Mitch?"

If a pair of eyes could frisk a person, hers would have patted him down in the first six seconds. Her name was Mira, and Mitch was impressed.

She seemed slimmer than in the pictures; her hair was shorter but it was blonde. Up close, he could see that she had perfect teeth, and her eyes were deep emerald green like her outfit. A fine gold chain circled her neck and dangled a large three-diamond pendant below her throat. A gold watch slid along her wrist. She opened her purse and reached inside for a tissue, and Mitch saw that she had just had her nails done.

She questioned him, but refused to answer any questions about herself. How had he found the website? How long had he been a member? How many other women had he contacted? He told her the truth, she was the only one. And everything else was exactly as he had written in his emails. He was looking for fun, same as she was. No drama, no games, no strings.

After an hour of talk she seemed satisfied with him and his answers, so she told him to meet her at the hotel across the street that evening.

Mitch whistled.

"The Craige? You know those rooms go for three and four hundred bucks a night don't you? And those are the cheap ones."

She gave him a look and sipped from the water bottle.

"I'll be here at six. If you're not here, I'll go home."

She carried a laptop that evening. An all-weather trench coat was draped over her forearms. She sat down on the bench and crossed her legs.

"Get a room on the front. I'll be up in fifteen minutes."

"How do I know you won't change your mind?" he asked with a smile.

She flicked her fingers dismissively but smiled at the corner of her mouth.

"You'll know in fifteen minutes."

When he opened the door for her, she told him to take a seat on the bed and waited at the threshold until he had moved away. Once inside the door, she looked the room over. It apparently met her approval, for she closed the door and walked straight into bathroom carrying everything —coat, laptop, everything—with her. He heard her lock the door and turn on the shower.

Ten minutes passed.

Fifteen.

Twenty-five.

When she reached the half-hour mark, he knocked on the door.

Silence.

He knocked again.

"Yes?"

"Are you okay?"

"Yes. Go have a seat."

He went back into the room and sank into a plush, winged chair. He had turned on the evening news and was staring through the open curtains when the bathroom door clicked.

He looked over his shoulder and saw her toss a thick towel onto the carpet. Speaking through a crack, she told him to take off his clothes and wrap himself in the towel.

This was getting silly.

"Why?" he asked.

"Do it or I'm leaving."

Mitch shook his head, stripped to his birthday suit, and wound the towel around his waist. Catching sight of himself in one of the mirrors across the room, he gave thanks to Bally's Total Fitness. Praise them with great praise.

"Anything else?" he said to the bathroom door.

"Keep your wallet. Put everything else in the wardrobe by the window."

'What?' he muttered to himself, then said out loud, "Are you serious?"

"Do it…then come over here…please."

He shook his head while he folded his suit and placed his belongings in a drawer.

You asked for it, dipshit.

He closed the drawer and called, "Now what?"

The bathroom door opened halfway. She took a tentative step into the room wearing the hotel's white embroidered robe and holding her own clothes in her arms.

"Come here."

When they were face to face, Mitch saw that he had overestimated her age. The stiff persona she wore in the park was gone, and she seemed much younger.

"Take a shower," she said. "I'll be here when you come out."

The television was off and the drapes were drawn when he came out minutes later. She lay across the bed on her stomach, her bare leg going up and down like a slow metronome. Her clothes were arranged on a chair near the door, and she had taken Mitch's suit out of the drawer and draped it over the valet.

He had felt a hell of a lot more cavalier sitting in his apartment, staring at what he thought was her on his computer screen. How recently had that been, the night he found that photo? Now they were in the same room and…

And what are we waiting for?

He reached back and turned off the bathroom lights. Her foot stopped, and she rolled onto her back. The lower half of the robe fell open exposing her thighs. He watched her sit up, undo the belt, and run her fingers down the lapels as if in invitation. The towel around his waist loosened and fell away as he walked to the bed. She took the robe off.

At eight-thirty she rolled away from him and climbed off the bed. She took her clothes and other items into the bathroom with her and showered again. When she came out, she insisted their exit be another complicated dance. She would leave first. He should wait at least fifteen minutes. She would take the stairs; he would take the elevator. She insisted he remain undressed until she was out the door. He rolled his eyes but agreed. When she was ready to go, she gathered her things and went out without a backward glance.

"Did you enjoy telling the guys about me?" she asked in an email.

'Sure did," he wrote back. "The fish congratulated me. The dog wanted to see pictures. You know how they are."

"Don't be too proud of yourself," she wrote the next day. "And don't think I'm a slut."

"Never crossed my mind. Will I see you again?"

"Maybe."

They met the following Thursday. He paid for the room and waited upstairs. She came up, carried all her belongings into the bathroom and showered. Again, she insisted he undress and stow his clothes before she would come out. After his shower he found her naked on the bed. When she left, she again went without a word.

They began meeting every Thursday. On their third rendezvous, she saw they were in what must have been the cheapest room in the entire hotel. When she asked him about it, he shrugged with chagrin and suggested she start coming to his place.

"I'll take care of it," she said and dismissed his protest. The following week she emailed him a room number and told him to go straight up and wait for her when he got to the hotel.

In January, she changed their meetings to every other Wednesday without telling him why. Five months in, she still tended to be bossy, but he sometimes glimpsed a warmer, more vulnerable side of her. They talked more, but continued to cloak parts of their personal histories in clumsy anonymity. When he suggested "Twenty Questions" one evening, she countered with "One-Too-Many" questions. He'd ask, she'd answer until he stepped into forbidden territory. Would that do?

"What's your last name?"

"One too many," she said.

"Tell me."

"None of your business."

Another evening, they opened the drapes and watched the snow come down.

"Are you still married?" he asked.

"Duh."

"Why did you join?"

She sighed.

"Don't know. Bored. My life's a bore. My husband—*he's* a bore. He loves me, I know. And I love him; I do. And our marriage isn't...*bad.* He's good to me. It's just...I don't know." She rolled away from him. "I don't know. Are *you* married?"

"Nah," he said. "Who'd want me?"

At the end of March, she changed the day again. Back to Thursday this time.

"Why? Wednesday's fine," he said.

"My class is on Thursdays."

She had signed up for classes in the business school at the University. She revealed to him that she had registered online and paid for classes, each quarter since they'd met. She dropped the classes once the schedule was mailed to her home.

"I still don't know what you do," he said to her one week.

"One too many."

"Will you tell me if I guess?"

"I already told you, one too many. What do you do?"

He was silent.

"Well?"

"Let's say I'm a public servant."

She looked at him and twisted her lips.

"You could be a cop, but you're not. You're not a teacher, or a nurse... not a garbage man. Not a fireman, not a mailman. A public servant.... You work at City Hall, right?"

Good guess.

"What do you do?" she asked.

"One too many," he said.

"Do you work for a Councilmember? City Manager's Office? Mayor's office?"

"Two too many."

"You can't take a chance on people finding out that you belong to an online swinger's club because the resulting embarrassment would damage your social standing and perhaps endanger your job?"

"You're very astute."

"So stop asking me my name."

"How long have you been married?"

She shifted on the bed and put her head under the blanket. When he was aroused, she took her mouth away and threw back the bedclothes to look at him.

"Unless you want to do this yourself, stop with the questions."

No further questions dear.

When they next met, she came in and placed her things on a chair before going in to shower. On her way out the door two hours later, she stopped and looked back at him.

"My last name is Collingsworth-Baden. Happy now?" she closed the door.

* * *

There was no sign of her the following Thursday. He asked for her room at fifteen after six and was told she had not checked in. He asked again at six-thirty, wondering if he could have missed seeing her. Nope, she still wasn't there. At seven o'clock he went home and emailed her.

"What happened?"

The turn-around time for her responses was usually short. He checked an hour later but saw nothing from her. She still had not responded by day's end, so he emailed her from home that night.

"Was it something I said?"

He checked for a response before going to bed.

Nothing.

He got up and went straight to his computer the next morning. With forced casualness, he logged in and checked for an email. Today was Saturday.

Still nothing.

He guessed the party was over.

A part of him wanted to say "so what?" So she had blown him off. It had been fun. He'd spent months screwing a great-looking woman with no strings attached. Maybe he should be glad she moved on without becoming a nuisance. He decided to put it out of his mind.

But when Monday morning came, he went unenthusiastically to his office and plopped down in his chair with a sigh. He stared at the darkened monitor on his desk. If he checked his email now and found no message from her, his entire day would already have been ruined. The disappointment would sap what little energy he had, and that was something he did not need first thing Monday morning. He knew, however, even as he reached for the mouse, that he needed to find out something sooner rather than later. Maybe she'd gone out of town and hadn't been able to let him know. That was a reach, but it was something.

The monitor hissed as it came awake. He logged onto the system and went straight to his inbox. Bill pay notifications, instant loan offers, "lose ten pounds in thirty days!"

No word from her. It was going to be a long day.

Thursday night he was slumped in his favorite chair, a beer warming in his hand while he watched Judge Judy. He flipped the channel every minute or two but kept coming back to the courtroom show because the babe at the Defendant's table had a pretty face, and her breasts were playing tug-of-war with the buttons on her shirt.

He raised the bottle to his lips and took a pull.

One insipid commercial after another. How the hell did people watch this stuff all day? The smiling face of a tv news anchor appeared during the commercial break.

"Hi I'm Nona McGill. Here are some of the stories we're working on at this hour…"

Maybe a Twilight Zone re-run was starting on the Sci-Fi channel.

"A local family appeals to area viewers for information about the hit and run accident that killed a Lake Stratford woman last Thursday…"

Lake Stratford last Thursday…. Lake Stratford was the swankiest area in the entire county. Something about that name pricked the inside of his skull. Something recent. Was that where she lived?

He stayed put while the woman rambled and while a tiny, absurd idea formed and quickly wormed its way through the circuitry in his brain.

Get real.

What, are you living a tv show?

He took another swig from the bottle.

And you drink too much.

Moist fingerprints lingered on the plastic casing when he

adjusted his grip on the remote. Why was his hand sweating? He placed his palms on the arms of the chair and sat up straight. Why did he feel like a patient waiting for the dentist to come in?

"This is Eyewitness News at Six," the woman said after another round of commercials. "We begin tonight with a public appeal from law enforcement and from the family of a hit-and-run victim whom police say might have lived had she received medical care in time."

The camera cut to a male reporter.

"It's been a week since thirty-one year old Mira Collingsworth-Baden, a local activist and fund-raiser, was found near her parked car at the downtown campus of Hancock State University." The picture switched to a high-ranking uniformed cop standing before a bank of microphones. Mitch seldom watched local news, but he noted the date in the corner of the screen. This footage was a week old.

"The victim," the cop began, "a part-time student at Hancock State University, was discovered by campus police at approximately nine o'clock last night following an apparent hit-and-run incident. Information gathered at the scene indicates that she was struck and thrown several feet by a car traveling at high speed..."

The cop was voiced over by the reporter, whose face reappeared.

"That driver, when found, will face charges of recklessness and vehicular homicide. But that was a week ago and police still have no clue as to what kind of car it was, let alone who was driving it when it sped through a narrow street and ended the life of this mother of two."

A daytime exterior shot of a lavish house in an upscale neighborhood appeared and quickly changed to an indoor shot of four people arranged on a sofa: a rotund man, two school-aged children, and a woman who looked remarkably like Mira.

Her sister?

A studio portrait of her family sat side-by-side with a wedding portrait on the coffee table. The camera zoomed in on the photo of the happy bride and groom as the man talked. The picture flicked back and forth between the kids, the family portrait, and the woman who was indeed her sister. A tearful plea went out to anyone, anyone who had any information at all, and was followed by the number to the local Crimestoppers organization. The program returned to the anchorwoman in the studio.

"Mira Collingsworth-Baden will be laid to rest tomorrow at the Trinity Gardens Cemetery in Lake Stratford."

He reached for the beer bottle but it slipped from his hand and sloshed beer onto the carpet.

Dazed, he looked at the remote in his lap and tried to pick it up, tried to turn the television off so that it couldn't show her or say her name again.

He called in sick to his job the next day and lay looking at the wall next to his bed. The dog came over and licked his hand, but he pushed its muzzle away and ignored its whimpers. At one in the afternoon, he sat up on the edge of the bed and put his head in his hands. He was still in that position at one-thirty. The dog shit in a corner near the front door and the smell followed it when it came back and whined to him again. His stomach gurgled. The dog barked at him and licked its whiskers. When he did not move, it whined more. He got up finally, when the urge to urinate overpowered him. Her face appeared in front of him, as plain as anything, and he tried to see past her as he made his way to the bathroom.

Trinity Gardens Cemetery in Lake Stratford, he thought.

Don't.

His best suit was a low-end Armani that cost him six hundred dollars on sale. But a six hundred dollar suit was good enough, even in Lake Stratford.

Dressed in his best clothes, he drove the streets of Lake Stratford until he came upon one clogged with parked cars. When he found the house he'd seen on the news the night before, he passed it and drove until he found a place where he could park his four year-old BMW.

His insides were numb. One stubborn part of his brain wanted to believe he could go home right now, check his email, and find a message from her. A miracle? A dream? Who cared? It would come from her—that was what mattered. The other side of his brain pictured her sprawled on the asphalt.

He got out of the car.

You'll be sorry...

He slipped inside the wrought iron gate and followed the trail of Malibu lights glowing beside the long driveway. A group of people

111

stood in a small circle at the foot of the walk that led to the front door. No one spoke to him as he cut across the lawn and passed by. The idea of ringing the bell occurred and quickly evaporated when he reached the door. He placed his hand on the brass handle and noted the tremble of his fingers. Taking a deep breath, he pushed the latch and opened it.

A marble foyer led directly to a plush Great Room where people stood in somber groups. He looked to his left and saw a wide, marble staircase lighted by a massive chandelier climbing to the second and third floors. A middle-aged woman standing at the edge of the room to his right turned as he stepped inside the entrance. He hesitated. There was no feeling in his legs now, and he wondered if he could walk without stumbling.

The woman walked over and extended her hand. He opened his mouth and extended his hand at the same time.

"I...uh. I'm sorry."

She took his hand lightly.

"Thank you. Thank you for coming. Dave's in here. Are you...?"

"A friend. A friend of her's. Of Mira's."

The woman nodded and turned back toward the huge room.

"You've met Dave then, right? Have you met the kids? Would you like to say something to them?"

You have lost your fucking mind. You have lost—

"Ye...yes. Yes I would."

The woman gave him a look, pleasant but quizzical, that reminded him of the way Mira had looked at him at the end of their last rendezvous.

"I'm Kelly. David's sister," she said and walked him into the room.

An elderly man stood near the magnificent fireplace at the opposite end of the room. He held a brandy snifter in one hand and a white handkerchief in the other, with which he wiped his eyes. A grand portrait of Mira hung above the fireplace and dominated the room.

"...If I had known that the good Lord would see fit to call away my grandchild before he did me...there is no height to which my prayers would not have been pushed if I might have been summoned in her stead." He wiped his nose. "It was not to be that my children and my children's children would all stand beside my deathbed when my time came. But in my heart, every single one of you will thrive for the rest of my waning days." He turned to the portrait on the mantle. "If a grandfather's love may speed you to your reward my dove, then Godspeed, and God be with us who stand in your wake and say…farewell." He raised his glass in a shaking hand. "Farewell."

The lump in Mitch's throat grew to golf ball size. Some in the room watched the woman lead him in, but most wiped at their eyes and comforted each other. He felt wobbly and disoriented. Before he realized it, Kelly was introducing him to Mira's husband.

The television had made him look rotund, fat even. But face-to-face, Mitch saw that the man was not fat at all but solid and powerfully built. He was a broad-shouldered grizzly with a receding hairline.

"This iiiiiissss…Mira's friend," she said when Mitch failed to insert his name. He looked at the hair on Dave's knuckles when the large man extended his hand to shake.

"How are you, ahhh…? What's your name?"

"M-Mitchell. Mitch. It's good to meet you."

"How'd you know my wife?"

People, including Mira's grandfather, turned their attention to the two of them. Dave was only an inch taller, but his hand covered Mitch's like a bear's claw over a rabbit's foot. He felt himself smile suddenly, a great big beaming smile of all things, smiling like a fool. Kelly tilted her head and looked at him, perplexed. He scanned the circle of people waiting for him to say something and felt his tongue weld itself to the roof of his mouth. His hand, buried in the catcher's mitt of Dave's grip, began to sweat like crazy. Someone moved up behind him.

He felt a sharp prick in his left armpit. Then he felt another and another and then it was both underarms. Sweat broke out on his forehead and wetness formed in the center of his back.

"So how'd you know her?"

His eyes darted to the fireplace searching for flames, but of course there was no fire. There had been no fire when he came in. Why did he suddenly feel like he was standing in front of a searchlight?

"I didn't know her well," he choked out. The man held onto his hand like he expected Mitch to run. Every sound in the room disappeared. "It was only short...a short time." He sounded like an idiot. Like a stuttering imbecile. Dave looked deep into his eyes, and Mitch felt the bones in his sweaty hand grind together. The woman who had led him in laid a hand on his shoulder.

"Would you like something to drink?" she asked.

"Where'd you meet her?" Dave asked, still gripping his hand.

He wanted to say "work," but "class..." came out instead. "A class at school...at Hancock State." His voice creaked like a dry-rotted shutter in a windstorm. "She was...very nice." His tie was choking him. He dug two fingers of his free hand into the band of his collar and pulled at it trying to give himself air. "She's...a very good person and I grieve for your loss."

He heard someone whisper. Stares bombarded him.

Another hand landed on his other shoulder, one that could have belonged to a gorilla. He looked back as best he could and saw a much taller man standing over him. The tall guy took the woman's hand off his shoulder. Mitch turned back to Mira's husband and imagined he saw a look pass between the two men.

"Thank you for coming," the husband said suddenly and perfunctorily, letting go and turning away as though Mitch did not exist.

Mitch's hand dropped, throbbing, to his side. Other people in the room began turning away.

"Would you come this way, please?" the tall man asked quietly. His hand was like a brick with fingers, and he easily maneuvered Mitch toward a door that led deeper into the house.

Mitch protested feebly. "Perhaps I should go."

"Perhaps you shouldn't have come."

When they were out of the Great room, two more men fell in behind the one who held him by the shoulder. He was pushed like a child through the ground floor of the house, her house, and he thought he saw glimpses of her everywhere, glimpses of the life she shared with someone else, her real life. Her place. Her life. The men shoved him down a short flight of steps, through a darkened room, and out through a door that led to the swimming pool.

Mitch stumbled over the threshold and turned quickly to face them. The house disappeared behind a bright blue flash and a spiraling trail of stars. The first blow loosened two of his teeth. He fell backward onto soft grass, but they hauled him to his feet, and the tall man buried a fist in Mitch's midsection. He doubled over behind the pain, but they stood him up again.

A fiery cramp ignited and spread through his midsection. Bitter slime bubbled up his esophagus and coated his lips; he thought he might lose control of his bowels.

Jesus…

"You're one slick motherfucker, ain't you?" one of the men growled. "The bitch tell you she had a family?"

It hurt so bad, so bad. He almost wished they had hit him in the face again instead.

The tall man cocked his arm and did just that. Mitch felt the jarring, stinging wallop vibrate through his skull and ring out of his ears. They let go, and he fell to the ground.

The looming figure seemed a hundred times larger than normal until it crouched and got close enough for him to smell its expensive, woodsy cologne.

"You ever bring your pathetic, faggot ass near this house or my brother's kids again; I swear to God I'll put a bullet in your fucking head. You understand me?" The man slapped him to drive home the point.

Mitch gagged on the plug of blood and saliva in his throat.

"Get him the fuck out of here."

The tall man rose and disappeared.

The two others grabbed him, dragged him around the pool and out across the grass to a six-foot wooden fence that ran the length of the property. Together, they hoisted him to his feet and dumped him over the fence headfirst. He landed in a row of shrubs on the other side.

Mitch found his way to the street, to his car, and drove away with his head and his ribs throbbing. The sky was black as he threaded his way through traffic and eventually found the empty row of parking meters along the western edge of Griffith Park. He pulled himself out of the car and stumbled toward the fountain, bolts of lightning still burning away his insides.

Christ…

He needed a doctor.

A homeless man was curled up on the bench closest to the statue of Tennessee Williams. Mitch eased himself down into a corner of the bench nevertheless. Across the street, warm, yellow light brightened the windows of The Craige. He watched the people—men, women, couples—pass in and out of the double glass doors that had become so familiar to him.

She had told him her last name finally, but she had never once said goodbye.

8.

H.E.R. and the Great American Famine

"Let me get this straight," Doctor Giovanni Musgrove said. The nurse to whom he spoke pursed her lips, ready to answer the same three questions yet again.

"The patient is a forty-four year old male?"

"Yes doctor," she answered dutifully.

"Alert, oriented times three, suffering dehydration and advanced malnutrition?"

"Yes doctor."

"And the ER doctor ordered a psychological evaluation because—"

The nurse nodded in anticipation.

"—he thinks the man is afraid of food?"

"Yes doctor."

His disbelief twisted out of him in a straight-faced, deadpan monotone that still, somehow sounded like biting sarcasm.

"He's afraid of food?"

"Yes doctor."

"He is *afraid…*of *food?*"

"Yes sir."

Musgrove's eye twitched. "That can't be right," he sighed. Perhaps the man was afraid of being poisoned, or maybe he was afraid the hospital's food would make him even sicker. God knew that was a rational fear. But a person simply could not be afraid of food.

"It's the truth," the nurse said.

"If I walked into that room right now and showed him a salad, he would…"

"Become agitated, fight against his restraints, hyperventilate, show general signs of a panic attack, et cetera, et cetera," the nurse said.

"If I showed him a bagel?"

"Same thing."

"If I offered him a ten ounce rib-eye smothered in mushrooms he would…"

"Shit himself probably and go right through that window, bars and all."

She shrugged under his gaze.

Musgrove could take a joke as well as anyone, but this was his third day on call, and he had slept exactly four hours and eight minutes in the last two nights.

"Nurse," he sighed and closed his eyes. "If this is Dr. Allen's idea of a joke…" Dr. Allen was the chief intern. Before the weary man could finish his sentence, a bloodcurdling scream sounded two doors away.

"That's him," the nurse said casually.

"Come with me," the doctor said.

They entered the room and found a horribly emaciated man fighting to get out of the bed. The hospital gown had worked its way off one shoulder exposing part of his upper body. His chest and arms looked like a birdcage with twigs poked into its wire frame. His collarbone stood out so distinctly, the doctor imagined he could see the subclavian artery running underneath it. The man's face, probably thin to begin with, was shriveled and haggard, skeletal. His eyes, surrounded by darkened skin, looked like they had been sucked backward into his skull. Except for the wild, bushy hair that covered his head, he looked like a holocaust victim. The padded wrist restraints were still fastened securely to the bed, but they and two nurses were scarcely able to hold the man down.

"It's herrrrrrrr!!" he howled, "get it away! Get...ugghk...get it away!!"

"Get who away?" one of the embattled nurses squealed.

"Her!" the man screamed in pointed horror. "Her! *Herrrr!*"

The doctor moved to the bedside and took the man by the shoulders. With the nurses' help, he gently but firmly repositioned the man in bed and covered him with the blanket.

"Get it away...get it away..." the man moaned, breathing as though he had just run a marathon. His thin skin was slimy with sweat, and Musgrove surreptitiously wiped his hands on the bed sheet. He then asked all three women leave the room, since it was impossible to tell which "her" the man referred too.

"Go, go," he said, urging them out. "It's okay."

He was careful to hide his disgust when the women were gone and he was alone with the patient. The man continued to squirm and wiggle toward one side of the bed, twisting and arching his midsection as though the bedclothes burned him.

A small container of orange liquid sat on the bedside table.

Musgrove leaned toward it and peered over the rim of his glasses.

The label was a small, irregularly shaped sticker, intriguing in its simplicity. It showed an amazingly realistic, three-dimensional picture of an orange so ripe and so succulent that he thought he could lick the label and taste its juice. Lined up alongside the orange were the letters H-E-R in emerald green. The three letters were the only writing on the container. No other information of any sort—not a date, not a barcode, nothing else could be found.

The light came on in his head, and he was annoyed that it had taken so long for him to fit the pieces together.

This was "H.E.R." brand orange juice.

H.E.R. Incorporated—a household word in the United States (and fast becoming a household word everywhere else)—was reputed to produce the healthiest packaged foods available on Earth, literally, period. The nurses had not made the connection because it was simple nonsense to think that a person would refuse a food product distributed by H.E.R. H.E.R.'s reputation was so strong in fact, they were the only US food producer allowed to show nothing more than the corporate logo on their products. During the last Presidential administration, the US Department of Agriculture had gone so far as to revise its quality standards upward, in order to keep pace with H.E.R. quality standards.

H.E.R. was a testimony to the endless possibilities open to a company offering products of supreme quality in a free market, and its unbreakable bond with the buying public had been long in the making. Originally a genetic research firm, H.E.R. had one day announced it would discontinue its medical research and instead commit itself to the campaign to feed the world's starving millions. Years more of research, experimentation, courtroom litigation, and public relations campaigns, had opened the door for H.E.R. to revolutionize the food industry through a series of breakthroughs in production techniques. It was proven again and again through a parade of independent studies that H.E.R.'s produce, even after processing and canning, retained more vitamins, nutrients, flavor, and just plain goodness than even the freshest produce presented in most supermarkets. Over time, H.E.R. had driven the frozen food industry giants into bankruptcy and had absorbed nearly every viable regional distributor into its colossal enterprise.

Its greatest asset, though, was also its greatest liability. Every food it developed and marketed was genetically altered, and that fact alone had regularly brought out protestors in the hundreds of thousands during the company's first months in the food business. It came to be said, however, that a simple garden salad made with H.E.R. vegetables was enough to turn any protestor who dared taste it into a shareholder.

Three years after it became the leading food producer in North America, H.E.R. fell victim to an internal squabble unlike any ever seen in corporate America. The corporation had begun packaging pre-cooked entrees and shipping them to Red Cross food distribution centers in the third world. No one in its upper echelons offered to explain why such delectable food was being shipped to Africa, India, Central America, and other such undeserving places, when people right here in the good ole' USA couldn't get it. The fight between shareholders and the Board of Directors over domestic marketing became so intense that most of the company's top executives resigned and the price of the company's stock began to slide. Those who remained gave in to shareholder demands and ordered the distribution of H.E.R. Meats in the fifty states and Europe. Without preamble, H.E.R. began marketing frozen dinners. The shareholders were happy, but the general public responded with mixed feelings.

Many who loved H.E.R. vegetables and organic products thought it sacrilege that the maker of such wonderful natural foods should start selling meat. Left-wing extremists called for a worldwide boycott of H.E.R. products, but the foods were simply too tasty, too nutritious, and the brand too popular to succumb. Some sworn vegetarians secretly began eating meat. Simply put, H.E.R. had been the best thing to happen to food since the discovery of fire. A year after they began showing up in stores, the only freezers that did not have H.E.R. frozen dinners and entrees in them were freezers that were on the blink.

Musgrove scratched his head.

Could the juice container have upset the man? Could a lucid and rational person have found fault with a H.E.R. food product? He picked the container up and sniffed at it.

Preposterous. Hell, H.E.R.'s was the only orange juice that would ever pass his lips.

"Mister...." He checked the chart for the man's name. "*Doctor* Woodhill," he corrected himself. According to the chart, he was a geneticist. "Can you tell me what's bothering you?"

"Her, goddamnit! Her!" the man rasped.

"You mean one of the nurses, one of the women who were just here?"

The man's chest heaved. He shook his head.

Musgrove held up the container of orange juice.

"This?"

The man screamed, and the hoarse sound of his voice was underscored by a raucous burst of gas that escaped from his other end.

"What's wrong with it?" Musgrove asked.

"Get it away! GET IT AWAY!"

Good God almighty. Afraid of.... what? Orange juice? And from the most trusted name in the business.

He placed the container in the wastebasket, placed the wastebasket outside the room, and tried again to get the man to talk.

The man ignored all questions related to his medical history, but rambled on and on about an island and the fact that everyone on Earth was going to hell.

It did not take long for Musgrove to decide that the man was hopelessly delusional and give up. Scribbling a quick note on the chart, he left the room. Nothing he could do for this nut except order him fed through a tube.

Leaving the Emergency Room that evening, he stopped in the waiting area long enough to watch a television commercial that showed the sun rising over a pristine valley. The sky was vivid blue; the grass was vivid green, the sunlight vivid yellow-orange. The trees were the color of dark almond honey, and their leaves sparkled like large, flat emeralds dusted with bits and pieces of diamond. As he watched, the landscape morphed into the figure of a woman. When her face and upper body were fully formed, she opened her hazel eyes, smiled the warmest, tenderest, most disarming smile imaginable, and raised her arms toward the camera. She was cradling a cornucopia that overflowed with fruits and vegetables. They looked so amazingly real, and so delicious, that Musgrove wanted to reach his hand through the screen and take one. The letters H...E...R appeared in a soft, shimmering, velvety color. The chirping of sparrows wafted from the speakers.

Musgrove felt a tweak of hunger in his gut.

He drove through the city to his home in one of its sprawling suburbs. Along the way he saw H.E.R. billboards, ads on the sides of busses, ads on benches. There was even a radio spot telling him to stock up on H.E.R. frozen hamburger patties and wieners in time for his Memorial Day cookout. The tiny twinges he had felt walking out of the ER turned into full-fledged, growling, tugging, sucking, hunger pangs. Only two miles from his house, he had to fight himself to keep from pulling over and buying a hotdog from one of those drive-through fast food joints. No, no, no, he chided himself. His wife was making his favorite tonight, H.E.R. Chicken Alfredo casserole. His mouth watered when he remembered the last time she had served it. Herbs and spices in a crème sauce smothering sensuous, beautiful H.E.R. egg noodles (perfect every time or your money back), all of it wrapped around those succulent chucks of tender white-meat chicken so moist and juicy they fell apart when you speared them with a fork. The aroma was as impressive as the taste. He could feel those tender chunks of meat melting in his mouth, caressing his pallet and sliding down his throat. He licked his lips and pushed down on the accelerator.

When he opened the front door, the cooking aromas enfolded him and drew him into the house. The smell of cinnamon and brown sugar was on the air, and nutmeg. A pie. She had baked a pie. Then he caught the scent of basil and thyme and butter melting with just a hint of garlic. His wife met him crossing the living room and pressed a chilled glass of white Zinfandel into his hand. He swept her into his free arm and planted a kiss on her lips. They walked arm-in-arm to the kitchen, sharing sips from the glass.

In the old days, in the time of his mother and grandmother, a woman who considered herself a great cook would use only fresh ingredients, nothing frozen or prepackaged. These days, a person couldn't call herself (or himself) a decent cook *unless* H.E.R. was a part of the recipe. His wife, tossing a garden salad in a glass bowl, told him to wash his hands and set the table. His mouth watering like a garden sprinkler, he very happily complied.

They sat down to a splendid-looking meal. The doctor was so hungry by now, and the food looked and smelled so good, he could not wait for his wife to say grace. Before he heard "amen," he grabbed a thick slice of garlic bread from the tray and bit into it. His wife smiled and spooned food onto his plate. She was glad to serve a man still so appreciative of her cooking after all these years. While he worked his way through the first helping, she remembered to switch on the small television set in a corner of the dining room, hoping they had not missed much of the evening news.

The picture rolled up the screen then came to rest on the ashen face of a news anchorwoman. Actually, the doctor thought, giving his full attention to the screen, the woman looked a bit green.

"…We are going to take you live to ABC World News Tonight in just a moment…"

The doctor savored chunks of seasoned white meat and soft,

buttery noodles on their way to his belly.

"...But first we want to update you on local reaction to this breaking story."

He saw footage of workers in a local supermarket racing through the frozen foods aisle, sweeping packages off the refrigerated shelves and hustling them to the back of the store.

"We're seeing this same reaction all over town as word comes..."

The doctor stopped chewing.

Was there some sort of terrorist threat against the supermarkets?

He swallowed the last bit of food already in his mouth. Then he took a long sip of wine.

"...as word comes from the Department of Health and Human Services and the Centers for Disease Control that there may be a serious health risk to consumers using H.E.R. frozen foods. We do not know if this concern extends to H.E.R. brand produce, but we expect the Surgeon General to clarify that and many other questions any minute now."

The doctor looked at his wife, who looked down at the dish of noodles and chicken on the table and slowly set her fork down. The doctor refilled his wine glass and drained it again.

The anchorwoman talked on, stretching her commentary until she got a signal from behind the camera.

"I'm hearing—"

She stopped.

Pause.

"We now take you live to ABC World News Tonight."

A voice vibrating with forced calm faded in. "...shocking, absolutely unbelievable news coming out of Southeast Asia tonight. We are live in the Nation's capital, awaiting the Surgeon General. Our correspondent David Richards is at the White House, where the Surgeon General has met with the President and is seeking an emergency Executive Order to stop the sale and distribution of H.E.R. foods. David can you hear me?"

"Yes," another voice answered, also with measured calm. The screen split, and the two men's faces appeared side-by-side.

"David, I imagine a lot of people are going to find it easier to diet tomorrow."

Dr. Musgrove glanced at his wife.

"No doubt, Sam. The real question is this: how much of an effect will we see on hunger statistics in the next few months? Right now..." Voices rose and there was movement in the room behind him. A bearded man in a black uniform appeared from a side door and walked to a lectern beneath the White House seal.

"Here is the Surgeon General," the correspondent said and fell quiet.

America's number one health educator looked as if he had spent the morning watching trains run over babies. He adjusted the microphone with a shaky hand and spoke.

"Good evening. I have a short statement; then, I will open the floor for questions." He cleared his throat. "At five-fifteen p.m. Eastern Daylight Time, I asked the Secretary of Health and Human Services to contact the President and request an order banning immediately and unconditionally the transport and sale of H.E.R. Incorporated meats, meat products, and any food containing meat or meat products. I am directing all Regional Offices of the U.S. Public Health Service, and all State and Local Departments of Health to monitor the immediate removal of these same products from warehouses, stores, restaurants, and all places that prepare and serve food. In addition, they, in cooperation with the National Guard, will monitor the destruction of these products by the most expeditious means available and ensure these products are not usable by the public. The Public Health Service is taking these steps in response to shocking information obtained just a few hours ago by this office."

Cameras flashed in the room.

A murmur spread through the gaggle of reporters.

"If you would please turn your attention to one of the monitors positioned around the room..."

There was a general shifting in the crowd as people turned and adjusted themselves to watch.

A jerky shot of what looked like the inside of a food processing plant appeared on the screen.

"This footage was taken six hours ago by Japanese naval personnel involved in an exercise in the Celebes Sea south of the Philippine Islands. The landmass you see here is located fifty nautical miles west of Mindanao Island. What you are looking at is the inside of a meat packing plant owned by H.E.R. Incorporated."

It was an assembly line of skinned limbs and gutted carcasses, some dangling from hooks, some chopped into pieces and strewn along a conveyor belt, all disturbingly unlike the carcasses commonly seen in butcher shops and packing houses. Long bones and piles of entrails lay near grated holes in the floor. Musgrove was no veterinarian; but it struck him right away that some of those bones looked too large to have come from pigs or sheep, and too small to have come from cows. Not knowing what to make of it, he simply watched and shook his head as the camera panned around the large, open space. So, all the excitement had to do with unsanitary conditions at a plant run by the world's number-one food producer. This was going to be a scandal of unprecedented proportions. Picking up his fork, he followed as the camera zoomed in on a discarded limb, and then he saw very clearly a human leg and a foot with four of its toes missing.

His mind put it all together an instant before warm sludge backed up into his throat. Before he could get to his feet, he hurled a mouthful of puree onto his plate. He gulped air, then his entire body convulsed and sprayed slivers of pasta and undigested meat into his wine glass, into the casserole dish, onto the bread tray, the table cloth, and his wife's arm. She held a napkin to her mouth and vomited into her lap.

"As you can see," the Surgeon General went on, "these appear to be human remains."

With white sauce bubbling out of his nose, the doctor gripped the edge of the table. Then he heaved with enough force to bend his body double before collapsing to the floor. At the back of his mind he marveled. Twenty-eight years in medicine, and he had never seen so much puke come out of one person. His eyes watered, his abdominal muscles ached from the violent contractions, and his throat burned like it had been scraped with a Brillo pad.

"Oh Gooodddddd…" he moaned.

He heard gagging and retching from the television.

"These pictures are quite disturbing," the Surgeon General said unnecessarily.

Musgrove heard his wife crying just before she vomited again.

A month later, he was down from one hundred seventy-nine pounds to one hundred thirty. His wife seemed to have stabilized at eighty-six pounds. She was unable to sit up by herself. For weeks she had taken nothing to eat except white bread and water, though he had offered her peanut butter, ice cream, broth, oatmeal…she would have none of it. He did not know how much longer she would last.

In a month's time, the weight of the average American woman dropped by seventy pounds, the weight of the average man by sixty-one and a third. Some managed to keep eating fish, but its skyrocketing price combined with the new distrust of flesh as food meant that even it could not fill the nutritional chasm that opened in the wake of the H.E.R. scandal. Supermarkets were picked clean of grain products, soy, fruits, vegetables, vitamin supplements, powdered nutrients; it was not enough. America became a nation of gaunt, hollow-eyed stick people.

An investigation of the processing plant in the Philippines showed it to be only the tip of the iceberg. A far-reaching operation had been put in place to recover edible human flesh from the uncounted, undistinguished, unknown and unwanted, unclaimed, unidentified, and unlucky individuals who passed each day without ceremony. The sharp rise in demand for H.E.R. Meats in the United States and Europe had forced the company to find another, cheaper source of livestock than the domesticated animals it raised on ranches and poultry farms in three countries. Looking at the vast, undeveloped and underdeveloped regions of the Third World, they had found just what they needed. Although it could, and nearly always did, cry out for help or mercy when given the chance, the new livestock, for the most part, had lacked either the means to resist, or a place to run too. Refugees mostly.

When the weekly death toll from self-imposed starvation reached into the hundreds, a rival US food group, seeing a chance to save the world *and* get back on its financial feet, gambled on a bold and controversial marketing campaign. In a series of disturbing, but ultimately effective ads, the Tech-Foods, Inc. Board of Directors told people to eat hardy and rest assured: "Our entrees are one hundred percent pure beef, pork, poultry, and mutton. We never package meat that can ask to be spared."

9.
Being a Hero

All SUVs looked good in commercials. Climbing boulders, rolling logs, driving on the sea bottom, they were all macho and muscle. But that last crater in the trail they were on had kicked his passengers around so violently, Justin Harvey thought he ought to quit before he broke an axle. He pulled off to what would have been the side of the road if the road had been more than a slash mark through the trees. They (he, his wife and their best friends) had set out almost two hours ago searching for the Sienna River Camp Grounds on a three-day outing in the wilds of Mark Twain National Park in northern Missouri.

Harvey and Terrell Williams were business partners as well as best friends. Former college roommates, the pair had finished ninth and tenth in their graduating class. They had scraped together enough capital to buy a small grocery store that specialized in organic foods. The insight that solidified the business and put it firmly in the black was to make their more popular products available online at the height of the dot-com craze. Because they were smart enough to channel the lion's share of profits into renovating, expanding, and upgrading their brick-and-mortar store and not into building a virtual super-warehouse and delivery service, they survived when the creeping death began to eviscerate online businesses in the late nineties.

Once they found the signs that led to the campground's entrance, they registered at the Ranger Station and walked across the clearing to the camp store and restaurant, where they had lunch, double checked the first-aid kits, and topped off the beer supply and other provisions. While the women enjoyed a final, civilized bathroom break, the two men stood outside the log cabin styled building and waited.

The clean, pine-scented air called to Harvey the way the bright sun called to a kid in a classroom in the third week of May. Hands in his pockets, he leaped up and down on the leaves and pine needles like a West African tribesman in a ceremonial dance. The morning sun lit the face of the hills to their north and created a sharp line of light and dark contrast across the forest canopy. The long line of hills undulated against the sky and marched away into atmospheric haze. It would be a clear day, slightly warm but not unpleasant.

Harvey picked up a pinecone and hurled it toward the trees on the opposite side of the clearing. The prickly seed whipped through the air with a sound like the flutter of wings.

"Boy this takes me back," he said.

Terrell Williams had grown up in urban East Saint Louis. He had gone camping before and now as always he wondered why people did it. There was none of this wannabe woodsman stuff in him or in anybody he knew besides Justin. For Terrell, the Rangers could have skipped the safety speech. He had no intention of feeding the bears or anything else that wasn't human, and no strange humans had better sneak up on him. He didn't mind the idea of catching a fish or two, however. He could even stand the idea of gutting them and slow-cooking them over an open fire rather than frying them. But beyond that, he planned to sit on his ass, drink a few beers, and keep the mosquitoes away for two or three days. Cheryl, his wife, and the other two could do all the hiking and bird watching they wanted to; he would stay back and guard the camp.

"Did you get that postcard?" he asked, picking up a pinecone himself and sending it spinning away. Their bookkeeper had said the closest he wanted to get to the great outdoors was a picture. Harvey had said he would be sure to send one.

"Be right back."

Inside the store, he found a small rack of postcards at one end of the counter. He chose one of a huge grizzly standing in a stream and tried to pay without staring at the half dozen earrings dangling from the clerk's left ear. The girl gave him his change and turned her back, giving him a glimpse of a gigantic tattoo that peeked out from the bottom and sides of her tank top. A page of postage stamps lay on the counter, half in and half out of a plastic bag. Without knowing why he did it, Justin tore off one of the stamps, licked it, and pressed it onto the postcard. He walked back outside and dropped it into the mailbox next to the door.

When the ladies came out, the couples loaded into the Cherokee and drove back out to the main road. They turned east and headed toward the dense woods and hiking trails that began a mile or so up the road. They followed the blacktop a while, then turned off onto a rutted track that disappeared into the trees ahead of them. Justin followed the track until the truck began to bob and weave like a punch-drunk fighter. After a particularly violent lurch, he parked and got out.

According to the map, there should have been a cleared area for parking nearby. He turned in every direction but saw no indication of it, then, as an afterthought, he got on his hands and knees and looked under the vehicle. Everything looked fine.

"Break something?" Terrell asked opening the passenger door.

"Nah. It's fine. Smell this air will you?" Justin picked up a rock and threw it.

"How about we stop here and hike the rest of the way?" he asked the group.

Inside the vehicle, the women looked at each other.

"Honey, is it smart to leave the truck here?"

Allison Harvey was equally anxious to get her feet on the ground after the long drive, but she was not eager to stroll away and leave their transportation all by itself in the middle of nowhere.

"I think it'll be fine," Justin said. "Nobody out this far except hikers anyway."

"I think we should go a little farther in and try to find that truck park," she said.

They debated, then the two men climbed back in and they drove—this time more carefully—for another ten minutes. A red-dirt clearing appeared as they rounded a bend in the trail. They parked, got out, and unloaded their gear. The weather was perfect, seasonally mild with clear skies and low humidity. Loaded down with backpacks, they set off at an easy pace, moving up the hill in a westerly direction.

After a half hour of slow walking, they heard the forest-filling hiss of the Sienna River. Another fifteen minutes and they came out onto a ridge that looked down on the torrent of brown water racing to join the Missouri. A half-mile above the ridge they found a perfect clearing, but two tents were already being anchored to the ground at its opposite ends. Families with children had claimed the clearing and then put as much of it between their respective campsites as possible. Disappointed, they moved on, following a rock-strewn path that cut in and out of the tree line.

"I hope you guys are keeping track of where we are." Allison called from the back of the troop. Justin took the palm-sized global positioning device from the pocket of his fishing vest and checked it. It was working fine.

"Not to worry, dear," he said.

The four made idle chatter as they continued to march and look for another open patch of ground. Climbing a small hill that carried them completely out of sight of the river, they came into an area that had been scorched by a forest fire. Charred logs lay on the ground, but the ground itself was covered with green shoots, and a sapling had begun to grow out of a stump that stood alone to one side.

Harvey loved every minute of this. Eight months with only occasional days off had about driven him crazy. He had not believed he could talk the other two into joining him and Allison, but he was glad he had made the effort. No one complained, but he sensed they were becoming impatient with the nonstop tramping, so he stopped a minute later and took out the map of the park. He judged that they were again moving toward the river and suggested they leave the trail and look for a clearing at its edge. The others agreed, and the four began picking their way through bramble weeds and low brush.

131

An hour later, longer that he had calculated, they came out under open sky and found themselves standing at the edge of a large, flat clearing bordered on three sides by the forest and on the fourth by the river itself.

"We're home."

It took another hour to set up the two tents and unpack their gear. When Harvey was done, fishing tackle, a hatchet, and a small pile of wood lay on the ground near a pit that would hold the evening's fire. He found four suitably thin tree limbs and sat down on a low stool to fashion a fishing rod for each of them. Sitting with his back to the women, he hummed while he tied the first lure and then fixed it to the end of a fishing line. Down at the riverbank, Terrell wedged the six-packs of beer and soda into the rocks just below the water's surface.

Harvey whistled as he looped the fishing line around the end of the second branch. If they caught no fish, the Bird's Eye boil-in-bag entrees would be tonight's dinner. He squinted and brought the line close to his face to knot it.

Then he heard the sound.

"Harrrrroughhh...hannnngghhhhhh."

It came from his left—a massive, hackle-raising rumble that was unlike anything he had ever heard.

A garden of gooseflesh bloomed across his neck and back.

*Hrrrrrrannnngggggggghh...*louder. Closer.

Harvey leapt to his feet and spun as one of the women screamed. In the strange way that insights often came to him, at the most inopportune moments, he realized he had never heard his wife scream. Yet he knew it was Allison.

His vision raked past a massive brown shape. If a Volkswagen could run, this is what it would look like. The thing moved *fast*; its huge head bobbed up and down along with its breakneck gait. Allison stood almost ten yards to his right. The bear pointed itself at the space between them as if it could not decide which one to attack first.

In the instant it took his mind to process *"bear,"* his bloodstream flooded with adrenaline. In the instant before he gained conscious control of his muscles, his knees flexed and dug the soles of his boots into the soil. He fled from the bear. Away from his wife.

In fear, there was no time to look. His foot caught in the frame of the tiny stool before he went a single step, and he toppled face first into the soft grass. The hand he threw out in an attempt to break his fall landed on something hard and smooth. Scrambling to his feet, he closed his hand around it. Allison screamed again and he wheeled, this time in her direction, holding the hatchet he'd used to chop firewood. The blade flashed in the afternoon sun. He saw the bear rise up and saw Allison crumple into an embryonic knot before it.

Harvey willed his body to move. The thing lowered itself to all fours as if to even the odds. It shoved Allison with its muzzle and rolled her over like a toy. Harvey shouted and screamed gibberish from the bottom of his soul. He glimpsed the tail of Cheryl's blue shirt streaking away from them as she sprinted pell-mell for the water.

He rushed in.

Time turned in on itself. It raced past him in a slipstream yet somehow slowed like the hands of a clock. He neared the great animal, then he was standing over his wife. It reared again and towered over them both, gigantic and smelly, blocking out the sun. Harvey knew it would hurt. The claws would break through the wall of his chest like pointed iron, splitting his ribs before piercing his organs. They would shred him. He knew it, but he swung anyway.

The hatchet lodged in the dark wall of hair. The bitter smell of dung and other excreta sickened him. The handle slipped in his palm and he almost dropped the hatchet when he yanked it back. He hacked again despite the roar that blasted his ears. Something as hard as a tree trunk slammed against the side of his head and knocked him to the ground. The green taste of grass filled his senses before darkness washed him away.

* * *

Strange voices circled him.

"Watch his head, goddamnit!" Terrell's voice, angry, telling someone to be careful.

Beyond a headache worse than any pain he had ever felt, there was nothing at all. From the neck down he had no sense of his own body.

133

"I think he's waking up," someone, a stranger, said.

"Sir, can you hear me?"

Justin opened his eyes and saw a sun darkened face beneath a Ranger hat. He tried to turn his head but could not.

"Don't try to move," the man said.

He could see the sky. There were other people nearby, but he could see none of them clearly.

"Allison? Where's Allison?"

"I'm right here darling." She leaned into his field of vision. Her face was streaked and smudged.

"Okay, let's pick him up," another voice said.

Allison leaned back and the world lurched as the basket he was strapped into was lifted. "What happened to the bear?"

"Your friend shot it with a handgun."

"Oh," he said, and drifted into sleep amid thoughts of a wounded bear lurking in the nearby woods.

The bear had walloped him hard enough to cause a concussion and dislocate two of his vertebrae. The resulting paralysis was temporary. A week after the incident, after being questioned by the Wildlife, Fish, & Game Commission, the Park Service, and a local reporter, he was on his back in a hospital bed watching Jay Leno while Terrell updated him on situations at work. His attention drifted between his partner's dry reporting and Leno's dry jokes until the talk show host mentioned Missouri.

"I kid you not," the comedian said. "A television station in Missouri ran a story about a man whose wife was attacked by a grizzly bear while they were on a camping trip."

Terrell stopped talking.

"Mark Twain National Park in Missouri, a couple was on a camping trip. The husband was building a fire when a grizzly bear bolted out of the woods and attacked the guy's wife. True story." Pause. "The man grabbed an axe and went after the bear. Now that's true love. Isn't that love?" He clapped his hands and drew applause from the audience. "I understand that couple's been married eight or nine years." Pause. "See, the average guy would *feed* his wife to a bear after eight years of marriage...." The audience groaned while Leno made chopping motions with his hand.

Justin Harvey rolled his eyes. Terrell shook his head and went back to his shoptalk.

"I think we should forget about the seafood counter and put wine racks in that area next to the meats. Matter of fact, I already called Graffen Inc. and asked them to come out and take a look."

Justin stared wordlessly at the ceiling. The doctor had said he could go home in another day or so.

"You okay?" Terrell asked. "Need the nurse?"

In his mind, Justin shook his head.

"Nope. Ready to get out of here."

Terrell nodded. "I don't envy you. Being a hero is bad for your health."

Harvey sighed. "I ain't no hero, man."

"According to Leno you are."

Another mental shake of the head. Another sigh. He closed his eyes again.

"What's up?"

Harvey pressed his lips together. "I tried to run, man. I didn't go after that damned thing. Not at first. I heard the noise, heard Allison…" He paused as if in pain then went on. "I jumped up, I saw it, and I tried to run, like a punk."

Terrell watched, amazed, as a single tear rolled down the side of Harvey's face.

"If I hadn't tripped, that damn thing would have killed her."

An uneasy silence settled.

Terrell shifted uncomfortably in the chair. "I don't know what to tell you my brother, except you ain't Daniel fuckin' Boone, and that wasn't no stray dog coming at you. I think anybody would've panicked, and you ain't no different. You did what anybody else would've done. Nobody with common sense would have attacked that thing if they'd had time to think about it."

Harvey kept his eyes closed.

"You don't get it," he said. "She thinks I knew what I was doing. She brought into all that…" with his eyes he indicated the television, and Terrell knew he meant the hype about the courageous husband who had saved his wife from a grizzly.

"You're being too hard on yourself," Terrell said.

He stood up.

"Get some sleep. You gonna feel better when you get out of here tomorrow."

When he was gone, Harvey stared at the ceiling. When the nurse checked on him at two, he was still awake.

After two weeks in traction, he began to feel his extremities again. A physical therapy nurse came to the house four times a week until he was able to travel by car, then he went to the hospital twice a week for months until the orthopedist gave him a clean bill of health.

He never talked about his conversation with Terrell. Six months after he was out of the hospital, and a full year after the incident with the bear, his wife knew there was something about the whole thing that still bothered him. She tried on different occasions to get him to talk. Each time he would change the subject or shut down altogether.

It was four in the morning, the pre-dawn start of a day in late summer when Harvey turned over in bed and thought he heard his wife sobbing. Enough blue-green illumination from the streetlight seeped through the curtains for him to see her sitting with her back against the headboard. Her face was damp and she held a crumpled tissue beneath her nose.

He sat up.

"What is it? What's wrong?"

She hiccupped and wiped her nose without giving him her attention.

"Allie? What is it?" He turned on the bedside lamp. "What happened? Did you…was it a dream…? Are you okay?"

"I'm a coward," she said after dabbing at her eyes. Her voice was thick. "I'm a fucking useless coward."

"What?"

She rolled onto her side and hid her face. "Turn the light off, please," she said, but Harvey leaned toward her.

"Why are you crying?" He touched her hair.

She sighed miserably. "The bear," she said after a pause. "You tried to save me…" Her words broke but she forced them out. "You saved me…but I tried to run. I didn't think about you, I just…wanted to run. It almost killed you—" He felt her body shake. "And I tried to run away. Left you standing there…" A heartbreaking sob this time.

He climbed out of bed and walked around to her side. She turned away

He sat on the edge of the bed and put his hands on her shoulders.

Without thinking, he said "I did too. I tripped over that stool, and my hand fell on the hatchet. That's how I picked it up."

There was no reaction from her at first.

Finally, she sniffled and wiped at her eyes. He moved to make room for her as she turned over and sat up. Her eyes were swollen and red.

"What?"

He stroked her hair, ignoring the voice inside that wondered if he had just done a wise thing.

"What did you say?" she asked.

"I thought I was seeing things," he said. "I don't know what happened. One second I was sitting on the stool, the next I was standing, the next I was flat on my face."

"You tried to run?"

He searched her face but said nothing. The silence in the room grew until it became oppressive. What was he supposed to tell her?

"Well…" he began.

"You tried to *run?* To leave me?"

It seemed he could suddenly hear every clock in the house ticking the slow seconds by. What was he supposed to say? They were still sitting there, looking at each other, when daylight started to show through the blinds.

10.

Neptune Rising:
The Return of Marty Larkmon

Jonathan J. Osborne III was a man obsessed with being first.

The Vice-President in charge of Programming for Special Delivery Home Entertainment Incorporated had never been the first kid chosen for a game of stickball. He had not been first in his graduating class. He had been no woman's first love. He had obviously not even been the first in his family to have the name Jonathan J. Osborne. But he was old enough to have learned that he *could* be first in some things—things that did not require athletic skill or good looks, things that were not preordained by God or Osborne's parents. He never took the easy (or the sensible) route, therefore, when he stood a chance of being first at something. Every Monday without fail, he locked himself in his corner office and feverishly covered one legal pad after another with hand-drawn organizational charts and complicated wire diagrams. This, he believed, was proof to others of his complete immersion, his total commitment to making Special Delivery first among the growing number of pay-tv entertainment networks.

This morning, Osborne paused and inspected the diagram he'd just drawn. The lines that joined the little boxes were forceful and dynamic, breaking at crisp right angles. The boxes themselves were neat and highly symmetrical. The handwriting was deft and precise and eased his eye across the page. It all came together with nuanced perfection.

He stroked the thick black marker in his right hand. A warm sensation spread through his fingers and up along his arm. To him, the sharp smell of colored ink was like the smell of flowers to a poet, or diesel fuel to a mechanic. He glanced at his door to make sure it was closed, and then he raised the felt tip to his nose and took a long sniff. A choking cough made his eyes water, yet he smiled and closed the writing implement with a slow push of his thumb, savoring the *snap* as the cap clicked into place.

The fax machine beeped itself awake. It growled and spit three sheets of paper into a tray beside the desk. He reached over and picked up the first one. It was from the offices of the Metropolitan Symphony Orchestra.

He grinned.

What the hell did they want? Another donation so they could buy more bowties?

He read the first paragraph and chuckled.

They wanted to perform live on television. What a novel idea.

He read further and broke into a belly laugh.

They wanted to give a *paid* performance on television, on the Special Delivery network no less! They wanted people to *pay money* to hear classical music on television!

He laughed again—harder this time—until he had to stand and lean over the desk. His hand hit the intercom and his secretary, hearing the strange sounds, got up and knocked on his door.

Ignoring the knock, Osborne read the letter again. This time, tears streaked his face and dripped from his nose.

On the third reading, he began to wheeze.

He managed, somehow, to pick up the phone and dial one of the numbers in the letterhead.

A polished, professional voice answered and Osborne exploded.

"Bhuh ha ha ha ha haaaaaaa!!! Uh he he he he he...!!"

He tried to loosen his tie, but his fingers lacked strength to uncoil the knot. His secretary pushed the door open and came in; certain he was choking, or having a seizure, or both.

Great, rollicking belly laughs bounced him up and down in the chair, sounds that were way too big to come from a man his size. He steadied himself and tried to speak.

"You wanna...tcc he heeee..."

It was no use.

His secretary took the phone and addressed the person on the other end. She listened and her eyes grew wide.

"It's him! It's him! It's *Marty Larkmon*!" she whispered in disbelief, pressing the phone against her bosom.

Osborne sat up.

In a matter of seconds he was stone cold sober. He straightened his tie and took the phone from her, shooing her away with his free hand.

"Who is this?" he asked, his voice tight with disbelief.

"Marty Larkmon," a casual yet distinguished voice replied.

Osborne's eyes widened.

"*The* Marty Larkmon?"

"Yes."

The secretary fidgeted and wrung her hands.

"You're kidding me, right? Manfred Phillip Morganthal Larkmon? The World's Greatest Living Composer? *That* Marty Larkmon?"

"Is there another?" the voice asked..

Osborne put his hand over the phone.

"Holy Jeezus! I think it is him! Hold all my calls; tell everybody I'm out of the building! Call Marketing, Legal, and Operations and get them down here now! Go! Move!" He turned back to the phone and plastered a smile across his face. In the warmest, friendliest voice imaginable he said, "Good morning Dr. Larkmon, sir. Why didn't you say it was you calling?"

"I did, and it still is me calling. Listen, I've got an idea. Are you sitting down?"

"Yes sir," Osborne said, a smile as big as a city block stretching the skin of his face.

Manfred Phillip Morganthal Larkmon was one of the most famous men alive. People all over the world—actors and entertainers, politicians and world leaders, even ordinary folk on the streets of any major city—knew the name "Marty" and uttered it as though they had grown up with the man. In addition to his international celebrity, the groundbreaking composer and virtuoso musician was rumored to have intermittent psychic abilities; moreover, he was nearly a certified genius.

Nearly.

The issue was still being argued in court by his lawyers and lawyers representing a well-known association of highly intelligent people. He had sued the group for defamation when it refused to certify that his childhood IQ had been so high it placed him in the top two percent of the population—a requirement for official recognition as a genius.

That IQ test (which was his pet obsession and the root of all ill feeling in his life) had been administered when he was nine years old. The clinician (a graduate student) had misinterpreted the results, and deprived Marty of a critical half point (which would have placed him in the genius-level scoring range). The fact that he had come so close and been robbed of the respect and adoration due a genius scarred him and filled him with bitterness and resentment that lasted well into his adulthood. Having one's greatness proclaimed around the world would have been vindication enough for the average person, as would a second IQ test, and the world-wide celebration of his music should have dispelled the animosity that lingered in Marty's soul. Paradoxically, it did not cure him at all, but only made him more determined to prove himself.

Eighteen months earlier he, Marty, had conceived a great composition and, with the financial backing of an eccentric billionaire, had staged a performance so unique and unorthodox it had earned him the unofficial title "World's Greatest Living Composer." While the title was unofficial, the prestige and recognition that accompanied it were not, and Marty soon found himself the envy of scores of mainstream celebrities whose fame he had eclipsed overnight.

Following his rise to stardom, he had moved into an elegant upscale home on the banks of Long Island Sound. Between concerts, rehearsals, promotions, and celebrity engagements, he would unplug his phone and lock himself in his studio for a day or two at a time. At one point, four days went by where he ignored all knocks on the door and neither emerged from the locked room nor answered the intercom. His personal assistant and his housekeeper began to suspect that he had died, and so they called fire and rescue. Firefighters had chopped the heavy studio door to splinters before Marty came out with a huge set of headphones cupped over his ears and a baton in one hand. He wore a canary yellow bathrobe and fuzzy brown slippers with little plastic claws on the ends. To him, this violent intrusion was a moving expression of concern on the part of his fans and the public at large. Rather than become angry, he grabbed a sheaf of papers and held them up for the camera that had followed the firefighters into his home. He proclaimed in a voice reverberating with drama, "I am well! I...am well!" And then he had his lawyers sue the city for the cost of replacing the door and cleaning the carpet.

The papers he'd brandished were the completed scores of several new works, a collection of short pieces inspired by a recent trip through the agricultural heartland of America. He had named the collection *Meditations on a Bovine Theme: Walking with the Spirits of Beeves,* and in it, he had attempted to capture his newfound sensitivity to the struggles faced by dairy cows trapped in a society hungry for milk and red meat. The music was subsequently recorded and—because it bore his name—shot right to the top of both the Classical and New Age recording charts. To the surprise of many, it crossed over to the Jazz chart and made a respectable showing there. To the absolute amazement of everyone (including Marty), it jumped to the Pop/R&B chart where it squeaked into the top ten, edging out a fourteen-year-old rapper who was also an ordained minister on weekends.

When all four of Special Delivery's Vice-presidents—Osborne and his colleagues in charge of the Marketing, Legal, and Operations divisions—were huddled in Osborne's office, his secretary put through a three-way call to Marty and Marty's lawyers. Osborne's enthusiasm burned bright for an entire hour while the composer explained in detail the bizarre, utterly ridiculous idea he had dreamed up.

"Uh huh, uh huh," Osborne said, grinning and bobbing his head as he listened, rolling his eyes now and then, and circling his temple with an index finger.

The Vice-president in charge of Marketing had asked Marty to hold on and muted the call.

"Is that man insane?" he asked in a whisper, just in case the line was still open.

"Is money green?" Osborne whispered back. "Does a bear shit in the woods? Do birds fly south for the winter?"

Of course the man was insane. He was a textbook case that no cliché could adequately describe. But he was Manfred Phillip Morganthal Larkmon, the World's Greatest Living Composer; a man smack in the middle of his fifteen minutes of fame. Anything he was even remotely associated with would draw a huge audience.

"But he's talking about *little green men from Neptune* for Christ's sake!"

"I don't care if he's talking about pulling a rabbit out of his butt! This lunatic is like King Midas. Anything he touches turns into market shares. He's *gold* baby!" And it was true. Even if Larkmon had been a less important celebrity, if he had been nothing more than a reject from reality tv, there were more than enough dingbats in the world to make his idea a huge success.

"You're a fool, Osborne," the Marketing VP said.

"And," put in the VP for Legal Affairs, "you don't have authority to approve this."

"Too bad," Osborne said, "because I'm approving it anyway."

He turned the speaker back on and listened to the rest of Larkmon's proposal. When they were done talking, they settled on a profit split that Osborne swore to with his very life. "In fact, I'm going to meet with our production department and some of our ad people as soon as this call is finished. I'll have them have their people start scouting a location and brainstorming the ad campaign." Around the table, the other vice-presidents shook their heads.

When the call was disconnected, the three men and the handsome, silver-haired woman (the Vice-president in charge of

Operations) remained seated and gave each other quizzical looks. Osborne tore up the charts he had made and started drawing new ones. He whipped out a few symmetrical diamonds, threw in a box or two, and then connected them all with crisply angled lines. As the marker flew across the paper, the vice-president in charge of Marketing asked, "How are you going to explain this to the old man?"

The old man was J. Neville Warren, Owner, President, Chairman of the Board, and CEO of Special Delivery Home Entertainment Inc. He was a blasphemous, cantankerous seventy year-old curmudgeon whose greatest love in life after Scotch, rum-soaked cigars, his horse, his dog, his gold-tipped walking stick, and Special Delivery was his wife of fifty-three years

Osborne thought a moment.

Although he was quite leery of Larkmon's premise, it seemed obvious to him that only a fool would pass up the chance to broadcast the first public performance of a new work by a major celebrity. Not only would it be easier to ask forgiveness than permission from the network's grizzled owner, the old goat would love him like a son when the show turned out to be a huge success.

"Indeed, the old man might want to know why *he* wasn't called in for the conference," put in the Vice-president for Legal Affairs.

"Don't worry about it." Osborne said, feeling his lower body go numb in the chair. "He'll be in by eleven thirty. Meet me at his office; I'm gonna give him the good news then."

The Vice-president in charge of Marketing, a man only slightly older than Osborne smirked.

"Wouldn't miss it," he said. "Hope your resume's up to date."

The head of Operations rose and gave Osborne a reassuring pat on the shoulder.

"It'll be all right." she said without looking into his eyes and then left the room.

"Of course it will," Osborne mumbled to himself. When they were gone, he turned back to his diagrams.

* * *

Osborne, like everyone in the entertainment industry (like

everyone in every industry, for that matter), was keenly aware of the popularity gulf that separated so-called "New Age" music from the more mainstream forms such as rap, rock, R&B, and jazz. Each of these more popular forms was being played on some television, radio, or internet station and listened to by somebody somewhere every minute of every hour, twenty-four hours a day, seven days a week, literally. The other type was heard mostly in bookstores or coffee shops, or in movies or commercials. Even devoted fans of the genre listened to it primarily when they were stressed out, or while trying to fall asleep.

Every other decade or so, an unconventional musician would come along and blaze a new trail, create a new sound that—through some magic—connected with the general public, even though it did not fit neatly into one of music's established categories. Marty Larkmon was just such a musician.

He had trained to become a classical composer, one who conducted and wrote music for a symphony orchestra, but he was the acknowledged progenitor of a whole new category of entertainment. It was a bizarre dream of helicopters and nuclear destruction that had inspired him to combine classical and archaic instrumentation with exotic and futuristic themes, and then couch the resulting motifs in ambient effects with digitized underpinnings. The first mega-successful example of this had been *"A Bloody Mess: Symphony #1 in A-Sharp minor,"* the work that catapulted him to international fame. Despite its form (not to mention its title), the work had inexplicably won approval from music lovers of every conceivable taste and from every walk of life. This, suggested one distinguished psychologist, was due to a genuine psycho-somatic affect. The sounds involved touched the listener at a subconscious, nearly a primal level. It actually stimulated pleasure centers deep in the brain, so the psychologist said, and was the auditory equivalent of a stiff drink plus a backrub with warm oil. The theory was not universally accepted, but no one else had come close to explaining eighteen million sales of a CD about the secret life of farm animals.

As eleven-thirty drew near, Osborne found his courage waning. Whispered hubbub about some "damn-fool idea" had made its way through every corner of the building. It had seemed like a great idea just two hours ago, jumping at the opportunity to broadcast the world premiere of a Larkmon symphony. Such a move might have guaranteed his future, put him in line for yet another promotion and for all sorts of bonuses, brought corporate headhunters out of the woodwork to court him.

If Larkmon had been only a little less weird.

Osborne, who was only twenty-nine, did not believe in making small mistakes, however. He had become a Vice-president at such a young age because he took risks and made decisions without waiting for someone to take his hand and tell him it was okay. He weighed options and assessed situations, and if his gut told him to move, he moved. It was how he did things, and—until now—he had never second-guessed himself.

He fingered a hand-carved plaque on his desk hoping, perhaps, to draw strength from the quote inscribed on it: *If we must die, Oh let us nobly die!* He stared out his office window and wondered if he would have a job an hour from now.

Then his innate decisiveness took over.

He stood up and cracked his knuckles. Placing his hands on his hips Macarthur-style, he sucked in his gut and grimaced. If he had to die, he would die big. He would die huge! If he went down on this broadcast, he would go down in the biggest goddamned flaming wreck Special Delivery had ever seen. He cracked his knuckles again and took up his marker and a legal pad. A surge of adrenaline swept through him. Marching to his door, he threw it open with supreme confidence. Then, striding across the threshold like a Titan, Osborne went to see the boss.

When he arrived at Warren's huge office, the others, including Warren, were seated around a long walnut conference table waiting for him. In the past, it had not been difficult to sell Warren on risky ventures. He himself had taken a small, insignificant television station in upstate New York and parlayed it into the Special Delivery colossus. Osborne had impressed Warren from the outset with his go-getter attitude. That, though, was not enough to protect Osborne if he screwed up, or if he rubbed the old man the wrong way.

Osborne strode in and bravely pulled out a plush leather chair, placing his marker and the legal pad on the highly polished table. If he were as good as dead, he told himself again, he would attack like a mad dog and go down fighting.

"Mr. Warren, it's a damn good thing you hired me…"

Warren cut him off with a growl and a hiss.

"You better have a damn good explanation for whatever it is that's got this place in an uproar." He bit down on a lit cigar and sucked fire into his lungs. A Great Dane with fur the color of gunmetal rested on its haunches beside Warren's chair. The big creature yawned, settled its large gray head on the edge of the table, and watched Osborne with suspicion.

Had they said something already?

Osborne looked at his colleagues, all three of whom averted their eyes.

"Well!" Warren thundered.

A pocket of gas in Osborne's colon chose that moment to force its way out.

"Um humph hum... I guess someone has already leaked the essence of…that is, I see that someone has already briefed you to some extent—"

"All right, who cut the cheese?" Warren glared at those seated around the table. When no one answered, he turned his attention back to Osborne. "Well don't just stand there wetting yourself! What in the name of Jesus-Mary-and-Josephine have you gone and done?"

"If I could be allowed to explain sir—"

"You damn well better explain!"

Thinking fast on his feet, Osborne began chronicling artistic *coups* that had taken popular culture completely by surprise. Beginning with the 1970's disco version of Beethoven's Fifth symphony, he gave a long and detailed list of unlikely hits, including Marty Larkmon's most recent album, and a curious album by a female singer that had unseated Larkmon from the top of the charts that very week. He talked at length about the tremendously popular "Hooked on Classics" albums of the previous two decades, about music videos based on Italian opera, about blockbuster movies spawned from classic novels, about the multi-platinum recordings of Gregorian Chant made by Benedictine Monks. These works had hijacked box offices, radio station play lists, and entertainment outlets the world over. His argument was logical, intelligent, and

147

surprisingly compelling.

"You just never know what people will take a liking too," he said. "We have been offered a golden opportunity to capitalize on the New Age market. Right now, New Age is the fastest-growing music genre in the country, thanks to a small group of exceptional musicians." He was thinking particularly of Marty Larkmon and the female singer he had mentioned.

"What the devil is New Age?"

Osborne explained that "New Age" referred to a relaxed, dreamy, esoteric style of music made with synthesizers, electronic devices, and unusual and archaic instruments from cultures all around the world. New Age lyrics, he added, usually involved inner thoughts, and evoked a spectrum of feelings associated with altered states of consciousness. Thematically, he went on, it dealt extensively with issues and concerns involving the natural world and sought a transcendent universe in which all things co-existed in peace and harmony.

"It's that goddamned yuppie elevator music my granddaughter does her yoga too," Warren growled, half to himself. Sensing disturbing news, he glared at the others. "Somebody tell me why this hippy-lover is tap dancing all over my office."

The Vice-president in charge of Marketing took off his glasses and rubbed his eyes to hide tears of laughter.

Osborne took a deep breath and stood up at the end of the table.

"I've asked Professor Larkmon to meet with us in perso—"

"Jeezus H. Christ! Will you quit stalling!" Warren, whom rumor said had once lost his temper even though he was sound asleep, slammed his hand down on the table. "For Jesus' sweet pity will you just cut the crap and tell me what it is you've done? Spill it, man!"

Osborne spilled. All the details of the deal he had made with Larkmon.

"The agreement," he coughed into his fist, "the agreement calls for Special Delivery to pay a flat commission of thirteen million dollars to the composer in exchange for exclusive broadcast rights to the unpublished instrumental work titled *Neptune Rising: The Call to Extraterrestrial Life.*" He took a deep breath. "Sp-Special Delivery will also create an exclusive venue for the first ever public performance of the work and guarantee its transmission into interplanetary space where it…where it will be received by intelligent beings from the planet Neptune." A deathly silence settled over the humans; the dog let out a groan. "All rebroadcast rights, movie rights, gate receipts, and broadcast revenues belong entirely and exclusively to Special Delivery. However. Sir."

When Osborne finished, Warren sat—mouth open and eyes starring, head slightly to one side—like a wax dummy. He gazed unblinking at the far wall, his face a disturbing shade of purple. The dog stood up and growled.

The four Vice-presidents looked at each other.

"Should we do something? Should we call an ambulance?" Operations whispered.

Marketing convulsed in a high-pitched snicker.

Osborne got up and walked around to where the old man sat. He waved his hand in front of Warren's face, then he leaned over and looked deep into his boss' eyes.

Warren came back to life with a howl. The dog jumped and began running in circles. Warren leaped to his feet and clamped his fingers around Osborne's throat, forcing the younger man to his knees.

"You stupid *bastard!*" he hissed through clenched teeth. "You've *ruined* this company!"

"Mr. Warren pleeeease!" the others wailed in unison. The dog growled and grabbed Osborne's pant leg in his teeth.

They tried to wrestle man and dog away from Osborne, but Warren held on with all the strength left in his aged body.

"You'll kill him! You'll kill him!" the others shouted.

"You're damn right I'll kill 'im! Idiot! *Sonofabitch!*" Warren pressed his thumbs into Osborne's Adam's apple.

"It's Marty Larkmon he's talking about!" Operations cried. "*Marty Larkmon!*"

Warren froze, and then his eyes widened to donut size. He let go of Osborne and clutched his heart.

"Jeeeezus H…*the* Marty Larkmon?" He leaned against the table. "*The* Marty Larkmon! The fruitcake! The nutcase!" Foaming slightly at the mouth, he shouted, "The schizophrenic psychopath *Marty Larkmon? That* Marty Larkmon wants to host *a celebration to welcome aliens! Because he dreamed aliens were sending him messages!* And you...you *idiot*, you obligated my network to broadcasting it!" He found new strength and reached for Osborne again.

Operations threw herself between them. The dog leaped backward then bared his teeth at the woman.

She showed the dog her own teeth, then turned to Warren and spat, "He's the *World's Greatest Living Composer!*" Appalled and disgusted by Warren's ignorance and lack of sophistication, she nevertheless left off the words "you idiot!"

"He's the *world's greatest fucking lunatic!*" Warren spat back, leaving off "you dumb broad!"

The Vice-president in charge of Marketing was doubled over in his seat, shaking uncontrollably.

"Sell...it...sell," Osborne wheezed, "New Age...top...of...the charts." He fell out flat on the floor. The dog lunged at him, but the woman stamped her foot and growled at the dog again.

"New Age, New Age!" Warren seethed. "Shoot me for Christ's sake! The next person who says New Age—"

"He's telling you the program will sell, because the number one album in the country is by a *NEW-AGE* singer!" Operations hissed with exaggerated patience, as if she were speaking to a six-year-old.

"Oh for the love of Satan!" Warren bellowed, throwing his hands up finally. "Great gods of thunder and lightning! Why don't we just hire every goddamn cocaine-sniffing genius hippy in the whole goddamn country?"

His gaze went around the room.

"Well! Why don't we?"

Operations scratched her head. She was a huge fan of New Age music and owned most of the albums Osborne had talked about, including the most recent, most popular ones.

"Arreonna," she said to herself. "Her name is Arreonna."

"Whose name is Arreonna?"

"The singer."

"What singer!"

"The one he's talking about. Arreonna."

"Arreonna who?"

"Just Arreonna. Like Cher; like Madonna."

"What the hell kind of a name is Arreonna?"

"It's from a book," Operations said.

Warren's eyes glinted.

"Does she dance and shake all her parts, like in those music videos?"

"Of course not!" Operations said indignantly. "She's an artist, not some ...exhibitionist!"

"Damnit!" Warren fell silent and scratched his own head in thought. "You said she sells lots of records?"

"Truckloads," Operations said. "Boxcars full." Silence.

Warren snapped his fingers.

"We need her! You!" He kicked the bottom of Osborne's shoe. "Get up from there! You get that woman. Offer her whatever you have to. Give her some nonsense; tell her we're all fans or some such, but you get her, or I'll crack your skull open and use it for a chamber pot! Now get out of here!" He kicked him again.

Osborne wobbled to his feet and hurried out of the room.

"Damn fool!" Warren muttered as the door swung itself shut. The dog barked in agreement.

* * *

Four weeks later, Warren, his Vice-presidents, a group of consultants, technicians, and others crowded into that same office. The center doors of a wall-sized armoire were rolled back to reveal a television screen the size of a sofa painting.

"Lights," said a voice. "Okay, here's the first one."

There was a lofty fanfare, followed by a powerful roll on a bass drum. A rich, tinkling wave of sound flowed from the speakers and filled the room. Elegant and dynamic script appeared on the black screen as if embroidered there by the music pulsing, raining, vibrating from the speakers.

There is only one Larkmon...the writing said and disappeared.

His image appeared in profile with rays of light streaming around it. His head and eyes were canted downward in a thoughtful, meditative look, his hands clasped as if in prayerful supplication. His vision turned inward, he seemed lost in contemplation, examining the landscape of his own soul. A beat, two beats, three...the picture and the roiling, hypnotic music faded.

...<u>But now, he has a partner</u>...

A delicate piano melody rose up in its wake, accompanied by the winsome, satiny voices of what sounded like a thousand angels. It was in fact the voice of only one woman, but it had been electronically manipulated so that by itself it sang echoing, angelic chords in perfect, six-part harmony.

The singer's face appeared as Marty's had. She had short, red hair (very stylishly cut) and liquid green eyes that stared into the camera. Her long and slender throat gave her the look of a fashion model; her lips looked remarkably soft and inviting. A white-gold glow shimmered about her head and bare shoulders and brought out a twinkle in her eyes.

The image faded.

The music stopped altogether and was replaced by the sound of a reed flute and waves breaking on volcanic rock. The cry of seagulls filled the room; underscored by the sonorous, hackle raising moans of an organ. A string of short messages flashed on the screen:

...<u>The World's Greatest Living Composer</u>...
...<u>teams with</u>...
...<u>the greatest singer of the New Age</u>...
...<u>to welcome voyagers from a distant planet</u>...
Warren shook his head. The others watched in total silence.
...<u>You owe it to yourself</u>...
...<u>to witness</u>...
...<u>the most important event in human history</u>...
A steady heartbeat sounded below the crashing surf.
...<u>Be there live with Special Delivery</u>...
...<u>when Larkmon</u>...
...<u>and Arreonna</u>...
...<u>hail the arrival</u>...
...<u>of non-terrestrial intelligence on Earth</u>...
All sound stopped.
...<u>*Neptune Rising: The Call to Extraterrestrial Life*</u>...
...<u>Saturday, May 3. Only on Special Delivery</u>.

The company logo faded in and out; the screen faded to black.
There was a burst of chatter and scattered applause.

"Knock it off!" Warren bellowed. "Show the next one."

A dimly lit laboratory scattered with complicated electronic devices and peopled by technicians in lab coats faded in on the screen. As they went busily about their work, the composer walked into the shot.

"I'm Marty Larkmon," he said. "In 1947, an interstellar vehicle carrying explorers from another planet crashed in the desert near Roswell, New Mexico. The craft's wreckage and the bodies of its operators were recovered and have been held in secret ever since." He walked out of the shot.

The picture changed to a wide-angle shot of the seashore. The camera found Marty on an outcropping of rock, gazing at the late-afternoon sky as waves crashed below him.

"What if there are more explorers out there, eager to visit Earth? Shouldn't humanity make contact?" He turned and looked into the camera. "On Saturday, May third, live from the coast at Santa Monica, I, along with my special guest, Arreonna will welcome extraterrestrial visitors who are traveling through our solar system at this very moment. If you are not a believer in extraterrestrial life, you will be on May third. This is one performance no human should miss."

The camera followed his gaze back into the sky, which darkened to a color-enhanced star field.

"Witness the most important event in human history," the voiceover said, "and hear the newest work by the World's Greatest Living Composer. Call your cable operator now." The words *Saturday, May 3rd Only on Special Delivery* showed on the screen. The picture faded to black.

The lights came up, and they all looked sheepishly at Warren.

"Has anyone actually *heard* the damned music?" he rasped.

There were headshakes and murmured "no's" all around the room.

Shaking his own head again, Warren turned to the Vice-president for Legal Affairs.

"There's no way I can get out of this?"

The man shook his head no and looked over at Osborne who, no longer allowed to sit at the main conference table, occupied a straight-backed plastic chair in the corner.

153

"If we breech the agreement, that psycho" he nodded toward the television "will have his lawyers all over us. We needn't fear, however," he went on, reading the look on Warren's face, "because no one's going to believe it. No reasonable person, that is, will expect an actual spaceship to appear. Thus our official position: The commercials are hyperbole; anyone who orders the program does so to see Larkmon and this...aureole—"

"Arreonna."

"—whatever—perform. Two popular artists with huge followings of devoted fans giving a televised concert. All perfectly legal."

"But what about the *intent?*" Warren persisted. "Lawyers and judges are always talking about intent. Either this fool, and by association *we*, expect space aliens to hear this music and land, or, we intended to fool people and take their money. Isn't that what some bloodsucking navel-picking lawyer'll say once we're inside a courtroom?"

"The intent behind the *commercials* is to sell subscriptions to a televised concert featuring two of the most popular musicians alive. The intent behind the *concert itself* is to entertain the viewing public for a profit. Both are within the letter *and* spirit of the law." He gave a nonchalant shrug. "Of course there's someone out there who'll cry foul, but anyone who has the means to cause us real grief won't want to look like an idiot by going into open court with a complaint about spaceships not appearing. We have nothing to worry about."

"You're absolutely sure?"

"Absolutely."

"You're positive?"

"Positive."

"I'll rip your balls off if you're wrong."

The lawyer shrugged again, confident in his assessment.

Warren spoke over his shoulder to the assembled group.

"All right, run the damn things."

But the lawyer was wrong.

The FCC, the State of New York, and the State of California all took the matter quite seriously, and none was prepared to write it off as simple hyperbole. A letter from New York's Attorney General arrived at Special Delivery the same week the commercials began airing. "Because of the sheer outrageousness" of the claims they made in the ads, he said, there were only three ways they could all avoid spending long years behind bars.

First, they could admit the ads were a hoax, call off the performance, refund any money they had collected thus far, issue a public apology, and swear never to do any of it again.

If they did any of that, the company's executives reasoned in turn, they would lose all credibility as a legitimate enterprise. Subscriptions would drop, the company's stock would plummet, and massive layoffs would follow, beginning with Osborne. If the public came to believe Special Delivery was crooked, the entire company might go belly-up in a matter of months.

Second, they could produce an actual, working, interstellar vehicle operated by intelligent, non-human, non-terrestrial life forms.

This would be a great deal harder than simply selling off the company's assets and filing for bankruptcy.

The final option—and here the Attorney General felt he was only doing right by the viewing public—called for the surrender to authorities of J. Neville Warren, Jonathan J. Osborne III, Marty Larkmon, Arreonna, the staff and management of Special Delivery Home Entertainment Inc., the Metropolitan Symphony Orchestra, and the ad agency that had produced the commercials. All would face charges of fraud, conspiracy, conspiracy to commit fraud, a host of FCC violations, and a list of other crimes that his office was still sorting through. But he would think about asking for blanket clemency when it came time for their sentencing.

Warren had not taken the news well.

* * *

On Saturday May 3rd, fifty-eight thousand spectators packed into a half-moon shaped amphitheater built overlooking the ocean just north of Santa Monica. An additional two hundred and fifty thousand or so covered the sands outside the amphitheater and cavorted along the beaches as far as the eye could see. Thirty minutes prior to the start of the performance, twenty million households had ordered the broadcast. At twenty-nine dollars and ninety-nine cents each, Special

Delivery was left with an eye-popping profit margin. This was an ironic vindication for Osborne. He had produced a hit.

He opted to watch the show from a hotel room and had brought his long-time girlfriend, a talent scout and contract negotiator for 20th Century Fox, along on the trip. They sat in a luxury suite at the Santa Monica Hyatt-Regency and sipped champagne while they waited for the show to begin. When she asked about the fax from the Attorney General, Osborne had shrugged, said, "screw it," and told her he would worry about finding a lawyer when the show was done and he was back in New York.

Warren stayed in New York at his Long Island mansion. He, his wife, his two sons, and half a dozen of his aides sat around the spacious indoor pool sipping Manhattans. Warren wanted to be near water so that he could go ahead and drown himself once the show was over.

The other Vice-presidents had taken front-row seats in the amphitheater. The Vice-president in charge of Operations was giddy because her spiritual counselor had told her he felt an awesome event just ahead in her future. This performance, the first official reception for extraterrestrial travelers, had to be the thing, she reasoned. For the occasion, she had made a gorgeous white dress with chiffon sleeves, and had let the silver mane of hair loose in all its glory. The Vice-president in charge of Marketing was there to prove himself a team player, something that would come in handy when he went job hunting in the coming weeks. He also wanted to witness Osborne's professional demise firsthand. The Vice-president in charge of Legal Affairs had been thinking about going back to private practice, plus, he had always loved dressing up, so he was there in a full tuxedo.

It was of no surprise to anyone that every crackpot group on the face of the earth had made a pilgrimage, or sent emissaries to Santa Monica. Every crystal-toting, sandal-wearing, green-tea-sipping, incense-burning, self-help-reading, horoscope-following, past-life pondering hippie, yuppie, mid-life-crisis and menopause survivor who could afford a ticket had turned out. Scores and scores and scores of organizations, from the Eurasian Consortium for the Study of Interstellar Physics, to the Yazoo, Mississippi Witches Coven, jostled for seats inside the amphitheater. Astronomers from the Moscow Observatory, orange-robed Buddhist Monks and Hare

Krishnas, teams of faculty from MIT, Caltech, the American Psychic Institute, the Foundation for Advanced Studies, and every other college or university in the country that had ever conducted any sort of investigation into the paranormal were present. A person could not swing his arms without hitting an Elvis. There was an ET, or a Spock, or a Kirk, or a Lieutenant LeForge every five feet. The annual Star Trek Convention had—in fact—been rescheduled and moved here. There were people who had survived the Bermuda Triangle, members of the Hemlock Society, the Near-Death Society, the UFO Society of North America, the Society for the prevention of Cruelty to Aliens, the Darth Vader Fan Club...and the list went on and on and on.

A huge radio telescope had been leased from the Johnson Space Flight Center in Houston and erected on a high bluff a quarter mile from the amphitheater. When the music started, microprocessors in the control station would convert it to binary signal. It would then be relayed to the dish via fiber-optic cable and beamed into space at a coordinate just above the western horizon, the place where the planet Neptune would rise above the curve of the Earth at exactly eight fifty-six p.m. Pacific Standard Time.

At precisely seven o'clock, three giant screens rose high into the air above the stage. An eccentric light display danced across the white fields, and synthesized music filled the air. An unseen announcer stroked the audience with a smoky, velvety, buttery voice. His mellow, intoxicating tone fit perfectly with the mood of the concertgoers. Thousands of scented candles burned, as did thousands of joints, bathing the air with the scent of paraffin and a potpourri of dried, organic smells. Vendors sold herbal teas, dried roots, extracts of every sort, tee shirts, horoscopes, and zodiac calendars. Fortunetellers and Tarot readers abounded.

The sky had begun to darken when the ten-minute documentary about the music of Arreonna began. It focused heavily on the stories and places in classical mythology that inspired her songs and original compositions, and when it ended, the announcer rolled out her name to deafening cheers.

She glided onto the stage, her silk kimono in peacock blue and gold brocade sweeping the ground behind her. Pressing her palms together in a prayer position, she bowed as graciously as she had at the Grammy awards earlier that year. The crowd did not stop applauding until she was seated at the piano and her background singers had started to hum.

She sang. And she played. And she wrapped the audience in beautifully abstract lyrics that carried them into another dimension. When she finished, the amphitheater and the surrounding areas floated on a blanket of peace and tranquility. Those who had not drugged themselves gave her a standing ovation and threw flowers. Picking up a long stemmed carnation that had landed at her feet, she walked to center stage and took a microphone from its holder.

"Before I bring out the man of the hour..." she began. There was applause and whistles. "I need to cleanse my spirit." She sat down on the stage and folded her legs in a full lotus position. Closing her own eyes, she said "Please close your eyes and say these words with me: ooooooohhhhhmmmm waaaaaaa mmeeeeeeettaaaaaaaa."

The audience joined in with gusto. In just over a minute it sounded as if all the world's insane asylums had been emptied into this one place.

When she stopped the chanting minutes later, an expectant thrill ran through the arena. The orchestra sat quietly behind her, but music, soft like running water, sounded from unseen sources and carried throughout the arena.

"Are you ready to enter a new age of human experience?" Her voice, all warm honey and gilded satin, brimmed with sedateness and mysticism.

There came back a roar which touched the low-hanging clouds.

Out on the cliff, the radio antenna hummed like a Porsche-990, sending the broadcast into outer space.

"Are we prepared as one race—the human race—to welcome those who have come to us from a distant world...?" Another roar in response. "Those who seek contact with other intelligences, those more rare and far more precious than every gem drawn from the deeps of the earth, await us beyond the gates of perception."

The audience shudderd like a giant pot on the edge of boiling.

"It is time," she said with enormous gravity. "We are come to the dawn of a new era, a new chapter in the book of human actuality." A soft *ting*, the sound a glass bell might make, was heard everywhere, and an exquisite tension came into Arreonna's voice. "It is time to welcome *The One*—he whose gifted discernment, whose genius and far vision made this unprecedented evening a reality."

A rolling wave of applause and cheers went up.

"It is time to meet humanity's ambassador, Earth's liaison to intelligent life beyond our world…"

Her voice quickened, and she went on building Marty up and up until the masses were ready to riot. In a final, breathless burst of praise that rang opposite her somber and mellow beginning, she called out to them, "Ladies and gentlemen, friends and loved ones, brothers and sisters, cherished members of the human race, I give you the one, the only…." The applause grew to ear-shattering and nearly drowned her out, "…the *World's Greatest Fucking*—I mean *LIVING—Composer!* Mar-teeee Lark-monnn!"

The howls mixed with screams mixed with shouts and whistles were so loud they could be heard in the Los Angeles suburbs. A galaxy of spotlights picked out a dashing figure surrounded by bodyguards. Marty made his way to the stage amid a blizzard of flower petals and gold and silver confetti. He mounted the steps and crossed to center stage where he and Arreonna shared a long, tight embrace. She kissed him on both cheeks before stepping back, taking a bow, and skittering off to one side. He directed the audience's attention her way and joined them in applauding as she moved to the sidelines. She did not leave the stage, however, but resumed her seat at the piano which had been moved to stage right. When she was settled, Marty faced the audience and bowed deeply, blowing kisses with both hands. Minutes passed during which the applause ebbed many times but always picked up again. When it finally lowered and seemed about to cease, he turned to the orchestra. The spectators began settling in for what they knew would be the musical equivalent of a sunrise seen from the edge of space.

There was shuffling as people skoonched down in their seats. Many of those who wore shoes removed them. Travel pillows and portable backrests were positioned behind heads and necks. Here and there, cups of steaming herbal tea were poured from thermoses and homemade fruit wine from leather skins. The announcer's voice wafted out of the sound system and introduced the work. Peace and tranquility, the likes of which many had thought impossible, settled over the teeming thousands.

Marty at long last, took the baton in his right hand, tapped it with a flourish, and began bathing the universe in his new music.

It began with a few simple notes on a bamboo flute like the ones heard in the commercial. It evolved quickly into a mellifluous, trance-inducing cacophony of sound, richly ornamented with trills and synthesized glissandos, underscored with the recorded sound of wind harps and whale song. A critic had once said that Larkmon's music was the sound of Waterford wind chimes and Tiffany strings stroked by golden hurricanes and platinum bows. Listeners proficient in the techniques of yoga, tai chi and transcendental meditation, began losing themselves to profound states of relaxation. A Hindu fakir and two dozen of his followers sat lotus-style in the buffer zone between the stage and the first row of seats. Television cameras panning the audience showed thousands of people slumped peacefully in their seats with eyes closed. They were not simply hearing the music; they were *experiencing* it with every facet of their being, reveling in it as it washed over them, feeling in their very consciousness this aural beauty in its purest form. As they reached and unlocked the deeper levels of their understanding, some already in contact with their innermost person, with the child inside them, all swiftly but assuredly on the road to actualization, the music slowed, faded, and came to a halt.

Marty Larkmon put down the baton and scanned the evening sky. Then he turned to the silent, puzzled audience and bowed deeply.

The spectators looked at each other through cracked eyelids. People sat up out of their relaxed slouches wondering why the music had stopped. Onstage, the musicians gave helpless shrugs in response to mouthed questions from listeners in the first few rows. A low buzz started near the stage and spread throughout the arena. When it was established that nothing technical had stopped the music, but that the piece was, in fact, *over*, the noise grew into a rumble of protest.

On Long Island, Warren eyed the television nervously. The drink in his hand had given him a buzz, so it took a moment for him to grasp what was happening. When it did hit him, he spat the rye mixture back into the glass and hurled it across the pool. He pressed his fingers into the bridge of his nose, and then he hefted a heavy ceramic ashtray and sent it crashing into the television screen. An aide was speed-dialing Osborne's hotel room. When Osborne answered, Warren snatched the phone and began cursing with all the fury he could muster. The Great Dane, lying beside him, lumbered to its feet and filled the air with savage barks.

"*Four minutes?* It lasted *four fucking minutes!* You paid that sonofa..." he spit the words out like bile and vinegar, "thirteen million bucks for *four minutes* of freaking goddamned sound effects? *What are you trying to do to me Osborne!* I'll kill you, damn you!" He was foaming at the mouth. "I'm gonna rip your balls off! If it's the last thing I do on—!"

"Shut your ass Warren!" Osborne shouted back, figuring he now had nothing to lose. "He promised you the *most important* concert in human history, *not the longest!!*"

Back on the beach, Marty kept on bowing despite the absence of applause. He motioned to the orchestra to stand and take a bow themselves, which some of them did with great uncertainty. He glanced at the sky again; then he commenced blowing kisses with both hands.

The booing started as if on cue and grew to a deafening roar. Hoots and vile curses competed with each other to drown out all other sounds. A chant began in the upper tiers—*Bull-shit, Bull-shit!*—and spread until it echoed everywhere. The air grew thick with ice, candles, and paper cups hurled toward the stage.

Out beyond the growing bedlam, the radio antenna began to glow. A green halo of St. Elmo's fire shimmered along the support beams. The parabolic dish threw off a shower of sparks and a cloud of smoke rose above it. The sky directly over the dish turned a peculiar shade of lavender. Out on the water, a wall of fog coalesced and rolled toward the shore. Bolts of lightning jagged across the sky in its path. A powerful surge of static electricity swept the entire area, raising goose bumps and causing hair to stand on end. The riotous noise lessened, and the crowds' attention turned from the stage to the metal structure a quarter-mile away pointing at the sky like a glowing finger.

In the amphitheater, on the beach, and in front of televisions, millions watched in fascination, and whole throngs of people jumped in unison when a fantastic, three-tailed whip of lightening lashed down from the sky and struck the antenna with a terrific boom. Its pieces blew apart as if made of plastic, leaving twisted beams pointing in all directions and a far larger ball of smoke rising into the air. The light from the explosion did not fade but somehow, as the crowds watched, grew brighter. Soon, a square mile of coastline was lit up like a movie set. As the people looked on, a mammoth ring-shaped object wider than a shopping mall descended from the clouds and hovered above the wreckage.

"Sonofabitch..." the genteel announcer said into his microphone.

The thing was black over most of its surface, but the irregular outlines of piping and tubing and various utilitarian geometric shapes stood out against its dark walls. It made no sound that those on the ground could hear, and people squinted at the sky above it in search of whatever it might be suspended from. Powerful pulses of static electricity swept across the area, and bolts of lightning, less frequent but still frightening, continued to zip about. After a few moments of confused denial, the crowds began to understand that the thing was operating under its own power. Some pointed in amazement while others shaded their eyes. The infinite rustlings turned into a great wave of noise when thousands began tossing questions at whoever was standing next to them.

A warm breeze blew across the stage and, without warning, the thing started to drift in the direction of the amphitheater.

No one knew what to do at first; then the screaming started. It was taken up in several places, and the final roar was heard almost as far north as Oakland. The exits were clogged in a matter of seconds with people scattering in every direction, like ants scrambling out of a trampled mound. Musicians who could carry their instruments did; others quickly abandoned anything that did not fit under one arm. All swore to themselves as they ran that they would never perform with Larkmon again.

Marty—meanwhile—watched in giddy amusement as the ship approached, and as the audience melted into a teeming, frantic, frenetic mass and clawed its way across the California seaside. The Vice-president in charge of Operations sprang to her feet and yanked a cord out of the hem of her dress. The hem fell, and the dress became a billowing, snow-white gown. She climbed over the man next to her and ran down the aisle against the current of panicked individuals coming her way. She stepped over the Hindus (all of whom had fainted), and made her way onto the stage crying, "Take me! Take me!" although she could not be heard above the cries of spectators.

Marty looked in Arreonna's direction and winked. Arreonna stood aghast, staring in open-mouthed wonder at the object, which came to a stop directly above the stage. As she gazed up, a blood-red column of light dropped from its underside and encircled her.

Marty's heart stopped.

He had seen every episode of the X-Files and every Star Trek movie and tv show ever made, and so he knew for certain what was about to happen. He tried to call out to her but his voice stuck in his throat. People stopped running and turned to look. To Marty's horror, Arreonna began to rise into the air. She was six feet above the stage in a matter of seconds. Marty raced toward her, vaulted onto the piano keyboard, and, with a desperate, life-or-death leap reached out to grab one of her sandaled feet. He missed, sailed over the edge of the stage, and landed face down in the sand.

Arreonna tilted her head back and looked up into the shaft of light as she rose. She spread her arms wide and so resembled a crucifix drifting steadily toward the unknown. Before thousands and thousands of live spectators, hundreds of television and video cameras, and millions of viewers across the world, Arreonna disappeared into the hovering object. The beam went out, and the ship began drifting toward the sea.

Marty spit out as much of the sand as he could and dashed across the beach in pursuit of the receding craft.

"Bring her back!" he shouted, he himself becoming a dot against the landscape before plunging into the ocean to swim after Arreonna's abductors.

Back in the amphitheater, chaos reigned.

The spectators, many of whom were in shock, shouted wildly and tripped over each other as they tried to find loved ones and purses or other belongings. The stage director shouted frantically to his men to safeguard the equipment. The teams of paramedics had their hands full with people who had either fainted or been trampled in the outward rush.

A panicked shout came over the sound system.

"IT'S COMING BAAAAAACK!"

The outward flight intensified. Even more people fainted. Some dropped to their knees and prayed in desperation.

Had anyone paused to look, he or she would have seen Marty (soaking wet) tearing back up the beach, the leading edge of the spaceship hovering high above him. When he got close to the stage, he dropped to the ground and rolled under a sound truck. The object continued moving until it was directly over the stage again. In his mansion, Warren (watching on a portable set) fainted. Osborne, in his hotel suite, bounced up and down on the sofa in joyful disbelief.

Marty stuck his head out from under the truck and watched as the shaft of light re-emerged from the bottom of the craft. To his joy, Arreonna reappeared, riding down the glowing beam with her kimono clasped firmly between her knees. Six feet above the ground the light vanished and she dropped the rest of the way, hitting the stage with a thud. Marty wondered briefly if they had come back to get *him*, decided he didn't care, then scrambled out from under the truck and raced to her side.

Beams of light sprang from the ship until hundreds crisscrossed the shoreline in a laser-light display. People hid under anything they could find; chairs, cars, rocks, umbrellas, even each other. The ship remained stationary for several terrifying moments. Then it went dark and drifted back toward the coastline. In less than a minute it had disappeared against the night sky, leaving the air behind it eerily still. Two Navy fighter planes and a Coast Guard patrol boat were immediately dispatched to search the area where the craft had vanished. They found nothing except a rusted oil tanker under tow and a few small pleasure boats.

Arreonna clung to Marty as people and cameras pressed around to ask her questions. She later told interviewers that she had felt sad, but somehow unafraid when the spaceship took off with her. Unfortunately, it had been completely dark inside the craft, so she could tell them nothing about the ship or its inhabitants. They signed a partnership agreement two weeks later in at a lavish party in Manhattan. Harcourt Books offered the pair a multi-million dollar deal for their combined recounting of the entire saga, from Marty's inspiration, to Arreonna's return to the California shore. Several Hollywood studios began bidding for movie rights.

Later that night in his hotel room, Osborne had drawn the woman to him and given her a passionate kiss. "If I live a thousand years I'll owe you everything I ever have," he'd said.

She nodded, smiled, and sipped Champaign from a crystal flute.

They'd been looking through a South American travel brochure and watching the Easter parade two days after the first ad for the concert was broadcast. Watching the giant cartoon characters drift across the screen, she had marveled that no matter what size or shape it was ("it could be a mile wide for God's sake!") a hot air balloon would still float if you could just get enough gas into it. Then as an afterthought, she had added that at night, if enough lights were attached to it, people on the ground would look right at it and still not know what the hell it was.

"Special Delivery owes us a heck of a lot of money," she'd said. "Will that be cash or charge?"

Any amount they could reasonably arrive at would be pocket change compared to what Special Delivery would clear once the night was over. Then there would be the profits from re-broadcasts, from soundtrack cds, home video and DVD sales. Osborne felt like a kid on Christmas morning.

"Tell me one thing," he said, "How in God's name did they make that thing disappear so quickly?"

The woman smiled slyly.

"If you took a circus tent, sealed up all its seams and filled it with helium, what would happen?"

"It would float."

"And if you could suddenly re-open all the seams at one time, what would happen?"

"It would drop like Internet stocks!"

"Right!"

Osborne squinted. "I don't get it. If the circus tent were as big as that thing, wouldn't it stay on the surface after it hit the water?"

"That would depend on what it was made of, and whether or not it had enough lights and smoke blowers and what-not attached to it to pull it under." She winked.

"Buuut…what about the woman?"

"She's in on it."

"How did they get her to float up a beam of light?"

"Hoisting mechanism."

"How come you didn't tell me?"

"If you had been all relaxed and confident, people would have known a hoax was coming. Now, will that be cash, or charge?" She winked again.

"It'll be cash, baby," Osborne said with a leer. "But first I wanna give you my personal thanks."

Special Delivery Home Entertainment Inc. saw a dramatic surge in its stock after Jonathan J. Osborne III was named its new CEO. In a special meeting with stockholders, Osborne laid out his vision for the network, saying that its first priority was to locate and hire a cadre of qualified psychics, and that he would personally negotiate a live interview with an Englishman who claimed the Devil visited him each Thursday for tea. Special Delivery reported record profits for the third quarter of that fiscal year, and Osborne became the first mainstream corporate CEO under the age of thirty to grace the cover of *Business Week*.

The State of New York indicted everyone it had threatened to indict even though the promises made in the ad campaign had, as far as the general public knew, been fulfilled. The State pressed forward its claim that the entire production had been a hoax and that the defendants were guilty of fraud. The Hyperbole Defense, however (as it came to be called), stood up in a way no one—not even Special Delivery's legal team—had anticipated. The judge who heard the case threw it out at the end of the first day of testimony. He sided with Special Delivery and said in his ruling that there were just too many stupid people in the world. Anyone who actually believed a spaceship would land should not have been trusted to cross the street alone, never mind been given money or access to credit cards.

Arreonna remained the preeminent artist of the New Age and continued to be a crossover sensation. Her next album, *Mother Earth: The View from Above* became one of the best-selling albums of all time. She was listed in the Guinness Book of World Records as the only human, living or dead, to have returned to earth after making verifiable contact with non-terrestrial intelligent life, a distinction which was not to be equaled in her lifetime.

After a special vote, the members of ASCAP and the International Society of Composers and Conductors jointly and unanimously proclaimed Marty Larkmon the Greatest Composer of the Modern Age, and one of the most important composers in Western history. He was made an honorary member of MENSA: The High IQ Society, and offered a starring role in the upcoming Broadway revival of the television series Buck Rogers in the 25th Century.

Marty and Arreonna were married in Times Square and lived happily together in creative bliss. Moreover and most importantly, for as long as Marty lived, no one ever, ever questioned his genius again.

11.
When I See Home

I am standing in the middle of an unpaved road beneath a stark blue sky and a sun approaching midday.

I am bewildered, because I am wearing an Armani suit and a shirt of white linen with a pointed collar and French cuffs. My tie is also an Armani, a handmade original in raw silk, and the cufflinks at my wrist are sapphires set in 24-karet gold. I am dressed for a televised awards ceremony, or a Broadway opening, but I am standing in the middle of a dirt road with ox carts and wagons trundling up and down on either side of me.

The smells are palpable. Each wagon that passes reeks of human sweat and animal feces. The aroma of dry grass, the smell of wood and leather hangs in the air. A warm wind blows and all are intensified.

I look down at the ground in disbelief, and when I raise my eyes, a horse and buggy is bearing down on me.

A horse and buggy?

Sweet Jesus...

"Hey! House nigger!" A gravelly voice breaks my revelry. The buggy veers around me and I hear the driver curse. It is good that he was able to maneuver the vehicle because I cannot move my feet.

"Get over there and help them other niggers load that wagon!"

I turn my head in minute increments, trying to locate the voice. My neck feels as though it is rusted in place. I manage to turn, and I watch and listen as a 'whoosh' ruffles the air. A short bullwhip bites into the shoulder of a mulatto boy. The boy scrambles away, raising his hands to ward off another blow.

"I said git!"

The man roars from high in the saddle. The boy hustles to a flatbed wagon where two other men—each much darker than he— pile bulging burlap sacks atop each other. "Doggone good-for- nothing son of a mongrel you," the man growls.

The three work feverishly. From where I stand, I can plainly see a large red welt rising on the boy's skin.

My feet, frozen at first, now turn me in a slow circle. All the buildings are made of hand-hewn wood, and hand-lettered shingles swing above the doorways.

Jesus H. Christ…

I look at my watch; the second hand still sweeps the dial.

An eerie feeling washes through me, and I think it would be more comforting if the watch had stopped completely. It might be easier then to tell myself that I am dreaming.

The voice roars again.

"You! Boy! Git over heah!"

I look all around.

"Dagnamnit, I'm talking to you! Get yo'…*get over heah!*"

Stunned, I look up at the menacing figure in the saddle. I cannot move, again.

He clips the horse and capers it to where I am. He raises the riding crop but I do not flinch. *Dear God what is happening to me?*

"What's yo' name nigger? An' what you all prettied up for?"

My mouth will not open. I try to make a sound, any sound that will communicate the caustic profanities boiling inside me. But no sound will come.

"Boy, if you don't open yo' mouth, I'm gon' strap you so yo' mammy'll feel it. Now, who you b'long to, and what in the *hell* is you all dootied up for?"

I turn my head and look down the dusty street toward a grand house at the foot of the distant hills.

I must be dead.

This is far too real somehow. Were smells ever so intense in dreams? So heavily layered one upon another that they overwhelmed the other senses? And could I even form that question if I were dreaming?

The man sighs and a look akin to understanding spreads across his face. "Goddamn worthless mute," he says to no one.

He gets down from the saddle and puts his face close to mine. His skin is red and pockmarked. White beard stubble grows on his cheeks and chin. His misshapen teeth are the color of hundred-year-old ivory, and tobacco juice fills the crevices between them. The sharp odors of unwashed clothes, of dried sweat and flatulence stab at my nose and cause my eyes to water. His breath is unimaginably foul. "Can't you talk boy? Or is you jest too scared to open them lips?"

He walks around me, swirls of dust rising where his cracked and worn brogans scrape the ground. Dust settles on the six-hundred dollar Bertucci lace-ups that enfold my feet and still hold their shine despite where I am standing.

"Ummph. You sho' is a good-smellin' nigger. Smell good as white folk damn near. Who you b'long to?"

Fury blisters the pit of my stomach. I open my mouth to curse him but the sound that comes out is strained and barely audible.

He inspects my clothes.

"You somebody's butler ain't ya? Must be them blue-bloods vistin' up yonder with the gov'nor." Then he speaks loudly and more slowly. "Is-that-yo-Marse-up-at-tha-gov'nor's?"

My mind spins, searching for the name of the science fiction writer who said that hell will be an individual experience formed from each person's worst nightmare.

"A deef and dumb nigger." The man scratches his head. "Well, boy, you must make one helluva cup-a tea for them to dress you up like some fancy Duke or somethin'." His regard—or fear—of the governor and his guest causes him to crank his hostility down, and I am amazed when he becomes almost civil. He even laughs, as if we are sharing a joke. "They might just put you up to serve the President of these United States!" He looks at me, waiting for some indication that I understood, that I shared in the joke. "I reckon they don't want they prized nigger getting' run down, though, so you best not go standin' in the middle of the road. Now git on outta heah." He points toward the gutter that runs along the wooden sidewalk. "Git."

He cannot understand the look on my face.

"Shheese," he says, climbing back into the saddle. I hear him mutter "damn niggers" as he walks the horse back to where the three men still load the wagon…

12.
The End

"Blessed are the dead..."

"Professor Todd?"

A soft hand shakes me and calls me back from the long nightmare I have been having. I sit up, startled, and look around at the walls of my office. A colorful abstract artwork woven from strands of plant fiber and given to me by an African diplomat hangs reassuringly on the wall above the filing cabinets. The woman, my tall, bespectacled teaching assistant, hands me a manila folder stuffed with carefully typed essays and her grade recommendations for each. I reach for it and fumble with the reading glasses that are now askew on my forehead. She gives me a quasi-sympathetic look, one that hangs somewhere between irritation and profound pity.

"You really ought to take a day off and just rest," she says. Her tone, along with the brown spots on her hands and the few gray strands visible at her temples make her seem more like my mother than a graduate student marking time until the end of the semester. She continues to speak as I glance over the papers. "You can't make that deadline if you're laid up in a hospital." I have almost finished my first work of fiction—a coming of age novel set in the urban south at the height of the Civil Rights Movement. My editor is pushing me to get the book finished so that it can be in stores before the end of the year. My other books, three collections of essays and short stories, were well received. Now I am trying something larger, something riskier and more demanding. The preliminary feedback has been encouraging, so much so that she (my editor) feels certain it will clinch an award in the coming spring if it can be gotten out in time to compete with this year's crop of new fiction. I am less preoccupied with the thought of winning something than with the desire to have the whole thing done so that I can concentrate on my class load. My contract says nothing about time off to write novels, after all. One could even argue that I am cheating the university and my students, giving them less than their money's worth when I show up late to class, my brain fuzzy and my lecture less than ideally prepared. My assistant continues to chastise me as I look through the essays. Oh well. By next quarter, all will be back to normal, and no one will have the slightest cause to complain—not my editor, not my assistant, not my students, not the university. No one.

"Everyone else has gone," the woman says. She resists adding "can I go now?" but her tone makes it clear she does not wish to wake me up again. Her own children are high school aged, but I have no doubt she would rather share their company than mine.

"Why don't you call it a night?" I say to her. The campus is dark and the night warm. The grounds and the dormitories are never completely still, but I can see no cars moving on the street outside my first-floor office window. Water droplets dot the lower half of the windowpane. The lawn sprinklers have emerged from the ground to moisten the parched flowerbeds and the grass, which will soon need cutting.

"Shall I walk you to your car?"

"That's okay," she says hurriedly, "thanks. I'll call for an escort. Goodnight." There is fumbling in the outer office and then quiet as the door closes behind her.

It is only nine o'clock so I decide to press on. I will stop in a little while and go over the notes for my eight a.m. class. My assistant is right, of course, but there is no rest for the weary. Or is it the wicked? Soon there are no sounds at all except the clicking of the keys and the buzz of the hard drive. It would feel so good to lay my head down and steal a few minutes of sleep. But I still have miles to go before I can justify sleeping. Soon, I remind myself. Soon this will all be over.

Before long, my left eye starts to sting, telling me it has gone from slightly red to completely bloodshot. For the next few days, everyone who sees me will ask if I have pinkeye, or if my allergies are acting up. I let go of the keyboard and sink into the soft leather of the chair, closing both eyes. Warmth and numbness wash over me in alternating waves.

Miles to go before I sleep…

Moments later, I heard the sound of rain, lightly at first, then loud and with increasing violence. Wind and water soon beat against the windows like poltergeists trying to shake loose the latch and force their way in.

I sat up and stretched.

In that brief moment, someone had crept in, turned off the overhead light, and turned on my desk lamp. I was instantly annoyed. Some undergrad student still clinging to adolescence might be standing on the other side of the door right now, waiting to jump at me when I got up to turn the overhead light back on. I sighed.

The outer office was empty and would have been totally dark if not for the orange glow of lights in the parking lot. I heard voices and saw the glow of a television set coming from a door further down the hallway. Leaving my office, I walked toward the door from which the glow emanated, passing as I went a pair of French doors that opened onto a small courtyard. Rain lashed against the panes with incredible energy, as if buckets of water were being catapulted at the glass. I stopped and, cautiously, moved the thin curtain aside to look out. The wind had bent an entire row of young dogwood trees to a near ninety degree angle. All would be shorn of their leaves and possibly uprooted by the time the storm passed.

Turning back toward the blue light down the hall, I made my way to the door and looked in. A handful of people were listening in stunned silence to a news bulletin. I listened for a moment, then turned, and walked back to the French doors. When I moved the curtain aside this time I saw that the rain had stopped. As suddenly and unexpectedly as it had come, the storm had vanished. I cracked one of the doors and looked out.

The air was still.

I stepped outside and looked down at the walkway. The concrete was jaundice yellow in the light of the gas lamps and showed not a sign of the drenching it underwent just moments ago. I stooped to touch it and, indeed, it was completely dry. I walked down to the edge of the grass and clutched a handful of green blades. They were dry as well. I looked up at the sky.

Three red stars glittered malevolently in the darkness above. As I gazed at them, my eyes drew the lines that formed them into a triangular constellation, one that I, an avid stargazer, had never seen. High above the western horizon, they stared back at me like the eyes of some immense beast. Murky black clouds, black as the soot from an oil lamp floated past at intervals and obscured their light. I went back inside and closed the doors behind me. More people were crowded into the room with the television. A white-haired announcer in a dark blue suit calmly broke the news that U.S.-China peace talks had broken down.

"The White House has confirmed..."

Two American aircraft carrier battle groups had taken up positions in the Philippine Sea off the coast of Taiwan, and a third was on its way. The tough-talking American President, a swaggering imbecile oblivious to his own fallibility, had ordered the fleet to deploy and provide a firewall in case the Chinese moved against the island nation. In response, the Chinese had massed an entire amphibious army in the southern Fujian Provence just across the Taiwan Strait. They called it a defensive force, but one word from Beijing, and it would become an invasion force. Now, each side was faced with backing up its rhetoric or abandoning the island to its adversary for all time.

I thought of the Cold War and marveled at how quickly it had become the stuff of abstract history. Why had world leaders allowed such a situation to develop?

Two things and two things only were certain: there was no place to hide, and, once either side pulled the pin, it would all be over very quickly. Unless cooler heads—or higher powers—prevailed, the approaching midnight might well be the world's last.

Some got up quietly and left; others continued to listen. More people came into the doorway behind me.

I turned back to my own office.

Two men stood in the hallway through which I'd come. Each wore a dark business suit with a pin of some sort in the left lapel. It did not register that they might be there to see me, but they stopped me as I walked past. They asked me to identify myself, and when I did, they followed me back to my office and asked me to sit.

Outside my window, the rain had started again.

One of the men told me why they were there, and what he said I could not grasp, let alone believe. He talked without stopping for twenty minutes, and when he fell silent I could only gaze at him dumbfounded. Rain pounded against the windows with gale force. My mother, he wanted me to understand, was alive. Again.

The other man opened a large leather case and drew out a thick gray binder which he offered to me as his partner watched. I opened it, and there at the very front was the death certificate I had first seen twelve years previously. The succeeding pages—radiology reports, progress notes, lab results—recounted in detail the slow progression of her cancer. Flipping through the items in her chart, I re-lived the long months of her decline. No ventilator for her, no serene crossing. She suffered as if God himself held a grudge against her. By the time it was over, I would have pulled the plug without hesitation—for my own sake as much as for hers—had there been a plug to pull.

Now, miraculously—no, tragically—a woman I watched die twelve years earlier was alive.

They had already told me how, supposedly, but I needed to ask again, and again, and again. They had anticipated my confusion and incredulity. The one who had handed me the binder did all the answering. He could only tell me so much, of course, something to do with national security. Fourteen bodies appropriated from hospitals in Washington D.C. twelve years ago. Each one deceased less than twenty-four hours at the time it was seized. Spirited away to an undisclosed location, they were experimented upon. Injected with something, pumped full of something else, the cellular decomposition had slowed drastically in all fourteen; in three, it had stopped altogether. Twelve years later, those three were comatose, but all three breathed on their own. She was one of them.

I rose and left the room, shaking my head and clutching the

binder like a live electrical wire. I needed to go to this place and see this for myself; I had to see if it were real, even though I knew it could not be. A voice inside me, a cordoned-off segment of my mind, decided on its own to play along with these men. Seeing her the way I last remembered, it warned, would make *me* want to die, just as I had wanted to die twelve years ago in her place. And what would she look like after twelve years...*twelve years*...in an unnatural sleep?

These men were lying, or I was dreaming. This was insane. A horrible prank perhaps. Maybe all of the above. Whose ashes had I scattered on the Potomac River if not my mother's?

One of the men followed me to the outer office. He told me that the decision to go public with this research had been handed down from the very highest levels of government. The families would be well compensated, but we had first to be told.

The rain had stopped again.

I found myself back at the French windows, opening them against damp air. The grass glistened in the light of passing cars. There was movement all over the campus now, people loading into cars and driving away. Overhead, the three stars, the three red eyes, seemed brighter.

I noticed right away that there was no panic. Everyone on earth knew the seriousness of the situation that faced the two superpowers. I had kept the entire crisis at the back of my mind, perhaps in denial, for days, yet a part of me had all along believed that if the talks ran into trouble, there would be chaos in the streets. As my mind struggled to make sense of all that I had seen and heard in the last hour, it noted no prayer vigils, no hysterics among the growing numbers of people emerging from the buildings. No one fled in terror. There was no violence; no end-of-the-world jubilation that I could see. People were quietly gathering their belongings and, in most cases, loading into vehicles. Some stood in groups and talked quietly; a loose cluster of individuals had started toward the highway on foot. One student whom I knew well, a young man who had confided in me on occasion, stood nearby with his arm around an incredible young woman whom he had not had the courage to approach a week before. The two of them gazed up at the strange constellation.

177

The modicum of faith that had survived in me until adulthood perished along with my mother. I had not worshipped, nor prayed, nor taken part in any religious celebration or ritual in over a decade, including Christmas mass. But no span of years can erase memories of the book of *Revelation*. Many such memories from that book and others surfaced in my mind. I recalled reading that the stars would fall, that the dead would rise up, that there would be unbelievable destruction and suffering, that panic would ensue on a scale unprecedented in all of history. *"Blessed are the dead in Jerusalem,"* wrote a Jesuit monk in the thirteenth century, *"for the day of suffering comes as a swift wind, and their tribulations shall be to ours as a single stone cast upon a mountainside."*

Hours into the night, I found myself walking the highway with a group of people going toward the nearby town. At an all-night diner, I sat and examined my life but found no answers. If tomorrow came, what change could I make to give meaning to my ant-like existence in a universe of ants? An unnatural hush hung over the world, as if a pool of invisible energy drew all extraneous sounds into itself. Every conversation, every door closing, every clink of glass or rattle of change was muffled. When dawn was near, I started back to the campus alone, not knowing what else to do.

The sun rose, and the grounds seemed deserted but for a handful of people in the main administrative building. I stopped in its rotunda and tried to take stock. The windows in the dome poured long columns of light down into the open space, highlighting the hundred year-old crest inlaid in the marble floor. I watched the dust motes floating in the yellow shafts. On the far side of the open space, tinted windows and doors looked out across a concrete balcony and down onto a large central courtyard where concrete walkways radiated outward from a bronze sculpture like the spokes of a wheel. Windows in the other buildings were dark and empty. A man with yellow hair and a cigarette dangling from his lips stood at a display table to my left and sorted through a pile of rags. He told me with a smirk that he was going to make bandages. As he mumbled to himself, I took note of the remainder of the group of people who had stopped here. Some sat quietly while others paced; some wandered into and out of offices. A small group sat in a circle on the floor and talked quietly.

A giant-screen television hung on a wall near the information desk. A live report on the deepening crisis came over the airwaves. The Chinese Premier had called home that nation's ambassadors to the United States and the U.N., announcing that all diplomatic ties between the two countries were suspended indefinitely. Here in the U.S., every Cabinet member and most of the congressional leadership had gone to "undisclosed locations." Every harbor was empty or near empty of merchant ships and naval vessels. Nowhere in U.S. coastal waters could an American warship be seen except for floating museums like those in Mobile Bay and Pearl Harbor, or those dry-docked in Mississippi and Virginia. The Vice-President's whereabouts were unknown to any outside the Executive Branch.

The report switched to a recorded image from the conflict zone. The picture—transmitted from a missile cruiser in the area—showed a wide-angled view of the heavens. Against a backdrop of washed-out sky and clouds on the horizon, a blazing meteor dived toward the East China Sea. It cut a blinding streak through the atmosphere and left a long white trail pointing backward toward infinity. A creeping cold enveloped me. Could this truly be happening?

One by one, others joined me in front of the set. There were murmurs and questions, and then one woman began to laugh. She snickered while the rest of us looked at each other, trying to discern the humor that was so obvious to her. Her mirth grew as the report continued, and then she was caught in a long, loud guffaw that rocked her body until she wiped away tears. Then she began to scream. Long, bloody, terrifying screams that unnerved the others.

The panic was beginning.

Another woman, a peculiar sparkle coming into her eyes, announced she would help the blond man make bandages. First, they had to find more rags. Within moments, most of those in the rotunda were gone, running through the ground floor of the building. The screaming woman fell silent and collapsed into a chair, her eyes fixed on the floor. Only she and I remained near the television. She did not speak again. My own uneasiness was still in check, but I felt it lurking at the back of my mind, pacing like an animal ready to bolt from a cage.

The report continued.

Russia's Ambassador to the United States had been recalled, but he and its Foreign Minister continued to act as intermediaries urging the White House and Beijing to negotiate a stand-down.

Though I was aware of it, I found myself unable to absorb all that was happening. The visit from the two men the night before was already distant and unreal. The news that they had given me was too incredible, too far outside of everyday reality, and my mind could not accept it, so I let it alone. In the very real world of international conflict, however, there was the truth that in a matter of hours, I and everyone I had ever known might be dead. The only planet upon which intelligent life was known to exist would be reduced to a scarred and contaminated rock. That in itself touched the bounds of unreality.

Yet that was almost nothing.

What of violent storms that appeared out of nowhere, and then disappeared without a trace in the blink of an eye? How had a new constellation appeared—a constellation made up of aged stars that no one had ever seen? How could a woman whom I watched die be alive again? How?

The sound of sobbing broke my rumination. I turned toward the glass doors that looked out over the courtyard. A brunette woman richly dressed and exuding an aura of wealth and status stood alone with her hands flat against the glass. Her body shook with the effort to silence her cries, but the glass reflected them into the lobby and they drifted to where I stood. She looked almost like a mime, her hands pressed against tinted nothingness as if shielding her eyes from some dreadful thing on the other side.

I went to her.

"What is it?" I asked quietly, wishing I could comfort her for no other reason than that there seemed so little comfort left in the world. She pressed her forehead against the door.

"The stars..." she said after a moment. "The stars are still out. I can see them."

The sun was up—high up—in the sky. How could it be that stars were visible? Were they the same stars, the same constellation that had appeared the night before?

Suddenly the fear, the very same fear that I had denied and held at bay the entire night, found its way through the cracks in my defenses and wrapped around me with hideous strength. I tried to breathe but felt the air being squeezed out of me. I wanted to run suddenly, to hide. I wanted to crawl into a sewer drain and keep crawling, down and down and down until I had lost my way in cold, wet blackness. But there was no place to hide.

The woman sank to her knees, her sobs bitter and profuse.

An overwhelming urge came over me then.

If I could see the open sky with my own eyes...

If I could see it, I might see that something held to normalcy. It was daytime, goddamnit! It was broad daylight outside. How could stars be visible? I had to see it in order to believe. This was why there had been no panic. The truth was too much for anyone to absorb, not just me.

Eeeeennnnkkkkk...Eeeeennnnkkkkk...Eeeeennnnkkkkk...

A stabbing squawk pulsed from the television.

The screen flickered for several seconds then displayed a network test pattern.

"My God," an old man moaned behind me, "my God, my God..."

A female voice, distorted by distance and unnaturally calm, crackling with static like an ancient analogue broadcast spoke from the screen.

"At 6:41a.m. Eastern Standard Time, the U.S. Joint Strategic Defense Command issued an alert to the National Security Agency, indicating an attack underway against the Chinese homeland—"

I turned away from the set and leaned against the door, chips of ice running up and down in my veins. I could not feel my legs, but neither could I withstand the compulsion to see with my own eyes whatever was out there.

I pushed the metal bar and felt warm air on my face and arms. My legs carried me out onto the balcony, out to the bronze railing that felt as warm as a stove when my hands clutched it. In the distance, a flock of white birds lifted skyward like an explosion of sea spray. I watched them rise and saw that high above, the cool blue of the troposphere was streaked and scored with violent orange and angry red clouds—a roiling field of molten lava spreading out to smother the sky. The sun was high above the trees, and the world shimmered in an eerie, golden, undulating light. The great clock, high in the bell tower across campus, had stopped at one minute past midnight.

And the birds.

The gigantic flock soared high into the air, wheeled, and flew around and around above the buildings in a perfect circle, golden light flashing through their wings. Like the inner workings of a machine, or the delicate gears of a celestial timepiece, the avian wheel spun against the horrific sky. They held to their positions so precisely that I knew this could not be a natural phenomenon. And high above the eastern horizon, I saw once more the triad of red stars glittering with nightmarish beauty, even against the morning sky. A panicked voice called from the doorway, begging me to come back inside, but I could not go. I could not turn back.

I had to *see*.

With my own eyes, I had to see what was happening, even though my mind complained that all of the things I now saw were impossible.

And I looked up, compelled to see the face of death as it came for me, and in that moment, all things became clear… I knew then that the awful weapons of man, fired from ships and planes and underground silos, would never reach their targets. There would be neither war nor peace, and the sun at long last had run its course in overseeing humanity's existence. The end of history, the end of all things was at hand, and I like so many, many others simply had not been able to believe.

People began appearing in other doorways and emerging from buildings I had thought deserted. I called out hoarsely, urging all to come out. A dizzying wave of emotions washed through me: numbing terror, a profound and inexplicable sense of relief, a loneliness more acute than any feeling I have ever known. I turned back to the doorway where the crying woman still stood and watched me. Then I, not wanting to die alone, held out my hand to her. Millions of white lights appeared in the sky overhead. As she hurried toward me, they began falling…

13.

Veteran's Day

Part I

The police arrived soon after I did.

Two cruisers stopped on the street in front of the house. Four officers got out, flashlights in hand; two went to the front door, two circled the house and went into the backyard. I was standing in the front room with a beer in my hand when the first loud, inconsiderate knock shook the front door.

I sighed, looking through the open curtains at the crowd gathering on the far side of the police cars.

They knocked again. Banged actually, with nightsticks or something that I bet had marred the paint on the other side of the door.

"Police!"

I heard a radio squawk police code and wondered why most police dispatchers seemed to be women.

Setting the beer on the bare wood of the coffee table I went to the door.

"Just a minute," I called, even though there was no reason to. It wasn't like I had to pull up my shorts, cinch my robe, or pour half a kilo of heroin down the toilet. Cops tended to be jumpy when they answered a call about unexplained gunshots, and I thought it might be a good idea to refrain from snatching a door open and surprising them.

"I'm coming."

I turned the knob and pulled the door open, trying to avoid both exaggerated slowness and an impression of urgency.

"Come on in," I said, "he's in the back."

"Would you step out here please," one of them said.

I sighed and though '*sonofabitch*,' but took it back as quickly as it had formed in my head. This guy was doing his job; a job I would not have volunteered to do.

I wasn't as hard on the cops as some of my neighbors, although I didn't trust them much. I'd always thought that being discreet with ones extra-legal fuckups greatly lessened ones chance of getting beat like Rodney King. And even so, it was possible for a law-abiding man to be shot forty-two times while reaching for his wallet. Best to open doors slowly and avoid driving ninety miles-an-hour while high on crack.

I stepped onto the porch.

"Keep your hands where I can see them."

"*Okay asshole*,' I said with my eyes, this time with no remorse. Doing his job was one thing, being obnoxious was another.

"Do you have any identification on you?"

I reached for my wallet but stopped when my fingers touched the leather.

"I'm getting my WALLET out," I said, loud enough to be heard by the spectators on the sidewalk.

The cop thought '*asshole*' at me.

Yeah. Whatever.

Wallet in front of me, I opened it and took out my driver's license, flashing the baby picture of my niece, just in case. The cop looked at the license (front and back), and when he was satisfied it was real said, "Mr. Douglas, is there anyone else in there?"

"Yeah, he's in the den."

"Who is?"

"The idiot who fired the shots. Nobody's hurt," I added.

184

"He's….just…." I shrugged, not exactly sure what was going on, but certain no one was dead or injured, and that I was not the one who had been doing target practice.

"You mind showing me?" He nodded for me to go first even though he was wearing the gun and the bulletproof vest.

I shrugged again. "Follow me."

I was at my house eating, listening to the weatherman of all people complaining about the forecast when we heard a muffled gunshot through the open window.

One shot…two….

Melinda, my long-time girlfriend, and I looked at each other across the table. A third rang out.

"Jesus!" she said. "What's happening?"

I shook my head, not because I didn't know, but because I thought I did.

"It's Clay," I said, pushing my chair back.

"Clay?" she said.

"Clay," I answered and stood up.

"Well wait, don't go out there!" she said. "How do you know it's him?"

"It's him," I said.

She stood up too.

"Oh man. You don't think…"

"I don't know," I said, moving to the door. "Let me make sure he hasn't blown his stupid head off."

"Luke…" she said as I reached for the knob. "Maybe we should call…someone…you know. In case…"

I turned around and kissed her.

"Be right back."

I crossed the narrow street and went up the walk of the house directly across from mine. I climbed the concrete steps to the front door, gave a loud knock, and shouted his name.

No answer.

People in the houses on either side had come out onto their porches. I knocked again before turning the knob (knowing it would be unlocked) and letting myself into the living room.

Clay's place was decorated in a common though maligned and

unappreciated style: contemporary Single American Male. It was accented throughout with knick-knacks and do-dads from the equally popular Who-Gives-a-Damn Collection at Wal-Mart The curtains hanging at the windows were lifeless, faded shears that looked like they were hung right after the windows were cut into the walls. The living room furniture was one of those imitation Ranch-style sets: a sofa, an easy chair, a rocker, two end tables, and a coffee table/ottoman with padded ends. Each piece was made of heavily lacquered two-by-fours and had hard pillows covered with fuzzy, Western-themed upholstery. The television sat on an old, prefabricated entertainment center whose imitation wood-grain was nicked in several places and showed the raw pasteboard underneath. There was something about modular furniture that attracted unattached men. Perhaps it was the challenge of assembling it, figuring out where all those screws and clips and color-coded dowels were supposed to go. Perhaps it was some sort of tree-house nostalgia. I didn't know one unattached man who would not drag a 150-pound carton up any number of steps and try to piece the contents together while drinking beer and without once looking at the directions.

The most modern thing in the room was the futuristic-looking AM-FM, multi-disc stereo CD player with automatic changer, Dolby surround sound, and a dynamic, multicolored, liquid crystal display. Melinda had remarked that that stereo cost as much as everything else in the living room combined, and she was probably right. But a man needed his music and so had a right to whatever system he could reasonably afford, or could hope to pay off in his lifetime. I walked through the kitchen (small, cluttered, the stove and microwave covered with a thin layer of grease), and into the den.

Clay was sitting on the legless sofa with one foot propped on a cinderblock. A thirty-eight revolver rested on his thigh. The smell of gunpowder hung in the air.

A forty-four magnum and two hunting rifles were disassembled on a sheet on the floor. Gun oil, rags, and steel-bristled push rods lay alongside the pieces. Clay wore denim shorts so ragged around the bottom they looked like the legs had been bitten off. An LA Lakers jersey and a black baseball cap completed his outfit. He sat there with his right hand on the butt of the pistol and a bottle of Miller

Genuine Draft in his left hand. His eyes were fixed on the far wall, on a row of citations, a picture of him in desert camouflage with an M-16 and rucksack, and another of him in his dress blues. The proud centerpiece of that display was an American flag encased in glass and walnut. Directly below the display case was a smiling studio portrait of a dark haired woman and a grinning, red-haired boy. A fresh bullet hole was punched into the glass and made spidery cracks where the woman's chest should have been. Two more holes were punched into the wood paneling between it and the case that held the flag.

"What in the hell are you doing?" I asked.

He said nothing at first. Then he grimaced and shook his head from side to side.

"You want a beer?"

I looked around for the cooler, which ordinarily sat against the wall with the fishing tackle. I scooped out a bottle, wiped off the bits of ice that clung to it and twisted off the cap.

"You want to tell me why you murdered that picture?"

He grumbled "sonsofbitches," and turned his own beer upside down.

"Well, that's a start," I said. "What happened?"

Clay McGinnis and I made an odd pair. He was a six-foot four-inch, thick-necked, muscle-bound country boy from the hills outside Anniston, Alabama. With his close-cropped blond hair, his blue-gray eyes, his tattoos and rosy cheeks, he could stroll into any Country Western bar on the planet and get hugs, handshakes, and the first round on the house just for showing up. I, on the other hand, had grown up in what we knew locally as Gate City—the largest government housing project in Birmingham. He stood well above my five-foot nine inch, toned but not necessarily muscular frame, and though we were both from the south, I noted a distinct difference in the way we spoke, even though few others did. Where I was down with hip-hop and Motown, could even tolerate Disco and 70's Rock, he was all Lynyrd Skynyrd and ZZ Top, confederate flags and *NASCAR*.

Yes, we were an odd couple. He wore his *X* and I wore mine, both with pride and without apology, even in places where one or the

187

other would seem to be asking for trouble. His "Southern by the Grace of God" tee shirt, for example, drew approving stares when we stopped for bait on our way up to Huntsville for a weekend of fishing. My own shirt, emblazoned with Malcolm X's pointing finger and defiant stare, was less appreciated.

But the oddest thing of all was this: Clay McGinnis and I were brothers.

It had nothing to do with made-for-TV hospital mix-ups (how could it?), exploited maids, or illicit affairs. Clay had saved my neck once and my ass twice (or vice versa) in the first Gulf War when we were ground-pounders attached to the 1st Marine Infantry Regiment in Kuwait.

To me, Clay was exactly like the other good-ole' boys who listened to country music cassette tapes. And I never cared what he or anyone else in the platoon thought of me, tending to keep to myself after duty hours. But every hour was a duty hour after we crossed the border into Iraq, and it was our battalion's distinct honor to meet one of the few Republican Guards units that didn't roll over when it saw the Stars and Stripes on the horizon.

We were in a dismounted firefight when our squad leader tasked me to move out past our flank and get eyes on a machine gun position that had us pinned down. It was Iraqi sharpshooters that I worried about as I low-crawled through the sand, but a fist-sized scorpion lanced my left thigh before I was twenty yards away from my own men. I had cover from the Iraqi position, but when that sand crawler lit into me, I jerked upright and exposed myself just long enough to get their attention. I flattened myself against the sand again and tried to smash the skittering sonofabitch with the butt of my rifle. That scorpion must have been Marine also, because it not only survived the blow I gave it, it regrouped and came at me again when I got down on my face. And then I saw that there was a whole nest of the damned things. I pushed myself away from the sand pit and got ready to spray the little fuckers with seven-six-two millimeter ammo, but the instant I raised my head, one of the other fuckers, an Iraqi, got off a shot that whizzed past my head so closely I felt hot wind on my cheek. I threw myself down before I could get off a single shot, at the scorpions or the enemy, and now I was face-to-face with an entire troop of them, led by the big, black motherfucker that had already scored a hit. It lifted its claws into the air and I smashed my fist down on it without thinking. I felt the mistake instantly. And then I was stung a third time by one of its brothers, just below the elbow. I figured I'd be home in three or four days. I'd be wearing a body bag, but I'd be out of the damn desert.

I lobbed sand at them with my good hand. Most skittered up the dune and away from me while a couple stood their ground. It took roughly a minute for my insides to start to feel like they'd been put into a blender. The air temperature was a few degrees above freezing that morning, but most of what I remember was the wave of heat sweeping over me, like I was a hamburger patty riding through the broiler at Burger King. I could hear small arms fire everywhere, and there suddenly was a looming shape above me that I could not make out because my eyes had gone funny. That shape, the heat, and a far-away feeling of something tugging on my right leg were my last sensory impressions until I woke up later—or half woke up—at the battalion aid station. I remember it taking all the strength I had to lay one hand over my closed eyes; Jesus, the light was bright in that place. The company First Sergeant, our platoon sergeant, Maniac Messner, and Clay were all standing at the side of my bed cracking jokes. Presumably about me, since they laughed harder and harder the more I tried to open my eyes or sit up. I got the last laugh though. I managed to lean over just far enough to get my head off the bed. Then I blew what was left of yesterday's chow all over the floor at their feet.

I didn't get to go home needless to say, and I also don't have to say the war was over by the time I got back to my unit. We celebrated like hell. The fighting was over and we'd won; I was alive; Clay had been given a medal for saving my butt. I bought him so much beer that week that he must have whizzed away ten pounds. There was still business to attend to after the initial burst of joy, however, so a week after So-damn Insane surrendered (Gil Scott Heron, the singer, had called him that), we were back doing the same shit we had done throughout the autumn months and that armies do while sitting in foreign lands and not fighting.

It so happened that after I came back from the hospital, Clay and I pulled guard together for the first time and drew the worst possible time slot, 2400 to 0200. Freezing our asses off in a listening post on the outer edge of the company area, we joked in low voices and soon discovered a couple of Twilight Zone coincidences. We had grown up less than a hundred miles from each other. His mother's name was Kathy with a *K*; mine was named Catherine with a *C*. I'd graduated high school with honors then dropped out of college after my sophomore year and gotten a job; he'd gotten a GED, done two years at a junior college, and then gone to work pulling wire on construction sites for his uncle. My new plan after college (and before joining the Marines) was to become a paramedic. His was to build a construction business. We'd both become disillusioned and signed for two-year tours with Uncle Sugar in June of '90.

We'd been out there an hour and a half when Clay excused himself to go and take a dump. Not more than two minutes after he was gone, I, dog-tired, began to feel as if someone had shoved a chloroformed pillow against my face. It was the longest part of the night. Long after lights out, and long before stand-to, or wake-up. This was the time when it was hardest to stay awake. If you had someone to shoot the shit with, it wasn't so bad. But the instant you stopped talking and listened to all that silence, then by God, the Sand Man would come waddling across the landscape and climb into your foxhole singing lullabies just like mom did when you were a baby.

As I looked out across the moonless, blue-black desert, the gnawing cold let go little by little until I no longer felt like I was crouching inside a meat locker. Melinda, ah my love, Melinda pulls her shirt over her head and grins at me with eyes full of desire and playfulness. The room is silent and dim beyond the glow of the tiny lamp beside her bed. I hear a voice, and then the cold snaps back with the force of a punch. I had slumped down to the bottom of the hole, and there were two voices talking above me.

I listened without moving and realized it was Clay and Staff Sergeant Messner. The platoon sergeant had been walking the company perimeter, checking on the LP-OP's. He had approached our listening post without being challenged, and had torn into Clay's ass when he reappeared at that very moment. I heard Clay tell the man that I had run back to get a fresh battery for the radio, and that he had run down the berm to take a leak.

Now, why the hell would he say that? I wondered.

Since he, supposedly, had been the last man at the post, he would be the one charged with abandoning it. So Messner told him and reminded him it was a court-martial offense. Sleeping on guard duty was also a court-martial offense, I knew, even punishable by death in time of war. I didn't think they would shoot me for going to sleep, but just like that, literally in the long, slow blink of an exhausted eye, a stretch in the brig became a very real prospect for me. But as I listened to the sergeant, I realized Clay was in even deeper. Whatever had been going through his mind, he had bit the green weenie when he opened his mouth. If Messner had shined a flashlight into the hole and seen me, or if Clay had said he didn't know where the hell I was, he would have been okay. As it was, he had lied to an NCO, and when Messner realized Clay had been lying to his face….

Oh.

Shit.

There was only one thing to do.

I had to stand up and take whatever Messner threw at me. I didn't want to go to jail, not for one fucking day, let alone the six months or even a year that I might actually get! And anyway, the fucking war was over! Any fucking Iraqi who came near us now was going to come with his hands out asking for food and cigarettes. It was over!

But there was the code. There was integrity to consider…

Jesus Christ in the starry sky, can't he let this shit go? Can't you give this pit-bull-looking sonofabitch a minor heart attack, or something else to worry about so we can get on with our fucking lives?

There was one right answer, and it presented itself to me again. I'd have to do my time. But what about Clay? What would Messner do to him for lying?

"Lance Corporal Fuck-up," I heard Messner say. "You will stand to this post for the remainder of the night, then you and that other ill-begotten, shit-for-brains, mindless, Bama, dickweed fuck will report to Company headquarters the instant you are relieved! Do you understand?"

"Yes Staff Sergeant!"

"Get your fuckin' ass in that fuckin' hole. If I were you, I'd get used to the taste of semen."

Two minutes later when Messner was out of earshot, Clay went off like a one-o-five howitzer. It got so bad at one point, I actually thought I might have to shoot him. I understood his anger, but my hand had not been up his ass working his mouth, now had it? He calmed down as the night wore on, and we sat wide awake in glum silence until daybreak.

I decided to see what the next day brought, and if worse came to worst, I'd tell them everything. Clay would still be on the hook for lying to an NCO, but they wouldn't send him to prison for that. Sgt. Messner would have a whole boatload of crap that he could mete out to Clay over the remainder of his tour. But he wouldn't send Clay to jail. Probably.

My mind was calm as half-past-four approached. That was the time we were to be relieved finally. My mind was calm but my gut was having thoughts of its own and made those feelings plain. I ignored what I first thought were hunger pangs, but then, great, ripping columns of gas began forcing their way out of me and suddenly I needed to shit like a madman. By the time our relief arrived, Clay was cursing like a homeless beggar who had lost a winning lottery ticket.

I wanted to laugh it off but couldn't. We could see two guys moving across the sand toward us, and for every yard they grew closer, the thunderclouds inside my gut grew more violent. Clay was on the verge of tears when they arrived, and I was ready to shit so hard I thought the next fart would light itself and launch me into the air. Finally, I scrambled out of the hole and ran for the latrine.

Ten minutes later, I had gotten rid of half a year's worth of MRE's, and Clay and I stood outside the headquarters tent trying not to think about the future. When Messner came along a half hour later, he told us to grab our entrenching tools and report back to him.

Over the next forty-five days, Clay and I dug a hole damn near to the center of the earth. Sgt. Messner took us to a spot near the ammo dump where the top sand had blown away and the ground was baked hard like the deserts of New Mexico. He marked off a ten-foot by ten-foot square and told us to start digging and keep digging until we struck oil or found hell. We were to report there every day after duty and stay there digging until he sent someone out to get us or retreat sounded, whichever came first. He said he was going to inspect that hole every week and if it wasn't deep enough, he was going to invite the whole battalion to come take a shit in it, and then make us dig with our bare hands.

In two weeks the hole was above our heads and we soon had to climb out with ropes. With help from the grease monkeys in the motor pool, we set up a shaky pulley system to haul up the dirt. On the twenty-first day, we decided to call his bluff, doubting that he'd be able to tell a difference in how deep the hole was compared to a few days earlier, even if he did come back out and check. Not only did the bastard come, he brought a long, wooden pole, measured the hole, and decided it wasn't deep enough. He made us fill it in and told us to start over the next day.

Before our forty-five days were up, half the company was coming out in the evenings to sit around the hole and screw with us while we dug. We handled that part okay—just kept digging. No matter what anyone said, no matter how many cigarette butts landed in the dry soil, we kept digging. I was wondering if the sides of the hole could cave in on us one evening when there came a sudden rain of red dirt. Tons of the stuff, it seemed. Clay must have thought the same thing because we turned at the same time and scrambled for the aluminum ladder Messner had gotten for us (he decided our rope system made getting ourselves down there too troublesome and getting the dirt up too easy). When we got to the top, panicked and caked with the mud of our own sweat, we saw that some asshole had actually brought out a bulldozer and pushed the top of our quite respectable mound of dirt back into the hole.

With shouts and guffaws ringing in our ears, Clay and I together dragged the guy off the dozer and started whipping his ass. This was a slight miscalculation.

Every other guy out there—we noted for the first time—was from his platoon. I was glad there were so many of them because it gave me ample room to work out my anger. I found out, however, that fighting three guys and putting them all on the ground was pretty much my limit, no matter how angry I was. Some Marine's knee was planted firmly in my chest, pressing my breastbone against my spine, when Clay came charging into the knot of men who held my feet and legs.

There were eight of them in all, and, as I said, my contribution was over after I knocked down my third, who got back up. Clay, however, went on fighting and fighting until they stepped back and called for a truce. The bunch of them backed away, then turned and walked off leaving us the bulldozer.

All eight came back the next evening. This time, they brought three cases of beer with them. They couldn't help us dig, but the beer was cold and the extra company, even their company, made the evening go a little faster.

On the last day of our sentence, Sergeant Messner brought the Company First Sergeant and some junior NCOs out to see the hole.

"Good fuckin' grief Sarge," Top told Messner. "We could bury your fat-ass momma in that hole."

Messner took the compliment in the proper spirit and passed it on to me.

"What's your girlfriend's name Private Douglas?"

"Melinda, sergeant."

I knew what was coming.

"Well Marine, your homeboys are gonna have Melinda Sergeant's twat stretched out just like this hole by the time you get back to the world." He then christened the canyon we had dug "Melinda's Twat" and spit an umber stream of tobacco juice into it. The First Sergeant whipped out his whizzer and took a leak. Then they told us to put the dirt back.

When we got out there the next day to start filling in the hole, we found a hand-painted cardboard placard stuck in the dirt and vaguely resembling a grave marker.

This hole courtesy
of two dicks from the sticks:
Pvt. Luther Douglas   Pvt. Clayton McGinnis
God help 2nd Platoon Bravo Company.

Part II

We remained in theatre with the occupation force after hostilities ceased and only rotated back home when the country was warming up for the presidential election a year later. Clay had grown accustomed to electric light and decided to move to Birmingham when his tour was up. We arrived in the Magic City within a month of each other and began the long process of turning back into civilians.

I had lost all interest in any career associated with mangled bodies, so I used the GI Bill to enroll in the City Planning and Public Administration program at the University of Alabama Birmingham. Clay was still determined to make his way as an independent contractor and went to work for his uncle's construction business there in the city.

Life settled into a comfortable if not exciting routine and stayed that way until Clay brought back an eye-popping souvenir from one of his regular visits home. She was a wide-eyed, long-legged brunette who glowed with health and sexual energy. Her name was Donna and she was smart and attractive, like Melinda, but she had little of Melinda's sweetness and none of her character it would turn out. Yet I knew that if I had found her up in the hills of Anniston, I too would have gone there every weekend.

And I might have lost my damn mind just like he did.

Something in a man makes him happy to stand on a trap door if he can get some sort of physical pleasure from doing so. This is true even if he sees the hand on the lever and knows it's just waiting for him to get comfortable. Clay and Donna Mae had known each other in high school. When he came home the decorated and rosy-cheeked Marine, the girls in the trailer park had put out their cigarettes, put on their shortest shorts, and gone after him. Donna Mae had him at the altar six months to the day after his plane landed, and Chad was born eight months after the wedding. With help from his folks, they purchased the three-bedroom house across the street from the foreclosed rambler I had bought with the help of the VA.

Donna proved herself an apt housewife but seemed to lack any other ambition. I thought of Melinda who worked full time and went to school full time, and I tried to imagine having a wife who did neither. It might not have been a fair comparison but it was the truth. She and I were always civil to each other, friendly even, although we both knew that Clay was the only reason we'd ever have spoken to each other. Had she not been his wife or I not been his best friend, the only exchange Donna and I might have had would be one letting the other go first at a four-way stop.

Their marriage followed what I imagined was the normal course. They tied the knot, had a kid, and after about five years were thinking about untying it. I knew most of the things they argued about but never offered him advice unless he specifically asked, and I hesitated to do it even then. It was better to let married folks sort out their own troubles. But there was one thing that had hung in the air since the day Chad was born.

I had been tempted to bring it up with Clay, because I knew he wondered, or he should have wondered, but I always decided at the last to keep my mouth shut.

When Chad was born, he had bright red hair that was like a scream to the whole world, and Clay seemed like the only one who couldn't, or wouldn't, hear it. One of his ancestors had had red hair he told me, so there was the possibility it had skipped generations. The combination of his blond and Donna's brunet colorings could have accounted for it as well, so there were two plausible explanations if you ignored the obvious. There had been enough play in the situation to suit Clay's mother, so she was satisfied, and Clay himself never had a single doubt about Chad.

I didn't know.

On my mantle is a picture of the two of them in a boat out on the Tallapoosa River taken the summer Chad turned six. Clay is sitting in the prow hunched over a tangled line while Chad, half-smothered by his life vest, watches intrigued. I had called out to Chad and he had looked back at me and straight into the aperture just as the shutter clicked. The late-afternoon sun made a flare on the lens and highlighted his hair, making the orange mop stand out with the clarity of an alarm bell next to Clay's blond crew cut.

There are some ideas you don't voice when all you have to go on is your own speculation. There are some things you leave alone if you don't have proof. I decided it was not my place to bring it up if Clay would not. Clay was happy; the kid was happy. Life went on, for a while.

It was at dusk on a Wednesday afternoon, two months after their fifth wedding anniversary, that I came home to find my television blaring and Clay asleep on my couch. A row of beer bottles stood at attention in the center of my coffee table, and dark gray smoke slid along the ceiling through the doorway from the kitchen. Clay had fried enough chicken to feed him, Melinda and me, and the family next door, and then he had gone to sleep and left the electric eye on under the pan. The blackened skillet, billowing smoke like a coal-fired locomotive, gurgled and spat when I dumped it—black grease and all—into the tepid dishwater in the sink. I turned off the television, opened the front door, and shook him awake. He was groggy and apologetic when he came to, alarmed when he saw the smoke hanging in the air. There was one beer left, and I drank it while Clay told me that Donna was gone.

She had called his job and said only that Chad was with her and she'd call again in a couple of days. He had punched out and gotten into his truck right away, but when he got home all he found were cleaned-out closets and emptied cabinets. It was a week before she called again. He said she'd told him she hoped he wouldn't waste time being mad at her but would go on with his life. She wouldn't tell him where she was, and she said nothing about the boy except "he's fine." Clay had called both her mother and her sister but neither would tell him anything. She had called again the following week and let him talk to Chad, and then they were gone again.

When Clay next heard from her it was through the Circuit Court in Charleston, South Carolina. She had filed for divorce. She said she didn't want the house or anything in it; support for her and Chad would be enough. He went to her family again wanting desperately to talk to her but again he got nothing. We even called the courthouse in Charleston to try and learn her whereabouts even though we knew it was pointless.

Clay didn't want a divorce, even after this. And it took his saying so to make me realize how little control he had over his feelings for Donna. He was still in love with her, probably the way he had been when he first saw her in eleventh grade. It took all I had not to say out loud the things that were circling in my head, not to point out to him the wreckage that had already begun to engulf him. If he loved her and thought he wanted her back, I supposed it was my job to help him get her. So we tried.

When he found out how much it would cost to hire a private detective who had nothing to go on except Donna and Chad's pictures, he was forced to reconsider. And when he gave in and talked to a lawyer in Birmingham, he was told that he'd have to hire a Charleston lawyer, since Charleston is where the petition was filed. The South Carolina State Bar Association referred him to a family law practitioner in Charleston who wanted two thousand dollars on retainer before he would even look at Clay's case. I chipped in and Clay sent the money off.

He conferred with his new lawyer via telephone for a half hour on two different occasions. Some weeks—I don't remember how many—after their first talk, Clay got a letter telling him a day and time to show up at the Charleston courthouse.

We left long before sunrise when the day came. I went along to provide moral support and serve as a character witness if necessary. He was silent for most of the ride up and we listened to the yammering of morning DJ's across Alabama and northern Georgia. I caught him bobbing his head when the Electric Light Orchestra came pulsing out of the speakers with a catchy melody that I had heard before and words that fit the occasion well. We hummed along as the truck crossed into South Carolina.

We went through the metal detector at eight-fifteen and met Clay's lawyer minutes later when we stepped off the elevator. I was almost thirty-one at that time in our lives, and in those thirty-plus years, I had never been required to set foot inside a courtroom. My idea of what we would see came straight from L.A. LAW and a dozen other television shows, as did his, I imagined.

The reality was altogether different.

Entering the courtroom, I saw no rich mahogany paneling on the walls, only sheetrock painted the same lifeless color as that which oppressed the waiting rooms at the unemployment office and the DMV. No swiveling leather chairs waited at cherry wood tables where plaintiff and defendant would sit. No swinging gate closed off the business end of the room from the rows of spectator seats. And no tiered jury box sat solemnly to one side. The bench was raised and the judge sat high above the rest sure enough, but there was a U-shaped arrangement of folding tables stacked with manila file folders immediately in front of his lofty perch, which itself looked like nothing more than a dark and fancy counter top. There was one folding table to the right of the center aisle and one to the left. Each table had a pair of folding chairs placed under it and a single microphone perched upon it. There was a waist-high wooden barrier with an opening at its center, and behind this barrier, there were rows and rows and rows of folding chairs for people waiting to have their cases heard. It was a warehouse where people's lives were processed, boxed, and thrown into bins.

We spotted Donna in the second row on the right-hand side of the aisle. A dark-skinned woman in a pinstriped suit with a hairdo that reminded me of a character from the Little Rascals sat to her left. Chad sat quietly in the chair to Donna's right. In the chair next to Chad sat a tall white guy in a black tee-shirt.

His hair was blond, like Clay's.

We found seats on the opposite side of the room and had just sat down when his Honor came in through a side door and all were ordered to rise. The entire room was sworn in at once, then the judge went down the docket calling names of plaintiffs and defendants, a roll call to see who was present and who was still looking for a parking space. He bantered with the court officials and made a few remarks to the assembled mass. Then he called the first case and the assembly line got underway.

I watched in silent disgust as he rooted around in these people's lives and then re-arranged each like it was nothing more than a drawer full of junk. Clay watched without comment until he and Donna were called at ten minutes to eleven. They and their attorneys went to the tables in the front and re-seated themselves. In a blazing, surreal examination, it was established that Clay, the solid, stand-up provider had been abandoned by his wife, but that he would still have to pay her for the privilege of having married her. I chewed my lower lip and realized I was sweating inside my shirt. I knew Clay wasn't stupid, and I knew he had not been blind all this time no matter what he pretended. Now that things had truly turned against him, I knew he would say something about red hair and how neither he nor Donna had any.

He didn't.

His Honor muttered some procedural bullshit while he examined Clay's last pay stub. He did some math on his countertop and then told everyone in the room how much of Clay's paycheck he would be allowed to keep from then on. I knew how much Clay took home to begin with, and I knew also that after hearing that ridiculous number, he would open his mouth and protest the railroad track that was being shoved up his ass.

But he didn't.

He sat there and didn't say a goddamned word. I shook my head and stood up.

Feeling that I'd let Clay hang once before I thought I had to say something this time.

I had too.

"Your Honor, that's child's not his." I said it loudly and plainly enough to be heard in every corner of the large room.

Heads turned to look at me.

Clay's lawyer. Clay. Donna. The twiggy-haired woman next to her at the table. Other lawyers. Spectators. Everyone.

"That's not his child," I said again. "It's not the kid's fault but he has bright red hair. Look at the hair."

Donna got halfway to her feet before Twiggy pulled her back into the chair.

"Bailiff, escort that man out," the judge said into his microphone.

"That's not his child," I said again.

Two men with badges on their navy blue blazers started toward me. One of them reached into the small of his back and drew out a set of handcuffs.

"Why don't you say something man!" I called to Clay as one of them took hold of my arm. "Shit, just say it!"

They walked me out of the room and stayed with me until, embarrassed and agitated, I was standing outside the main entrance.

'Sonsofbitches' I though over and over while people passed me going in and out.

The two men stayed inside the building and I could see them talking to the guards in the lobby. I knew there was no way I'd get back inside, so I crossed the street and walked back to where we had parked the truck.

It took only fifteen minutes for the two of them, Clay and Clarence Darrow, to show up at the front entrance. Seeing them, I crossed the street again and walked back toward the courthouse entrance. When Clay saw me coming, he gave me a look that I never was able to decipher. The lawyer stopped talking as I approached and looked at me as if he wanted me to disappear. I looked at Clay and asked, "What's wrong with you? Why the hell did you just sit there?"

Before he could say a word, his counsel weighed in.

"He should be asking you questions. If there *had* been grounds for a ruling in his favor, your outburst wouldn't have helped. All you did was irritate the judge and make your friend here look like an idiot."

"I ma—what do you mean *I* made him look like an idiot? I was telling the damn truth! Why didn't *you* say something about it?"

"You acted a fool in that courtroom because you wanted to slander his wife. But you undermined what little chance he had for a reasonable settlement."

"*The boy ain't his!*"

"Luke shut the fuck up," Clay snapped.

Clarence Darrow went on. "Misterrrr…" He waited for me to fill in my name but I just looked at him. "In the eyes of the court," he said calmly, "the child of a married woman is the child of her husband. Period. From the moment she conceives, not the day that she gives birth but the instant she *conceives,* that child is automatically her husband's child. Automatically."

"Aww that's bullshit. What if her husband was in the Persian Gulf when she conceived? Huh?" It was a desperation curve ball, and Clarence, after looking sideways at Clay, sent it sailing over the fence.

"He could have been on the moon. He was married to her, so it makes no difference. And by the way, consider that for six years he's raised that child and told the whole world he was the father."

"He didn't know!"

"It doesn't matter."

"It doesn't matter *whose* dick she was sitting on when she…?"

Clay walked away.

Clarence Darrow pressed his thin lips together and shook his head. "Listen to me," he said. And he had the nerve to point his finger as if he meant to poke me. "You are out of line and totally inappropriate. I cannot believe you aren't locked up and facing a contempt charge. Do your friend a favor and stay home the next time he has a court date."

I was about to swing on that four-eyed prick when he stepped back on his heel and hurried away.

"Fuck you too," I said to the back of his head.

The drive back from South Carolina was the longest trip Clay and I ever made together. Silence crowded into the cab of the truck like a husky, reeking hitchhiker. Clay looked straight ahead through the windshield and I gazed out my window at the endless acres of trees whizzing past us. We were no more than an hour outside Charleston when we spotted a roadside bar and he yanked the wheel toward it.

It was exactly the sort of Rebel honky-tonk where Clay's blond hair and blue eyes won him instant friends. I looked sideways at him as he slammed the break and skidded to a halt in the gravel lot. We had gone together into places like this before and gotten the same type of mixed reception that we sometimes got at strip clubs in the black neighborhoods of Birmingham. I wondered if I was going to leave this place without fighting, either him or some toothless fuck already inside pounding on the bar and yodeling *Sweet Home Alabama*. Feeling like Eddie Murphy in *48 Hours*, I asked myself if I should wait in the truck. The answer was obvious and came quickly. I undid my tie, threw it across the seat, and traced his steps to the weathered wooden door.

Once inside, I was relieved. The single waitress on duty and the three patrons seated at one of the tables looked at us as we entered but went immediately back to whatever they had been doing. The bartender greeted us with a "Hi y'all," as in 'how are y'll doing?' and then said, "Two fellas come in here wearin' suits this time of day must need to do some serious drinkin'." He set up two bottles of Coors Light and told us they were on the house. The worst beer in the world is light beer, but the best beer in the world is free beer, so we drank it. And then we had a few more.

A Confederate flag hung above the jukebox. While it undoubtedly meant much to the regulars, the place seemed to welcome whoever wanted to come in and seemed to care little about where they came from, as long as their money was green. It was three in the afternoon when we tottered out to the truck singing *"Slo-ow down, sweet-talkin' wo-man... So fuc-kin' sad be'cuz it's over..."* Clay hauled himself up onto the tailgate and threw one leg over. He raised the other leg, teetered for a moment, and then fell forward. He was asleep before he hit the bed of the truck. I climbed into the cab, somehow got the door closed behind me and collapsed across the front seat.

We slept until dusk.

* * *

Because he lived so far away, Clay had been allowed two weeks of supervised visitation each summer, something the court would consider revising if he moved to South Carolina. He called Chad or Chad called him every day those first two months. Over time it dropped to every other day, then a couple of times a week and finally to weekends. He said that they seemed to be running out of things to talk about. Their conversations had gone from could he, Chad, come back home, to would Clay come live with them, to Chad describing whatever toy he had discovered that week and wanted. Chad did talk excitedly about his first day at school and his new teacher. Soon he was telling Clay what he wanted for Christmas and asking again if Clay would come live with them.

Melinda had refused to believe the explanation I got from Clarence Darrow. Clay had had no chance of coming out ahead even though it seemed clear he was a chump who had been cheated on. Because his name had been on a marriage license when Donna got knocked up, he got the bills. Melinda opened the phone book the next day and called the first law office in the listings. After speaking to a divorce attorney, she told me that a number of states had passed tougher paternity laws in the last decade. In a situation where a child's other parent was known or reasonably suspected, it was better to take money out of that one person than to spread the cost of raising that kid to taxpayers. Well, that much made sense. But the rule also said that once a guy started paying he was locked in, even if DNA later proved he was of no relation to a child he had thought his own. People were amazed to find out how many men were paying for kids who were not theirs.

Along with that revelation came an insight that had eluded me before. Once I was able to think calmly about it, it was obvious why Clay had not spoken up in the courtroom that day. A man who spoke out against a shitty deal like that would be called a punk. The first thing people would say was that he wasn't a real man. Clay had been meat on the hoof from the moment he found Donna gone. The fact that she had cheated on him and deserted him meant absolutely nothing. The fact that he wasn't Chad's biological father meant nothing. He had been married to her so the kid was his, no matter whose kid it was.

That day outside the courthouse had been almost a year ago.

The evening Melinda and I heard the gunshots, Clay had gotten a letter from his South Carolina attorney. Donna had gone back to court and asked for an amendment to the divorce settlement. Originally, the court had accepted Clay's offer to buy her half of their home's value. A few hundred dollars had been tacked on to the monthly alimony and child support, but after a year, she decided she couldn't live with that arrangement. Clay had been given ninety days to sell the house, and the lawyer had told him the paperwork for his appeal could be initiated as soon as he paid a mere two thousand dollars up front. Clay was on his third beer when he opened the letter, and with the gun sitting there beside him on the sofa, he gave in to his frustration and held target practice.

It was dark when the cops finished questioning the two of us and searching the house. After talking to the neighbors, they wrote Clay a citation for improperly discharging a firearm, and then confiscated every piece of ammunition they could find. I had come up clean when they ran my driver's license, so the cop who had pounded on the door with his nightstick accepted my assurance that I would stay there and not let Clay leave the house until morning. When they were gone, Clay ripped the letter to shreds and went back to cleaning his guns.

We talked about the good old days, eons ago in the Kuwaiti desert, when we had only Staff Sergeant Messner, the Iraqi army and scorpions to worry about. Clay wasn't the type to feel sorry for himself. I was surprised and had no answer when he asked me what the hell a man worked and saved and sweated for, when the odds were that he'd wind up paying bills so some other guy could fuck his wife in comfort.

I knew he no longer had two thousand dollars to stuff into an envelope and mail away, so when I finished my beer, I wrote a check which he refused to take. I didn't want to add to his aggravation, so I didn't ask him the obvious question—how are you gonna pay the man? Instead, I let him nod off and then left the check on the kitchen table on my way out. I knew he'd consider selling his truck because he wouldn't get two thousand bucks unless he pawned his guns and sold everything in the house. The truck would bring him enough cash to pay the lawyer and pick up a second-hand vehicle that would get him back and forth to work. I hoped he'd see the long-term disadvantage of that sort of heroism and just take the money.

The weekend after Clay shot her picture, Donna was back in Alabama visiting her folks. She had talked to Clay that Friday morning and told him Chad could spend the night if Clay picked him up, but that he had to bring him back Saturday so they could get back to Carolina before nightfall Sunday. I asked Clay if he wanted me to drive to Anniston with him (I suspected the new guy would be there and figured I'd go along to serve as either the buffer or the backup, whichever was needed). He said no, assuring Melinda and me there'd be no trouble. He had something special he wanted to talk over with Chad and wanted to spend all the time he could with the little boy.

This was strange.

If Clay had had a change of heart and decided to move to South Carolina he had said nothing about it to me. That was my first guess, because the only change in his life that I was aware of was a pretty, green-eyed cashier at the new Food World six blocks over in a shopping center near the university. He'd brought her over and introduced us, and my impression was that they looked like all-American sweethearts lifted from the pages of a high school yearbook. They looked good together, and the smile on his face as he went out the door was genuine.

I was glad something good had finally happened to the man. He had dropped fifteen or twenty pounds in the year since Donna had taken off and now looked more like a receiver than a linebacker. He ate at our house a couple of times a week now and hung out with us most evenings. Melinda and I had both worried about his sanity, and she had tried fixing him up with her friends. Nothing had worked out until he met the girl at the grocery store, and it was still too early to make a prediction about that. It felt like a good thing, though.

It was late that afternoon when my mother called and told me my grandmother had been taken to the hospital down in Montgomery. I left work and went to my house to leave a note for Melinda. Clay had already left for Anniston so I spoke to neither of them before I picked up my mother and sister and the three of us drove south toward the capitol.

Catherine was nervous all the way there and chattered about anything and everything with my sister who sat in the backseat while I drove. My mother insisted we call her by her first name. She said it made her feel younger now that we were grown. Her mother thought it was abhorrent for children to address their parents by their first names, even after those children were grown-up and had families of their own. I remembered how grown up I had felt the first time I called her Catherine and she answered. That had been almost ten years ago. I had thought at first that I would never get used to it, but I did in time. And my grandmother had warned us that no matter how old we lived to be, if either of us, including her own daughter, ever slipped and called her Bernice, she would take off her shoe and beat the snot out of us.

A mini-stroke had caused her to pass out in the kitchen and rendered her unable to speak for several minutes after my aunt found her. My aunt called an ambulance, and she was taken to the hospital and admitted for overnight observation. Several family members were there when we arrived, and it looked for a while like a full-blown reunion. By nine o'clock that evening, it was clear grandma was in no danger, and when the nurses came around to clear out visitors, she gave her blessing to everyone who needed to leave and might not be able to visit the next day. Catherine decided to stay the night, so my sister and I got two rooms at the Red Roof Inn nearby.

Catherine stayed with grandma until the doctor showed up to sign her release order at one-thirty the next afternoon. We took her to my aunt's home where a flock of people waited and got back on the road at five.

I had been gone only twenty-four hours.

When I turned onto my street I knew something was wrong.

The people who owned the house next door to mine, and others across the street watched my car as I pulled into my driveway. A white van sat in Clay's driveway and the front door to the house was open. I noticed his truck was gone and was at a loss to explain why that was. There was no way he would have traded his beloved pickup for that plain white box on wheels that could have belonged to the phone company.

They watched me get out of the car. A man and a woman seated side by side on a gliding porch swing nodded almost imperceptibly when I raised my hand and waved. It was a quiet street normally, but today it seemed eerily so.

I shrugged and walked into my house.

Melinda sat in a corner of the living room sofa and stared out the open window. She turned as the screen door swung shut behind me. Her eyes were red-rimmed and her hair was pulled back in a tight ponytail. She looked up at me and said nothing as I placed my keys on the table beside the front door.

I stopped moving and waited for her to say hello. When she went on starring at me without speaking, I turned my head to look back over my shoulder then brought my gaze to her again.

"What is it?"

A crumpled tissue in her hand disappeared into her pocket when she stood up. She walked across the room to where I stood and, wordless, put her arms around me.

When I awoke the following morning, Sunday, I could not move. My body was a distant, vacant thing bound to my bed by misery like the unbreakable chain that bound Lucifer in the pit of Hades. I felt Melinda's hand touch my cheek and I wanted like anything to roll over and hide my grief from her. I managed to turn onto my side and pull my knees up, but that was as far as I got. After awhile she got up and left me, and at some point I found my way to the bathroom and washed.

She had food on the table when I made my way to the front of the house. I could see it but my sense of smell was gone. I went to the front door and looked at the house across the street, at the yellow tape that now sealed the entry to Clay's home. The truck was still gone from his driveway.

It would stay gone, I knew, but I looked anyway.

"Luke..."

I turned to the sound of her voice and went into the kitchen.

She asked if I wanted coffee and I nodded and thanked her. I sipped away half the cup and then gazed out the window while my hands picked over the food on the plate. She sat in the chair next to me and stroked my hair.

"It's gonna be all right baby."

There was a story in the paper that Monday.

"Gulf War Vet Dies in Police Custody"
—AP. Birmingham.

"A thirty-three year-old Marine veteran who saw combat in Kuwait died Saturday after police arrested him on a charge of parental kidnapping. Clayton McGinnis, a native of Anniston who lived and worked in the Birmingham area, was taken into custody after a violent struggle with police who were sent to his home after receiving a phone call from his ex-wife.

"Donna Mae Lilly, also of Anniston, called police after McGinnis drove away with their eight year old son whom Lilly has custody of.

"Lilly was visiting family and had agreed to allow McGinnis to pick up their son for an overnight visit. The arrangement fell through when McGinnis got into a violent exchange with her current companion. Allegedly, McGinnis had also been drinking before he arrived to pick the boy up. When someone noticed empty beer bottles in his vehicle, Lilly refused to allow him to take the child. Family members who were present say McGinnis became enraged and threatened several of them. He then carried the boy bodily to his truck, where a loud argument ensued and blows were traded between him and the mother's friend who tried to prevent him from leaving. He was able to drive away despite attempts by several others to stop him. He then made the two-hour drive to his home in Birmingham where he found police waiting to arrest him.

"Neighbors who witnessed the arrest said that several officers fought to subdue McGinnis before shackling him hand and foot and lifting him into the back of a patrol car. According to a police spokesperson, McGinnis developed breathing trouble and exhibited choking sounds as he lay on his side in the rear of the police vehicle. Officers transporting him to the municipal jail detoured to HEALTH SOUTH Critical Care Midtown where McGinnis received emergency treatment but was later pronounced dead. The cause of death is thought to be asphyxiation; however, an official cause has not been given pending the outcome of a report by the medical examiner.

"McGinnis had been cited for improperly discharging a firearm one week earlier when neighbors reported the sound of gunshots coming from inside his home. No one was hurt in that incident…"

There was more but I couldn't stand to read it. I called his mother, Kathy with a *K*, that night and talked to her briefly, telling her I would be there on Saturday. And then I sat for most of that night with Melinda's arms around me.

We have all seen flag-draped caskets.

Pulled through stony fields on caissons, they call out the soldier's final deployment to the hinterland of eternal honor—his ascension to the ranks of those whose virtues only are remembered. In the green hills of Anniston, I watched the days of my youth evaporate forever in the blustery sunlight of an autumn morning. The stiff collar of my uniform was a blessing because the hard-won Eagle, Globe-and-Anchors upon it kept my chin from lowering to my chest and thus my face from falling down in grief. It lent me strength that day, strength that I did not own and which I had no hope of mustering. It protected me from the outpouring that reason told me must come at some time. Not today, I thought, not yet. The Chaplin reads from the book of Matthew and I hear him clearly at first. Then his voice recedes until it is replaced by the hollow whistle of the wind. Rifle shots echo across the field and I remember the weight, yes, and the *smell* of my own M-16 rifle firing in rain, in freezing woodlands, and finally in the sands of the desert. Six pairs of white-gloved hands lift the flag and draw it taut. They fold it with rehearsed precision, and it is presented finally to his mother. I stand next to her chair, dry-eyed and stoic and I rest my hand on her shoulder as she receives the flag. She breaks down immediately and weeps into its folds. I squeeze her shoulder gently then take my hand away.

The slow cry of taps fills the hillside as the echo of gunfire did moments ago. When the color guard moves off, so too go the mourners in a slow wave. All but Melinda and me. I find my voice and ask her to give me just a moment. She kisses my cheek and walks toward the car.

Now it was all done, I thought. I would go back and pick up my life in the place where everything had paused. We all would.

I laid my gloved hand on the sloping lid of the casket and felt its shape beneath my palm. There was movement to my right, and when I looked up there stood Donna in the place where the Chaplin had been. We looked at each other, and I both wondered if she would say something and fervently hoped that she would not. I had no room for forgiveness for her. Not for she who—in my mind—had set all this in motion with her faithlessness and her perfidious ways. I turned my back to her and fixed my gaze on the American flag fluttering a stone's throw from where we stood. A fresh gust of wind rattled its chain against the aluminum pole and lifted the fabric against the blue. While I watched, its colors and those of the sky and the trees ran together in a jumbled blur.

Semper fi, my friend. *Semper fi....*

14.
The Thing

I am a grown man.

  I work in an office, but I change my own oil and perform my own tune-ups. I do my own taxes, and I can re-shingle a roof if necessary. I own fishing rods and a set of power tools; I get all sixteen ESPN channels. I play football and softball, and I do pushups on the bedroom floor. I drink out of the carton and straight from the bottle. I sleep in my boxers, and each time my girlfriend buys me pajamas, I lose them. I have turned entire loads of laundry pink, or baby blue, or mint green. I shine my shoes with an old tee-shirt. When I barbecue, the grilling fork becomes a weapon in my hand, and I use it to swat at flies after I've opened my fourth beer and made sure the ribs are dead. I read *Playboy* and *Men's Health*. I am a grown man. I am not afraid of spiders.

  I had lathered up with shaving cream and then stepped into the bedroom to turn up the volume on the television. The morning traffic report would be on any second, and I needed to hear it. It was seven-fifteen and I had to be dressed and closing the door behind me in eight minutes if I wanted to get to work on time. Actually, I should have been on my way out the door already, just in case there was a traffic tie-up somewhere along my route. No use worrying though. The best I could do was to shave, get dressed, and go running out of the place like I did most mornings.

I adjusted the volume and hustled back to the bathroom, the countdown timer in my head spooling off the seconds. Before I was completely inside the bathroom door, I spotted it crouching in the corner next to the shower stall.

I live in a modest, single-family home surrounded by trees and flowering plants. I liked the trees, and I didn't have a problem with the other plants before *it* came. I think the trees are where it came from, and that makes me distrust them now, despite my liking them.

I stopped with one foot on the tiled floor.

I had never seen anything like it, but I knew it was alive because parts of it were moving.

It was shaped like a squash, and it was as long as my hand from wrist to fingertip. It had six legs: four short segmented legs in front, and two long folding legs in back. Two hairy antennae quivered and probed the air in my direction. Its body was gray-brown, but alternating bands of brown and yellow marched along its abdomen and along the giant legs. It had scales, and it looked like a monstrous, mutated cross between a huge praying mantis and a gigantic scarab beetle.

My skin crawled in all directions at once. Goosebumps sprouted on every part of my body including my forehead and probably my palms. The hair on my neck, my arms, everyplace where it was not held down by the towel, stood on end.

'Ho-leee…' I thought. 'What the hell is that?'

My mind answered back in a dry croak: '*ssspiii-derrrr.*'

But that was ridiculous. There was no way it could have been a spider.

I have seen spiders. I know spiders. Spiders are ugly, and they are menacing. They are sinister and they are disgusting. *Spiders* are God's real punishment for the misdeeds of Adam and Eve. But spiders are from *this* planet. What stared at me from the corner beside my shower stall was…well…a *thing*.

I stared at it, thinking that maybe I ought to step backward out of the bathroom; then it jumped at me.

I moved involuntarily, lurching sideways the instant the thing twitched. Its body thunked against the shower door and fell back to the tiles with a plop. It stretched it legs two at a time, as if stunned. Then it waved its antennae all around. A bubble of darkness obscured my vision while an oily, queasy feeling slid down the sides of my stomach.

I must digress a moment and make a painful confession: I am among the chronically late. Movies, dinners, doctor's appointments, you name it; I can get there after it starts. My boss and my colleagues looked the other way because I am exceptionally good at what I do, and because I make up for it by working well into the evening and volunteering for crappy assignments which everyone else avoids. Still, this had been the great shame of my life until recently, until I talked to one of those time management people and got some invaluable tips. I made some adjustments here, changed a few thing there, and *voila!* I had arrived early or on time for work *every day* for nearly two months, an accomplishment that had my co-workers buzzing. I was on a hot streak. Last night, I'd gone to bed an hour late because the Steelers went into overtime. Now I was paying for it. My exit window was closing fast. But there was no way I would put a razor next to my throat with that thing watching me, hot streak or no hot streak.

No sir. That bathroom was not big enough for the two of us.

To make things even worse, my pants were on a hanger just outside the shower door. I (foolishly) thought that I could shave another minute off my time by putting them on in the bathroom, as soon as I was out of the shower and dried off. That timesaving shortcut—it turned out—had been a huge mistake.

I went back to the bedroom and got on my knees beside the bed. Not to pray, but to find a shoe. A woman had told me that the farther a shoe was under the bed, the less likely one was to ever pull it out and wear it. Way, way back in the corner, in that area under the headboard where the dust bunnies were mature and highly aggressive was a pair of old bedroom slippers I had forgotten I owned. I lay down on the rug, careful to keep my lathered face from touching the carpet. A minute later, I had fished the slippers out and picked up a few pieces of lint with my cheeks. That was okay, I thought; I was

213

now armed.

I marched back to the bathroom door with a dusty slipper in each hand and bloodlust in my eyes. I meant business. I had a healthy respect for living things, but I was not above murder if I could save a few minutes this morning. Besides, I couldn't leave the house with that thing still alive. Where would I find it crouching when I came home this evening? How did I know this thing would not wait until I was asleep and then crawl into bed with me? There were insects that killed people, I thought, bolstering myself for what lay ahead. The fact that those insects had to work in large groups to kill a man (or woman), or that they were widely identified and lived in remote corners of the globe didn't seem so important at the moment.

When I entered the bathroom a second time, I saw something that sent my blood pressure rocketing out through the top of my skull.

The thing was on my pants.

I should have put those pants on the instant I was out of the shower. I should have left them in the bedroom, carefully draped over the foot of the bed, and gotten dressed out there, like I always do. Routines evolve for a reason. We establish patterns in our behavior because of innate instructions that nature gives to us for a reason. It is not good to haphazardly change established routines. I had gotten dressed in the bedroom for years; I should have continued getting dressed in the bedroom. While I looked for a shoe, it had climbed, crawled, or jumped onto my pants and attached itself to the waistband.

This was serious.

Those pants had been carefully ironed. They matched perfectly with the shirt (which was also ironed) and tie (not ironed, but carefully rolled) that I had already picked out. There was no way I was going to iron something else, allow myself to be late for work, or leave the house in a towel.

I tossed the slippers into a corner where they gave off a puff of dust. It was time to take it up a notch.

Chemicals were called for, I decided. Or fire. At the very least I needed some real muscle.

I went to the bedroom closet and searched until I came up with the biggest, heaviest, thickest-soled hiking boot I owned. I could have killed a small deer with a solid *whump* from that baby. Clutching it by the toe, I went back to the bathroom.

The thing hung in silent repose on my pants, so I took a good grip on the shoe and advanced.

But wait.

I would get only one shot. The thing would counter attack if I did not crush it with the first blow, and it would be ground into the fabric if I did. Catch-22. To pulverize, or not to pulverize? That is the question. Whether it is smarter to smash the living hell out of an alien crea—

It moved. It started crawling up my pants.

Holy mother of pearl, it was climbing my pants like a drunken yuppie on a rock wall. My vision dimmed again and I heard a powerful whoosh inside my head. Pulled by the thing's weight, the pants started to slip off the hanger. Horrified, but transfixed, I moved closer, screaming at it telepathically, begged it to stop moving, to stop climbing, to stop pulling before…

My pants fell to the bathroom floor in a heap.

A hot wind brushed over me.

The thing showed itself atop the heap of fabric, and now I wanted to kill like I had never wanted anything in life. I wanted to destroy. I wanted to desecrate and murder. Bug filth or no bug filth, blood or no blood, I wanted death and destruction for this incarnation of disgust and evil. I took an angry step…and then another…and then I found out it had wings. A loud, angry, scary buzz—like a cinder block being scraped along a sidewalk—echoed off the tiles and filled the bathroom. Beads of sweat appeared on my palms and on my forehead.

Fire, I thought in desperation. I needed fire!

No.

Fire would burn the pants too.

Damn the pants; they were beyond saving.

Okay, fire. I'd have to go out to the shed and find the acetylene torch. Time. What time was it now? How much time did I have left?

I heard the doorbell. Then I heard the front door open and close. Footsteps in the hallway, and then the jingle of keys in my bedroom. I looked out.

It was Jeanine. She must have driven by to see if I was out of the house and then stopped when she saw my car still there.

Jeanine.

She gasped when she saw me.

"Why aren't you dressed?"

She looked at her watch and her eyes fell into a sorrowful, Basset-hound droop. "Ooooh sweetheart, you're gonna break your streak." Compassionate. That was one of the reasons I liked her. "Why aren't you dressed?" she asked again as she walked toward me, a curious gaze going back and forth between the patches of white foam around my mouth and the boot in my hand.

I pointed toward the corner.

Jeanine stepped through the door and looked at the pile of fabric on the floor next to the shower. "Are those your pants?" she asked, and then gasped when the thing—having hidden itself—crawled back up to the highest peak of fabric.

"What is that!" she asked in amazement.

"I don't know. I…"

She took off one shoe and moved past me.

"What are you doing?" I asked and placed a cautioning hand on her shoulder.

Jeanine scares me sometimes. One would think that the money she spends on manicures and pedicures and facials and graduate school would elevate her above some behaviors. The woman smokes cigars, however, and downs cognac with the best of us. More reasons why I like her, and fear her.

"I'm killin' that fucker!" she said in a voice suddenly dangerous, maniacal even. Her eyes gleamed, and her body exuded murderous intent.

"I don't think you'd better do that," I warned. But she had already kicked off her other shoe. She slid the skirt up past her knees, and got into a combat crouch.

Inching forward, feet apart and hands poised, she cornered it, so to speak. Her shoe, a shiny black pump with a wide, thin heel, would not be heavy enough to break the armor on that thing's back, I thought, and so I called her name again. She ignored me and continued advancing.

Don't do it Jeanine. Don't. That thing's a killer! I'll shave in the kitchen. I'll wear khakis! Don't throw your life away…

216

But she was locked on—she was focused so acutely she could not have pulled back if she had wanted to. Like a lioness stalking a gazelle, she closed in. I heard the loud, unnerving drone of the wings again.

Good God woman! Does life mean nothing to you!

Jeanine raised the shoe above her head, paused, and then lunged with a samurai yell. I watched the shoe start down and turned my head away. There came a solid, echoing *thwack* followed closely by a piercing scream. I turned to see Jeanine backpedaling towards me on her butt. She had missed.

The thing went after her; crushing the fabric of the pants under its immense weight as it climbed over the dips and folds and came down onto the tiled floor.

Good God! It was going to get Jeanine!

She backed into my leg, and I bent, hooked an arm around her body, and lifted her to her feet in a single fluid motion. She scampered behind me and wrapped her arms around my mid-section, afraid to stand where I stood, but also afraid to let go. The thing came brazenly across the tiles meaning to drive us back through the sheer panic it induced. Its large body wobbled, and its gruesome legs clawed at the grout while its antenna fanned the air. Dizziness swept over me, but the thought of Jeanine, helpless and dying in the clutches of that vermin ignited my protective rage. The boot was feather-light in my fist, the fear had drained out of me, and a flood of adrenaline fired the muscles in my arm. I raised the boot above my head and brought it down in a blinding flash. The walloping sound it made could not hide the crunch, or the sickening squish that followed it. Something moist splattered against my bare feet.

My lip curled downward in disgust, but I turned quickly to Jeanine and wrapped both arms around her. "Oh darling…" I murmured.

She squealed with laughter and buried her face against my shoulder.

"I thought I had lost you," I went on.

When she regained her composure, she used those long, beautiful fingers of hers to wipe away her tears. "You need an exterminator," she managed to say.

"Or a lumberjack, to chop down those damn trees," I added.

She went to the sink, where she used my face cloth to wipe flecks of shaving cream off the ends of her hair. "To prune them at the very least."

I allowed the adrenaline shakes to subside before I leaned over and gingerly lifted the shoe. The bug looked a lot smaller now that it was dead.

"What is that thing?" she asked again.

I had no idea, I told her, staring at it the way one stares at a car wreck, disgusted, sickened, but mesmerized. It looked a *lot* smaller now, not quite as long as my hand from fingertip to wrist. Not even as long as my thumb, in fact. Not entirely. But it was still frighteningly large for an unidentifiable insect that had gotten into my house from God knew where. The scaly armor plating on its back was actually a design on its wings.

It twitched.

I dropped the shoe and jumped backward. Jeanine flinched, and then gave me a look of both pity and rebuke. I cleared my throat, stepped boldly to where the shoe was and picked it up again.

"Guess I'd better clean this up," I said in a manly baritone.

She came over to me and took my head in her hands.

"It's okay. Mommy will protect you from all the bad buggies." She rubbed her nose against mine and giggled. Then, glancing at her watch, she let out another, longer "oooooh."

"You were doing so well. Two months, wasn't it?"

I grunted deep in my chest and thought to myself, 'so what?' So I'd be late for work. What were they gonna do, toss me into a volcano? Feed me to the animals at the circus? If they didn't like it, well that was too damn bad. I'd get there when I got there.

I am a grown man, after all.

Breinigsville, PA USA
08 September 2009
223689BV00001B/3/P